THE MAID

A PSYCHOLOGICAL THRILLER

RACHEL HARGROVE

Copyright © 2023 by Rachel Hargrove

All rights reserved.

No part of this book may be reproduced in any form or by any electronic or mechanical means, including information storage and retrieval systems, without written permission from the author, except for the use of brief quotations in a book review.

ISBN: 9798399122465

Imprint: Independently published

GET THE NEWSLETTER

If you'd like the latest news on my upcoming novels and advance copies before release, please sign up for my free author newsletter at rachelhargrove.com/newsletter

PROLOGUE

They'll come for me soon. There's still time to leave the country. I'll steal my neighbor's car and head south. Once I hit the border, I'll keep running. I'll disappear to some corner of the world.

Or maybe I'll go north. Canada's only two hours away. Blending in will be easy enough. My only problem is my driver's license. It's flagged. They'll arrest me unless I find another way in, which should be possible. Not every single mile of the border is protected.

A thrilling jingle plays on my laptop, the sound yanking me to crushing reality. A live feed of NBC news loads. Two grim news anchors stare into the camera.

"Rumors have surfaced that Grace Williams, the former maid for the Hamilton household, is a prime suspect in the murder investigation. Police have not confirmed her involvement, but sources say she is under heavy scrutiny. The victim's family—"

I click out of the window. My mugshot disappears, but the sensational headline blazes in my head. All week,

I've been glued to social media and cable broadcasts, reading the toxic discourse of keyboard detectives as they rip apart, stab, and deface every detail of my private life. Like this murder investigation is a *game*.

My hand falls to my swollen belly. The baby kicks, a gentle reminder of what's at stake. If the police come for me, I'll lose my child. I'll be stripped of the chance to hold my baby girl, see her first smile, hear her first word. The thought is more terrifying than any jail cell.

My phone rings. I slide it to my cheek, thumb stabbing the green button.

"Hello?"

"Are you that maid on TV?" a woman demands.

Not again.

"You should be ashamed of yourself," she snarls, my ear pulsing with her Philly accent. "What kind of woman does what you did?"

I picture a girl draped over a recliner in Boston Bruins sweatpants, hammering her chipped red nails on her phone's keys. Why do these people think it's a good idea to stalk and intimidate me? Aren't I a prime suspect in a murder case? Shouldn't they be scared of me? I lick my dry lips, resisting the urge to hang up. If I do, she'll call back. Again and again.

"I don't know what you're talking about."

She scoffs. "Yes you do, you evil, murdering witch."

Her nasty tone sends a wave of irritation through me, but I don't react.

"You have the wrong number."

"We all know you did it."

We? You mean the internet detectives online? I could

scream. They're delusional. They have no idea what really happened. A flood of heat claims my neck as I grip the phone. "Please stop calling me. This is harassment."

"You need to start telling the truth."

I raise my voice. "You need to stop. This is my private home."

"I'll stop when you give that poor family closure. You ruined that beautiful family," she shouts, her venom lashing my cheeks. "How could you?"

I run my hand over my burning face. "I'm hanging up now."

"You do that. And then do the world a favor and jump off a cliff."

Jesus. She's vicious enough to be the perpetrator of the crime *I'm* accused of committing. I hiss through my clenched teeth. "Thanks for the suggestion."

"You're a monster. You're a *murderer*."

I hang up and mute my phone. A pang stabs my aching stomach as the screen flashes with another call. This is the third time I've changed my number, but sleuths keep digging up my personal information and posting it online. They won't leave me alone. They call me the most disgusting names. Threaten me. According to the court of public opinion, I'm guilty. Those who believe I'm innocent are vocal, hence the trending hashtag #freethemaid, but most people cheer for my demise.

A stabbing pain hits my chest.

I never should've taken that job.

ONE

Naomi Hamilton leans forward on the wingback chair, her oval face white and bright, like a pearl. Her platinum hair, cut in a chic bob, completes the image. She's right at home in Bellevue. Earlier, she opened the door to her mansion wearing a garish Versace robe and a full face of makeup, apologizing for her state of undress. Everything about her screams luxury, but small wrinkles form near her eyes, a fracture in her carefully manicured appearance.

"Are you available to work next week?"

I take out my phone, pretending to swipe through a schedule. "Let's see...yes. I *think* I can make that happen."

"Wonderful. We're looking to fill the position immediately. We've had a weekly cleaning service for the last few years, but they recently switched jobs and our needs have changed."

We're looking, she says, as though Jack Hamilton has ever managed a household. Women like Naomi exist to pick out shiny objects for the built-in shelves of her husband's office—which she has done perfectly.

"Great. I'm excited to live here. It's such a gorgeous place." I gesture at a matte black vase with sticks poking out from the top. "I love how you've decorated the office."

Naomi smiles. "I'd love to claim credit, but an interior designer picked out everything."

"Well, they did a fantastic job. I'm really into the East Asian theme you have going on here." I sip the floral tea, inhaling the jasmine scent. "I noticed the canvas wall art with cherry blossoms in the entry hall, and there's a jade sculpture on the console table. You're wearing a jade necklace, too."

Naomi beams. "You seem like a detail-oriented person."

"Oh yes. I'm a jewelry designer."

"That's right. I checked out your Insta—stunning work."

I nod and smile. "Thanks. I hope to get back to it someday."

"How did you learn to do that?"

"My parents. When you spend countless summers setting stones, you cultivate an eye for detail."

I notice things. Like the white lab coat hanging over the chair like a stage prop in a drama. I have no idea what it's doing in her husband's office, but she wants me to see it. *I'm not some trophy wife—I'm successful.* Her posturing is unnecessary. I know all about her.

"That's a great quality to have," she says, folding her hands in her lap. "I'm the same. I have a photographic memory, which helps a lot when you're a primary-care physician. I don't have to look up a patient's history, diagnoses, or treatment plans. I remember everything. And I'm very nitpicky about cleanliness. I can be a bit high-maintenance in that regard."

"The way you want it is exactly what I'll do." I stare into Naomi's unblinking gaze. "Can I ask what will my duties be?"

"Oh, the standard stuff. Vacuuming. Dusting the baseboards. Washing the cars. I'll have a list. And I might ask you to run errands, so you must have reliable transportation."

"That's fine. Any preferences for cleaning products?"

"Organic only. I can't have any harsh chemicals in our home."

"Of course." I tap my knee, itching to get into the drawers of her husband's desk. "Do you have kids?"

I already know the answer, but I figure I should ask. Naomi blinks and stares down at her hands, the shift in mood so abrupt that a pang of guilt hits me. She looks off, like her confidence has taken a hit.

"No," she says softly. "We're not ready. We wanted to wait for more...opportune times."

You're thirty-five. What are you waiting for? A geriatric pregnancy puts her baby at risk for all kinds of disorders. She's a doctor. She knows damn well she's running out of time.

I smile. "Makes sense."

"How far along are you?"

"Thirteen weeks."

Naomi leans forward, the grin back on her face. "So past the first trimester, then. How exciting."

Yes, but I have mixed feelings. Raising a newborn without support will be terrifying. I'm not looking forward to navigating motherhood completely alone. Something on my face must show my anxiety, because she grasps my shoulder.

"You'll be fine. You'll see. It's the best thing in the world."

"I guess I'll find out soon."

Her warmth drops from my arm, and ice spreads through my stomach. Her brows knit together in an expression I hate—pity.

I know what she's thinking. *This girl can't handle working for long. Then I'll be stuck paying for maternity leave.* Who wants to hire a pregnant woman as a live-in maid? I sent my application on a desperate whim. I never thought I'd hear from her, but she called me the next day.

She taps her chin. "I'm guessing you'll be able to work up to thirty weeks."

"I bet I'll last longer. I'm a hard worker."

"I don't doubt that, honey. But eventually, your belly will be too big for certain tasks."

I shrug. "A little discomfort won't stop me from doing my job."

"Well, it's more than that. Our master bathroom has very slippery tiles. If you're just wearing socks, it's dangerous. You could fall." She shuts her eyes, and a shudder runs through her.

"I'll keep that in mind."

She makes a thoughtful sound. Then she lifts a teacup from the end table near her elbow and sips, staining the porcelain with her peach lips. She sets the cup down and wipes the rim with a napkin. Then her brown gaze dives into me. "Would you like a tour of the house?"

"Sure."

A crease forms on her powdered cheek. Then she stands, her robe fluttering like angel wings. She leads me out of the office and shows off her Pacific Northwest–inspired waterfront mansion. It's two floors, not including the basement. Lavish rich woods. Bamboo flooring. Bluestone. Amazon River granite countertops. She points out each feature like a real estate agent. She takes me upstairs, past the master bedroom and various rooms. We stroll through modern bathrooms with marble walls and black sinks, and then we head back to the main floor, through a home theater, then a masculine-looking bar attached to a round billiards room with giant, mounted fish.

"This is Jack's mancave," she says, giving the swordfish a rueful glance. "I wasn't in charge of the decor, as you can tell."

Their beady eyes stare at me. *Creepy*. I wrap my arms around myself as a chill penetrates my body. Naomi prattles on about what she would've done with the space as I shiver.

She slaps her forehead. "Where are my manners? You're *freezing*."

"I-I'm fine."

She takes my wrist and drags me out of the room. "I'm so sorry."

"No, I'm okay."

"You're not. You're shivering." Naomi sighs, climbing

the stairs to the second floor. "This house doesn't retain heat because of all the glass. I told Jack we'd be better off with something else, but he insisted." She shakes her head, still wearing that strained grin. "I'll get you a sweater."

My cheeks flush. "I'm fine. Really."

"It's no trouble. I have too many clothes."

She whisks me into her walk-in closet. It's the size of my kitchen. She gestures toward the bench in the middle and rakes through a rack of cream clothing until she tears a sweater off its hanger. It resembles a twenty-dollar sweatshirt you can buy at any gift shop.

"Here. Wear this."

She's being nice because she pities me, and I'm clinging to the slim hope that it will be enough. I desperately need this job. I take the sweater and pull it over my head. It's small and cropped too high.

"It's Anine Bing," she states with gravitas, but I have no idea who that is. "It looks great on you."

I don't agree, but I smile and nod.

"Want to see where you'll be staying?"

Does that mean I'm hired? "Yes, please."

On the phone, she mentioned separate living quarters, but didn't elaborate. I follow the sound of Naomi's heels clacking the floor as she guides us downstairs to the kitchen, behind the butler's pantry to a door. She opens the door to a carpeted staircase.

"After you."

A naked bulb illuminates the way down. My ankles wobble as I descend. I grip the wooden railing, which rocks under my weight. My feet sink into the cheap carpet of a room no bigger than the place I rent. It's cold. No windows aside from a tiny one over the kitchenette, which gives me a view of grass and not much else.

Still, it's functional. There's a chest with linens. A dresser. A bathroom with a glass door shower. The world's smallest fridge and freezer. A double bed is crammed underneath a curtained-off area under the stairs.

"Isn't it lovely?" Naomi palms the pale blue cabinets in the kitchenette, smiling. "I thought the color might brighten things up."

This dungeon needs a lot more than bright paint. I force on a grin. "You did a good job. It's...well, it's cozy."

"I think so, too. And you can bring any furniture you like. We're limited because the staircase is so narrow, but I can talk to Jack about fitting a couch in here. And maybe a TV, though we don't have cable and Wi-Fi is spotty. The guest network doesn't always work."

That's another bummer. I'm disappointed, but not surprised. If these are the accommodations she's offering people, no wonder the position has been open for a while.

"I know it's not much, but it has everything you need. There are plenty of linens. Extra blankets. And of course, you're welcome to the rest of the house." A slight edge creeps into her voice as she opens and closes the empty fridge. "I have no problem giving you a guest room, but my husband is...very particular about who we let in our home."

"No worries, Mrs. Hamilton."

"Call me Naomi. Mrs. Hamilton makes me feel like an old lady."

I chuckle. "Deal."

Naomi's touch drifts over my back as she ushers me upstairs. "Now, I can't *guarantee* you the job. I have to discuss it with Jack. He's hesitant...but I'll try my hardest to beat him down. I'll call you."

"Sounds great."

Becoming the Hamiltons' maid will put me one step closer to achieving my goal. I talk Naomi's ear off about how excited I am, like cleaning her toilets is an amazing opportunity, and it is. I'm not lying about that.

"Thanks for inviting me to your home. I'm honored that you're considering me for the position."

"You're very welcome." Naomi guides me to the front door. She clasps the handle, but hesitates. "Do you have any other interviews lined up?"

I bite my lip. "Some."

"Well, I wish you good luck."

"Thank you," I say, shimmying out of the sweater. "I should give this back."

I hand it to her, but Naomi refuses to take it.

"I meant for you to keep it."

"But it's yours—"

"Keep it. I insist."

Naomi's sympathetic gaze travels down my baggy shirt, down my faded blue skirt with its embarrassing frayed hems, to the heels I picked up at Goodwill. An ocean of privilege separates us. She's probably never stepped into a used clothing store.

Her eyebrows draw together. "What will you do if you don't get this position?"

I try to keep the fear out of my voice. "I'll apply for more jobs."

"But you're having a baby soon. What are you going to do? What's your backup plan?"

"I'll manage," I whisper, even though I have no support system. "There are programs I can sign up for."

"Let's hope it doesn't come to that."

A disturbing amount of optimism swells in my chest as Naomi opens the door. I step into the chilled air and descend the long staircase. Naomi stands on the porch, her arms crossed, her stare sizing me up. As I walk to my car, I wave at her. She waves back.

Once she hires me, everything will work out. I'll be in their house, earning a decent salary, getting close to his family. Best of all, he can't escape me.

TWO

I'm desperate to break out of this prison. Every night, I try to get comfortable on someone else's futon. It sucks. I never feel rested and I'm constantly battling low-grade nausea. Not knowing where you will sleep for the evening is stressful, and I've run out of sympathetic former coworkers. Now I rely on the kindness of strangers, like Janice.

She's a twenty-three-year-old I met on social media. I'm active there. I make and sell jewelry. Nothing fancy because I can't afford a jeweler's studio, but I've been to the farmer's market a few times. She asked why my booth wasn't at its regular spot, so I told her about getting kicked out of my parents' home. She offered me a room in her place. I'll repay her generosity someday, but right now, I'm scrambling to put my life together.

I drag my battered laptop over my knees, checking my email for the thousandth time. I've received zero responses to my applications, which isn't surprising.

Nobody wants to hire a twenty-one-year-old without a college degree. I was beginning my junior year of college when I had to drop out because my parents cut me off. No matter how many summers I've toiled setting stones or resizing rings, I can't get a design job without someone vouching for me, and leaving Dad's number as a reference isn't an option, so I've been applying to everything.

I pull out my earbuds, my oatmeal forgotten as nerves knot in my stomach. She should call me back today.

My eyes land on Janice as she pauses near my curtain's opening. She's in all black, from her beanie to her chunky combat boots. Purple streaks weave through her thick brown hair. A burlap bag decorated with beer brewery stickers hangs off her tattooed shoulder. Her soft brown gaze creases. "How'd the interview go?"

I open the curtain wider, sighing. "I think it went okay."

"What's their place like?"

"Amazing. Must be worth five or six million. Maybe more. The location is incredible. Their house is right against the lake. They can jump in if they wanted."

"Do they have a yacht?"

I laugh. "Of course."

The Hamiltons are one of Seattle's richest and most prominent families, famous for their luxury yacht cruise line, Luxe Pacifica. Everybody has seen their ships gliding in Lake Washington during Seafair. Jack Hamilton, Sr., the owner of the company, is pushing seventy and on the brink of retirement, which means his sons will soon take over the multibillion-dollar empire.

Janice drops her bag and throws herself on the couch. "So what are they like?"

"I've only met Naomi, but she seems nice. She's...not what I expected."

The moment I got home, I looked up the sweatshirt Naomi gave me. It retails at a hundred bucks, which is ridiculous, but it's free money. It's already listed on Facebook marketplace. "I can't go into too many details. I signed an NDA, but I'm feeling much better about my chances."

Her eyebrow quirks. Janice takes off her boots, sliding her feet over the coffee table. "Well, don't get too hopeful."

Too late. "I'm getting the job."

"You might not," she states, her voice kind but firm. "I can't imagine a wealthy family employing a pregnant woman for a live-in housekeeper."

"Naomi said she didn't mind."

Janice makes a discouraging sound. "People say all kinds of things."

I swallow hard. This is true. My parents turned on me after professing to love me for decades. I close my laptop's lid, my throat burning.

"This baby is coming. He can't ignore it forever."

"Are you sure he's the father?"

She keeps bringing up my baby's paternity. It's annoying. "Yes. I am."

"You weren't with anyone else?"

I glare at her. "*No.* I've told you that."

"Right. Sorry, I forgot." Janice trails off as I stab the keys on my phone. "But it's easy to assume someone's the dad before the third-month ultrasound. Have you had that yet?"

"No, I haven't, but I am one hundred percent certain it's his." I stare at her, gritting my teeth. "You think I'm lying?"

She chews on her lip. "I think you *believe* he's the dad."

My hand twitches with the need to slap her. "Now I'm inventing this pregnancy?"

"No...but this is so unlikely."

"What is that supposed to mean?"

"Don't get upset. I'm not the devil for questioning that a man like him...crossed paths with a waitress."

"A rich guy screwing the help is a tale as old as time. Ask Arnold Schwarzenegger."

"That makes sense because she lived in his house. You didn't."

"He was a regular at the restaurant where I worked, and *he* suggested we go somewhere."

Her skeptical gaze narrows as I recount how he took me to a hotel bar. We rode the elevator to a room with lots of mirrors and enjoyed a wonderful night that I'll never forget. I still have the frayed business card he scrawled his number on. When I show it to her, she squints as though trying to detect a forgery.

I exhale loudly, taking it from her. "I don't need to prove it to you."

"You're right. Sorry."

"I need to get his attention. You have no idea what I'm going through." I rub my sweaty palms on my jeans. "I don't have a job, a home, or health insurance."

"That must be difficult."

"It's *terrifying*. I'm having a baby in five months. Nobody will help me. My parents don't give a damn about me. They threw me out like I was garbage."

"Okay. Try to relax."

Easy for her to say. She's not surviving on the gratitude of strangers. I twist the hem of my shirt, struggling to breathe. "I'm not asking for the world, here. I just want him to do his fair share."

I bow my head in my hands. My lungs are on fire. I press my lips together, holding back tears. I'm scared of the future. I love this baby. I want to protect them, raise them to be a good person, but if I can't get their father to accept their existence, how will I manage that?

I've tried everything. He's blocked me on all social media accounts. That's why I need this job. It's the only way to get to him. I have zero support. Panic constricts my throat. I wipe my face, standing.

"Where are you going?" Janice asks, her expression guilty.

"I need some air."

She grimaces. "Don't go too far."

Her apartment isn't in the safest area in the city. It's called the Blade for a reason, but a short walk takes me out of danger and into Pike Place Market.

I descend the cobblestone road and weave through tourists, heading to the strip of grass behind the vendors. I sit on a bench and take in the amazing view of the waterfront. Ships head to and from Bainbridge Island. The chill permeates my skin, settling in deep.

My jacket chimes. I grab my phone and glance at the

screen. Naomi Hamilton. I answer the call, my heart thundering.

"Hello?"

"Hi, Grace. How are you?"

I grip my phone tighter. "I'm doing fantastic. And yourself?"

"Oh, I'm fabulous. Thank you for asking. Is now a good time for a little chat?"

"Sure."

"I wanted to let you know about the decision we've made. We were leaning toward another girl, but after some discussion, we decided to hire you."

My lips part but no words come out.

"Grace? Are you there?"

"Y-yes...yes, I'm here."

"I'm glad. Can you start Tuesday?"

"Absolutely." Everything inside me boils, and I can't think clearly. "I'd love to!"

"I'll be at work, but Jack will be there. Is that okay with you?"

"Perfect," I choke out. "I look forward to meeting him."

"Are you all right? You sound upset."

"I'm not. I'm very happy...just a bit overwhelmed."

"You don't need to be. We just want someone nice who works hard and is pleasant to be around. You can do that. Can't you?"

"Absolutely."

"Wonderful. We'll see you on Tuesday, then."

"Bye," I whisper before she hangs up.

I walk home, but I'm barely aware of the journey.

THE MAID

Adrenaline surges in my veins as I leap up the stairs to Janice's apartment. She's still lounging on the sofa, digging into a box of leftover Chinese.

"I got the job," I shout, opening the door. "Just now. She called me."

Janice puts down her chopsticks. "You're joking."

"Nope. It's happening."

She beams, standing up to hug me. "I'm so excited for you. When do you start?"

"Tuesday."

"That soon? Wow."

We disengage. Janice rushes to the kitchen, returning with a bottle. "We have to celebrate. Or I will, at any rate."

I smile, picturing the future. This position is a steppingstone to what I *really* want. A house in a safe neighborhood. A husband who will take care of me and our kids. Soon, I won't have to struggle for every red cent.

"It's disgusting how hard it is to find affordable rentals on a tight budget." Janice pours alcohol into a glass. "It's a Catch-22. If you're poor, you're stuck with places that are dirty and unsafe."

"Preaching to the choir." I clink my water glass against her tequila. "Thanks a lot for letting me crash here. I owe you."

"No worries."

Janice inhales the shot. Grimacing, she wipes her lips. My roommate is my only family. My parents haven't contacted me since they kicked me out. I'll never forgive them for that. It's fine. I don't need them.

All that matters is that I'm inside that house. Once

I'm there, I'll have the opportunity to do so much more. He won't be able to hide from me. He'll have to accept this baby. The Hamiltons are my gateway to a better life. I need to hold my nose and do whatever they want.

I just hope they're decent to me.

THREE

I'm safe. I've got a job and a place to stay. Okay, it's not a five-star hotel or anything, but at least I have it to myself. And I get to explore the city on my days off.

Bellevue is gorgeous. I never pictured myself living here. It's where people like me travel to work at jobs that barely pay the bills. I don't know the area well, but I'll learn. My baby's father will want me to move here. No doubt, he prefers his neck of the woods to mine. Bellevue is safe. Cleaner streets. The public schools are great. Local cops eyeball everyone pretty hard. A police officer stopped me on my way here.

Dragging my suitcase, I walk up a flight of stairs to the front door. Their house is a modern, glass-fronted building with cedar siding and a dark roof. It blends in with the rugged surroundings, almost like it sprung from the earth among the evergreens. It's huge, with a spacious balcony on the second level overlooking Lake Washington.

As I approach the front door, it swings open. A

broad-shouldered man in a Patagonia vest and jeans steps onto the porch, sipping his coffee. This must be Naomi's other half. He has this boss-like vibe I've encountered with many six-foot-something men. His strong jawline and sharp cheekbones only add to that impression.

His espresso-brown hair magnifies his pale skin. He raises his chin, sending a cool glare in my direction. It's as though he's sizing me up. How he carries himself is so different from his younger brother, Blake. Blake is soft, with rounded features and a friendly smile, but Jack looks like he could carve out a living in the Pacific Northwest with nothing but his bare hands. I hope my presence won't disrupt his life too much.

"You must be Grace," he deadpans, holding out a hand. "Jack Hamilton."

I shake it, his unsettling stare diving into me. "I'm looking forward to working for you, Mr. Hamilton."

"Call me Jack." He relinquishes my hand, his thick brows furrowing as he gestures at my luggage. "Is that all you brought with you?"

The way he emphasizes *all* sends a ripple of heat through my body. *Not everybody has a trust fund, Jack.* "Yeah," I say brightly, burying my annoyance. "I've downsized my life to a single suitcase, which is convenient when you're couch surfing."

His mouth curls. He backs into the house, leaving me enough room to squeeze inside. I follow Jack through the mansion, taking in the tasteful art and the views of Lake Washington through the many windows I'll have to wash. I head toward the basement, but I'm jerked back by my suitcase.

"I'll take that," Jack says, his fist around the retractable handle. "Naomi will be home any minute. Let's get you settled in."

"Sounds good."

I accompany him to the butler's pantry with the door leading downstairs. He opens it, gesturing inside. I descend the staircase, the steps groaning with Jack's weight. It's like plunging into a damp chill. It's freezing, but Jack makes no apology. He slides my suitcase beside the bed, which is weighed down by a bundle of fresh linens.

"There's a space heater if you're too cold."

He gestures to a tiny black rectangle standing upright by the only plug in the room. Judging by his tone, he doesn't give a damn whether I freeze to death.

I turn it on, holding my palm to the lukewarm air. "That's thoughtful of you."

He nods, his expression indifferent. "There are towels in the bathroom. And I've created a separate wireless network for you. The password is on the bed."

"Great. Thank you."

"Don't put any food down the sink. It clogs. I've been meaning to hire a plumber, but they're booked out for weeks. Make sure you open the window whenever you shower, because there's no fan, and it gets moldy."

Perfect. I follow him to a loveseat facing a flatscreen TV. Naomi probably tried to spruce it up. A luxurious throw drapes the cushions. I settle into them and wince. It's like sitting on a rock. Jack's as observant as a bat in daylight when it comes to comfort.

Jack crosses in front of me, hands on his hips. His

intimidating presence sends a dark thrill down my spine. He's not an easy person to share a small room with, especially when he's glowering like I've stolen the silver. Disapproval carves merciless lines in his face.

"The question I'm about to ask you is a very delicate one, and I need you to answer me honestly. Can you do that?"

"Totally."

"I hope so," he growls, eyes boring into mine. "Because I don't tolerate liars."

"Got it."

His heated gaze flicks to my belly. "Is the father going to be a problem?"

"What do you mean?"

"You know what I mean," he says, shooting me a twisted smile. "I don't want him in this house. If you need to hash out child support, you do it somewhere else. Not in my house."

I swallow the burning bile, imagining how satisfied I'll feel when the baby's paternity is revealed. "I'll honor your rules."

Jack's forehead ripples as he studies me. "I'm serious. I don't like strangers in my home, especially around my wife."

"No worries. He has no idea where I am, and I'd never dream of inviting him here." *Most likely,* you'll *do that for me.*

"Does he have a record?" he asks.

A pulse beats at the base of my throat. "I have no clue."

He glowers at me. "How could you not know?"

"Not everyone is as inquisitive as you."

He winces. "You're having a baby with this man, and you didn't look him up?"

"I'm still working on my mind-reading skills. Besides, I didn't think asking about a criminal record was a standard part of getting to know someone."

His eyes narrow. "Don't talk back to me. It's unprofessional."

That's rich. But I don't want him to convince Naomi to fire me, so I bite my lip, struggling to keep my mouth shut.

"You're right. I'm sorry. I'm a bit sensitive about my pregnancy."

"You should consider running a background check on him. You can't afford to be more careless."

I clench my mouth tighter. "Thanks for the tip."

"Who is he, anyway? A bartender? Some rando at the club?"

I flash him a sweet smile, my insides boiling. "I'm sorry, but I don't think it's any of your business."

"What's his name?"

"I don't see how this applies to my job."

"You're *living* here. It *is* my business if some guy shows up wanting access to you." His sharp tone whips my face, and I shift in my seat. "Whatever sob story you sold to my wife won't work on me, so don't even try. I don't care what you've been through. Every drug addict in a tent could drop dead."

"I'm not a drug—"

"*I wasn't done talking.*"

Okay, geez. My heart pounds as Jack stares at me like I'm vermin. That alone sets the alarm bells clanging.

"I did my best to talk her out of hiring you, but she wouldn't listen. So here I am, entertaining her latest whim. Again." The bridled anger in his voice spills over, and his expression clouds. "If I kick you out, Naomi will pitch a fit, and I have no time for that. So I'll let you stay here on *one* condition. When you give birth, you and the baby are out."

I swallow, managing a whisper. "Fine."

"This situation is temporary. I don't want you to get the wrong idea and think you've landed a forever home. Naomi thought it'd be a nice gesture to help you out. I'm willing to put up with you for her sake, but we're not getting stuck with your kid. We're not babysitters."

"Right. I get it."

"We want someone young and fun who doesn't look like she crawled out of a homeless shelter." His gaze slides up and down my body, his mouth curling. "There should be something in my wife's closet that fits you. I hope. I'll have her lay out a few things for you to wear."

His words wash over me like an icy waterfall. I can't believe what I'm hearing. So much for hoping Jack is as sweet as his wife.

"You'll start at seven to cook me breakfast. I like scrambled egg whites with ham and cheddar. Or oatmeal with blueberries, homemade scones, and buckwheat waffles. I'll send you our meal schedules." He opens his phone and flicks through screens. "We're having people over in a few days, so everything will have to be cleaned. Linens. Windows. Floors. The grout in the master bathroom needs a good scrub. And we need groceries." He pulls out a credit card from his wallet and hands it to me. "This has a monthly limit, and I check the statements."

I slip it into my pocket, fuming. "I'm not a thief."

"That's the second time you've spoken out of turn."

Shit. I can't make an enemy out of Jack.

"Oh, and another thing. This is important." He points to the ceiling. "There's a room that's off-limits to you. It's on the second floor. It's the only door that's locked. Don't go in for any reason."

Why not? I'm curious by nature. Telling me not to do something is like giving an alcoholic a six-pack and telling them not to drink. What's inside? A massive shrine to a boy band? A hidden theatre of sappy romantic comedies?

"All right," he murmurs, turning around. "I'm going upstairs. Do your job, and we won't have any problems."

"Yes, sir."

He waves his hand in dismissal and disappears up the stairwell. He's unbearable. How can a person be so bossy and cold? I'm overwhelmed by the idea of working for this terrible man. This job was bound to be difficult, but I never imagined Jack would be so hostile.

I'll survive.

I have to provide for my baby, no matter how awful my boss is.

FOUR

I lay low for the rest of the day. My mind races with a million thoughts. The urge to explore the estate's grounds, poke in Jack's office, and start collecting information on his family is overwhelming. But I need to tread carefully and build a rapport with this man. One wrong move and I'm out on the streets. I can't let that happen.

So I tool around on my phone, riding a wave of frustration at the slow internet speeds. The signal is weak. Their wireless router is probably on the second floor behind a cage.

The tiny window above the sink is dark when Naomi comes home. The *click-clack* of her heels echoes through the ceiling like the scuttling of a metal spider. I'm not working today, but I can't stand much more of being shut down here. So I race upstairs and open the door to the butler's pantry.

"Grace?" calls Naomi. "Come join us!"

"Okay. I'll be right there."

I follow her voice into the kitchen. Jack stands near

the stainless espresso machine. My stomach twists as he glances in my direction. Naomi sits at the island, dressed in slacks and a blouse. She watches Jack, as moon-eyed as a teenage girl.

"Thanks, sweetie." Naomi accepts the cup he hands her. "Jack makes the best lattes. Would you like one?"

I'd love to say yes, just to stick it to him after that insulting conversation, but I shake my head.

"I would, but it's late for coffee."

"We have decaf, don't we?" She wheels toward her husband, who shrugs. "Can you make her a latte?"

Jack sighs as he grabs a cup from the shelf. "I thought you hired her to do that for *us*."

"So? She's not on the clock."

"She's an employee," he grinds out. "Not one of your girlfriends."

Naomi's eyes flash. She sets down her cup, chinking the marble. "It's coffee. Get over yourself, please."

Curses fall from Jack's mouth as he shoves his drink into the sink. He rifles through bags in the cupboard, stuffs the lever thing with grounds, and turns the machine on. A trickle of dark brown liquid spits from the spout into a ceramic mug as Naomi leans over, speaking in a stage whisper.

"Don't mind him. He's in a mood."

Jack seizes a milk carton from the fridge and slams the door closed. If that's him in a mood, I'd hate to see him when he's really upset.

My throat tightens. "No, he's right. I'll get out of your hair...I'm intruding."

"No, no, no," Naomi chimes, imprisoning me with a

hand on my wrist. "This is *your* home. We want you to be comfortable."

She might, but that's not the case for her husband. Jack pours milk into a small metal container. His brow furrowed, he foams the milk, not bothering to back his wife's comments.

"Are you finding everything okay?" she asks, her sweet voice invading my thoughts. "Jack says you kept to yourself the whole day."

"Yeah...moving always takes a lot out of me. Even if I didn't have much packing to do." I tap my fingers on the marble. "So I stayed in my room and relaxed."

"Do you need anything else?"

"No thanks."

I *almost* throw Jack under the bus, but one look at Naomi destroys that impulse. Her smile has so much light and affection. It reminds me of my mother, when she used to pick me up from school—"*So what did you learn today, Grace?*" Before she turned into a tyrant, my mother was a decent person.

Jack is more like my dad. Domineering and harsh. His movements are precise, almost robotic. He frowns in concentration, or maybe irritation. It's hard to tell. It's as if he's carved out of an icy mountain—beautiful to look at from a distance, but harsh and unwelcoming up close.

Naomi beams at Jack as he walks over. He slides a mug over the counter, barely looking at me. The rich aroma of the coffee wafts up, soothing my nerves. Maybe working for the ice man won't be so bad. After all, even the harshest winters eventually give way to spring. I just have to be patient. And smart.

I smile at him. "Thank you."

He grunts.

I clasp the mug and sip the murky liquid. A potent bitterness cuts into my tongue. *Disgusting.* It tastes like burnt rubber, but I smack my lips and pretend it's amazing.

Naomi smiles. "Good, isn't it?"

I try not to grimace. "Best latte I've ever had."

As Naomi crosses the kitchen to put her mug in the sink, Jack smirks at me. Flames eat my stomach.

Naomi plucks an apple from the bowl. "I'm a latte addict. During med school, I drank eight cups a day. *Eight.* And I was always frazzled, running around like a headless chicken. Now I'm down to six, and I feel much better. But when I'm on vacation in Italy, all bets are off. Aren't they, baby?"

Jack makes a sound as he buffs out the stainless steel espresso machine.

She rubs his arm. "How was your day, honey?"

"Not bad," he bites out, folding his rag. "Blake's driving Dad and me nuts, as usual. He's still on his environmental kick. He's obsessed with installing solar panels, wastewater recycling systems, and custom blade propellers to reduce noise pollution."

Blake. This is the first time they've mentioned him. My heart pounds as I cross the room and open the fridge, pretending to be interested in its contents. I grab a few things—a wedge of cheese, sausage, and fruit.

"Well, what's the harm in that?" asks Naomi.

"He keeps saying we're missing a chance to attract an expanding market of eco-friendly consumers," he booms as he rinses his cup. "But we're a luxury yacht cruise line, for God's sake. Our clientele doesn't give a rat's ass about saving orcas."

"I understand where you're coming from, but Blake might have a point." Naomi opens her phone, scrolling through social media. "People are becoming more environmentally conscious."

Jack scoffs. "It's stupid."

"It's marketing, and it wouldn't hurt to consider his suggestions."

"Consider them, sure. But actually implement them? That's a different story." He slams the cup on the drying rack, his voice growing louder with every syllable. "It's going to cost a fortune, and for what? A few hippies who want to feel good about themselves?"

"It's not just about appealing to a certain market," I blurt, unable to stop myself. "It's about being responsible and doing your part to protect the environment."

Jack turns to face me, seething. He says nothing for a long moment. The silence suffocates my chest. Then he speaks, his voice like a clap of thunder. "Did I ask for your opinion?"

I bow my head. "No."

"You live in my house," he bursts. "You eat my food. But you do not get to chime in on our private conversations."

My cheeks burn hotter with every lashing word. He sounds like my father.

"Jesus. She didn't mean any harm by it." Naomi socks him in the arm, and his blistering glare flicks to her. "Lighten up."

He grunts.

"She's right. You can't walk a block in Seattle without bumping into a business that gives back to something. Who knows, maybe it'll attract new customers looking for a company that cares about more than profit."

"Donating a percentage of profits isn't what he's suggesting."

"What's wrong with retrofitting a couple of boats to see what happens?"

He shakes his head. "Naomi, I love you, but you aren't running a multibillion-dollar business. It's not as simple as flipping a switch and making everything eco-friendly overnight."

"I know that," she replies calmly. "But you have to start somewhere. And with the proper research and planning, I'm sure you can make it work without breaking the bank."

"I'm finished with this discussion."

Naomi sighs as Jack storms out of the kitchen. A distant door slams, and I flinch. My heart hammers as I face Naomi.

"I'm sorry. I shouldn't have said anything."

She waves a hand. "Don't worry about it."

"But he hates me."

"Of course he doesn't. He just has the worst temper. He's like a fire-breathing dragon when he's stressed, but that has nothing to do with you."

I smile, but I can't shake the memory of the conversation in the basement. He doesn't want me here, but maybe it's only because he's an uptight jerk. He'll calm down. He's an eccentric businessman who throws tantrums like a toddler. That doesn't make him evil.

Naomi grabs my hand in her firm grip. "You're going to be just fine."

I'm not sure about that, but I nod anyway.

I'll do whatever it takes to get along with him.

FIVE

> I'm at your brother's house.

I'm dying to tell Blake about my new job, but I don't send the text. He's easily spooked. After I told him the good news several months ago, he ghosted me. He probably thinks I'll disappear if he never responds.

Unfortunately for him, I'm not going anywhere. That's why I took this position. Living here is the only way to get in contact with him. He needs to stop ignoring me if he ever wants a role in his child's life. But not right now. I can't set him off when I've just found a place, so I won't reveal that I'm his brother's live-in maid.

Though I'm not sure for how long. Judging from my accommodations, Jack hates my guts. The mattress is harder than a morgue slab. My shower doesn't work. Water comes out, but it's lukewarm. I can't figure out why. They can't be using all the hot water in the tank. Complaining to Naomi is an option, but it'll escalate the tension between me and Jack. I want to avoid that. Especially since he's taking his authority over me to another level.

YOUR UNIFORM.

I peel off the sticky note attached to a black dress and white turtleneck. I woke up to this hanging on the doorknob, along with a pair of ballet flats, at the top of the stairs. Who got me this?

Jack, I'm guessing. I lay the clothes on my bed. Apparently, I'm starring in Jack's fetish for Edwardian maids. At least the turtleneck he picked is tasteful. I put it on. It's itchy and chokes my throat. Then I pull the dress over my head. It's belted at the waist and covers my knees. The bodice is too big for my chest.

I walk in front of the bathroom mirror. *Yikes*. I look like a kid who raided their mom's closet. I put on the shoes. They fit, but the sole is nonexistent. Zero cushion. It's probably part of his plan to make me miserable. If he thinks a silly outfit is enough to drive me away, he's delusional. Then I climb the staircase, breezing into the kitchen. I bolt down yogurt and granola.

Jack walks in, wearing jogger pants and a tight gym shirt. His brown hair gleams with sweat. His bleary gaze scans the kitchen. Instead of a greeting, he barks, "Where's my breakfast?"

His air of entitlement razes a hot line down my spine. I've met plenty of his type in Seattle. Tech bros loved the coffee shop where I worked before my restaurant gig. They'd order one cappuccino, take out their laptops, and work the whole day. They think purchasing a single five-dollar coffee entitles them to sit at a table for hours. I'd love to give him a piece of my mind. Instead I plaster on a smile and use my brightest voice.

"Coming right up."

"I thought I told you to have it ready by seven."

"It's six-thirty," I say.

He grunts a response, shuffling to the espresso machine.

I grab a carton of eggs and scramble three egg whites with chunks of ham, spinach, and onion. When it's cooked, I dump it all onto a plate. I slide it over the marble, along with a fork. He takes it without thanking me. Or looking at me. What is *wrong* with this guy?

"Is Naomi eating with us?"

"No. She's out on her run," he says tonelessly, stabbing bits of egg. "She'll expect you to be working when she comes back."

"Okay. Will do."

"Today will be very busy. You'll have to clean the entire house. Top to bottom. We're having my brother over for dinner."

I inhale a quick breath. "When?"

"Thursday."

Two days. *Perfect*. That gives me enough time to prepare for what I'll say to him once we're face to face. My heart pounds in an erratic rhythm. "How many people total?"

"Four," he answers. "We'll need appetizers. Sliced meat. A cheeseboard. Whatever. And something for the main course. I'm thinking filet mignon medallions. Can you do that?"

"Yes."

"Also, the grout in my bathroom is filthy. I need it scrubbed."

"No problem."

Jack skewers me with a glare. "Supplies are in the closet."

I zip from his side and open the closet door, grabbing them. I start in their kitchen, which is a mess. Biting my lip, I wipe the counters and sweep the floors. Cleaning the place doesn't worry me, but I'm not sure I can pull off a fancy dinner.

I watch cooking videos as I finish wiping every surface. It takes forever. Naomi comes back from her jog, her forehead slicked with sweat, and takes a shower. Then she leaves in a whisk of designer silks. Hours later, I finally reach the second floor. As I enter their bedroom, I come across a framed photo of Jack and Blake standing on a yacht next to their father. Even their smiles look tense. I snap a picture of it and set the frame down.

The front door opens and closes. Naomi's singsong voice echoes as she returns from brunch. While I'm scrubbing the sink, Naomi's pumps click the floor.

"Great job so far. Everything looks—" She pauses in the middle of unpinning her earrings, gaping at me. "What are you wearing? Is that my dress?"

I meet her anxious gaze, taken aback. "No idea. I found it on my doorknob with a note saying it was my uniform. I figured you or Jack picked it out for me."

"Oh, Jack," she laments, rubbing her forehead. "Jack, Jack, *Jack*. Those shoes don't even fit."

"They're a bit big."

"And you've been working in them all day." She tuts, dropping her earrings in a jewelry case. "I'll order something for you."

"No, that's okay."

"Don't be silly. I can't have you walking around our home looking like *that*. I'll get your measurements and have your uniform delivered immediately." Naomi lets loose another frustrated sigh as she stares into the mirror, primping her hair. "My husband can be such a rebel."

I laugh awkwardly.

"Have you had your lunch?"

"Um—not yet."

Naomi flicks her wrist. "But it's eleven."

"I know, but I'm not hungry."

"You've been working for five hours. You have to take your scheduled breaks. Your baby needs nutrients. Come, I'll fix you a smoothie."

I wave her off, flustered.

"Don't be shy. You need to eat."

She's right, so I let her pull me downstairs and into the kitchen. She throws powders and vegetables into a giant blender. Once it's all blended, sharp regret hits my chest. It looks disgusting. She pours the green goop into a tall glass. *Please don't make me vomit.*

I chew on my lip. "So what's in it?"

"Bee pollen. Flax seeds. Protein powder. Kale. Some banana." She gives it a stir and slides it in front of me, staring at me.

It smells terrible. I force a smile. "Thank you so much."

"You're welcome."

I sip it, just to be polite. It tastes as appetizing as it appears, but I pretend to love it. God, it's awful.

"Wow," I say, swallowing it down. "It's very fresh."

"I'm glad you like it. Superfoods are so important for us. It's astounding how off dietitians are when they recommend meals for pregnant women. It's all carbs, carbs, *carbs*. The baby needs protein and fat. That's what you'll eat from now on." She powers on, not giving me a chance to comment. "I've stocked the fridge with healthy snacks. Cottage cheese. Greek yogurt. Salmon burgers."

"That's so thoughtful of you. Thanks."

"Of course. You're working for me. I want to make sure you're healthy."

I'm touched that she cares. It's sweet. I drink more of the smoothie, and her expression softens. "Thank you for this, but I should get to work."

"All in good time. Finish your smoothie."

Her concern is so refreshing that I obey her without complaint. I choke down as much as I can. She went through all that trouble just to accommodate me. It's the least I can do.

When the glass is finally empty, Naomi gives me a quick hug before disappearing. Then I return to the master bathroom. I fill a bucket with hot water and scrub the tiles. It's difficult. My knees ache. The grout is so filthy, I change the water in the bucket five times. After fifteen minutes, I take a break, dizzy from the fumes. Approaching footsteps make me rub the bristles over the floor with renewed vigor.

Jack storms into the bedroom, opening and slamming drawers I've polished with wood cleaner. Scowling, he enters the bathroom, holding a shirt and jeans. "What are you doing? The floor is soaked."

I pause, my back bowing with fatigue. "Scrubbing."

"You're still not done?"

"You just asked me to do this."

"Well, hurry up. I need a shower, and I have guests coming over later. And what's that *smell*?" Jack inhales, his nostrils flaring into wings. "Is that bleach?"

I glance at the bottle. It's clear aside from the word etched onto the plastic—*tiles*. "You told me to use whatever I needed."

He raises his eyebrows. "That's not what I meant at all."

I gape at him. "I shouldn't use the bottle marked 'tiles'?"

"It was empty. You were *supposed* to fill it with an organic solution. Instead you cheap out and use bleach."

A ripple of anger runs through me. "What are you talking about? I didn't *fill* anything. I picked it out of the closet."

He rolls his eyes, crossing his arms.

Heat steals into my face. "Seriously. I didn't do that!"

His jaw clenches. "You did."

"I'd remember if I bought a bunch of supplies."

"You did. Yesterday, you drove to the store and bought some with my card." He pulls out his phone and taps on the screen. "See? Here's a twenty-five-dollar charge at Target."

He shows me the screen, which confirms the purchase. Except I didn't set foot into Target, which means *he* bought those items.

I hate this man. "I never left the property."

"Yes, you did. You headed out at around two."

"No. I was downstairs all day!"

Jack lets out a sigh. "A woman in your position should be exceptionally grateful for the opportunity you've been given, but you're already lying and cutting corners. I have to say, I'm disappointed."

I throw the brush in the bucket. "I didn't go to Target."

"It says *right here* that you did."

I snort. "It says that *someone* made a purchase."

"Are you accusing me of something?"

I hold up my hands. "I'm just saying, I'm not the only person with the ability to buy things on that card."

"You went to Target yesterday." He shuts off his phone, stony-faced, and shoves it into his pocket. "Lying only makes things worse for yourself. I don't appreciate it."

I'm not winning this battle. As long as I have the card, he'll use it to blame me for all kinds of frivolous purchases. How could I defend myself? What would I say to Naomi? That her husband went to Target and filled bottles with cleaning solutions that she hates to get me fired? Even to me, that sounds nuts.

I grit my teeth. "Then what do you want me to use?"

"I could do without the tone, and I shouldn't have to instruct you how to clean," he says, sounding so reasonable that I feel insane. "Nor should I have to keep reminding you not to talk back."

I swallow the rage building in my chest. He's trying

THE MAID

to get a rise out of me, and it's working. "Right. I'll remember that for the next time you sabotage—"

"What's going on?" asks a sharp voice, the bedroom door flying open to reveal a frazzled Naomi. She throws up her arm as though to shield herself. "Oh my God. That smell."

"The maid used bleach in the bathroom," Jack mutters.

Naomi pinches her nose shut. "Are you sure?"

"Yeah," he sighs, shrugging. "I saw a purchase on my credit card."

Naomi slaps the switch for the fan and faces me, frowning. "Why would you do that? I told you this household is organic products only."

I didn't. Your jerk husband set me up. Unfortunately, I can't tell her that. It'll start a whole he said/she said debate that I won't win. So I bow my head and murmur an apology to the floor.

"Sorry. I must've forgotten."

"You're not supposed to use bleach on marble. Surely you knew that? Bleach is a powerful chemical. It's damaging to tiles. Look at this." Naomi points to a wet spot near the toilet. "You can't let it sit in puddles like that."

"I wasn't—"

"This marble is from Spain. It's very expensive. You'll have to mop that up."

"I will. Right away."

Naomi glances at her husband. "Can you do it? She shouldn't be breathing in these fumes. It can't be good for the baby."

Jack glowers at her. "You want *me* to clean up her mess?"

"No, I'll do it. It's my job." I grab a towel and soak up the puddle.

Naomi hesitates, halfway out the door. "Are you sure?"

"Yes. Let me fix it."

Naomi sighs, her disappointment replaced by resignation. "Thank you. You did a great job cleaning the rest of the house, though. It looks amazing."

Jack's stinging criticism blasts the warmth of Naomi's praise. "If that marble gets bleach stains, it'll need to be repaired. And I'm taking that out of your paycheck."

Naomi bristles. "Jack."

"What?" he snaps, his head jerking toward her. "I'm not allowed to hold her to a high standard because she's pregnant?"

Naomi grabs Jack by the elbow and drags him out of sight, hissing in a low voice. "Stop acting like a jerk. You're embarrassing me."

"Questioning her judgment is acting like a jerk?"

"She made an honest mistake."

He laughs. "Pretty big one for a professional."

"I know what you're doing," she hisses. "I will not let you scare off another maid."

A bead of sweat rolls down my cheek.

Jack leaves the bedroom, slamming the door. He'll get me fired. He'll plant evidence to prove I'm incompetent at my job, and if that doesn't work, he'll accuse me of stealing. It'll escalate until I end up like...the other maid. Whatever that means.

A chill spider-crawls my spine as I wipe the floors.

Naomi returns to the bathroom, pink patches high on her cheeks. "Are you okay?"

"I'm a little mortified, but I'll live."

Her brow furrows. "I'm so sorry about Jack. He can be...temperamental."

"That's fine."

"No, it's not. His whole family is...well, they don't exist in the same world as us." Naomi reaches into her purse, handing me a few bills. "For your trouble."

"Thank you."

I take the small roll of cash, queasy. She knows her husband is abusive to staff. He's already run off one maid. Why? What did he do to her?

And will it happen to me, too?

SIX

Jack is out to get me.

During the next two days, I keep my head down. I don't touch the locked door on the second floor, though I'm dying to know what's inside. I memorize everything's location and adjust to my new job, taking care of everything from dusting the bookshelves to sweeping the porch. Every night I go to bed exhausted but satisfied.

Jack doesn't make it easy. He constantly reminds me of the items on my to-do list and berates me if they're not done perfectly. Yesterday, I washed the windows three times before he was satisfied. It took the whole day. I try to entertain myself at night, but the Wi-Fi guest network is inconsistent. It seems to work better in the early mornings. I entertain myself by writing nasty notes to Jack he'll never read and fantasize about pouring laxatives in his drinks.

My back aches from lugging a garbage bag filled with pine cones. Jack demanded I remove them from the lawn. I've stuffed four giant bags already under his watchful eye. He stands behind the wall-to-wall glass, sipping his coffee. He's always there. *Watching*. Even if he's in a business meeting. He'll stick earbuds in, stroll his house like a lord in his manor, and glare at the peasants sharing his oxygen.

Panting, I lug the bag across the lawn. A hole rips in the plastic. Before I can stop the damage, it tears, and a mountain of pine cones spills over my shoes. *Great*. I kick the pile and let loose a volley of swear words. Jack must be having a good laugh. I look for him, dangerously close to flipping him the bird, but he's vanished.

The distant hum of a power tool switches off. A bearded man in his sixties jogs over, wearing a plaid jacket and a Huskies beanie. His bewildered stare slips down my dress, my muddy galoshes, and my aching, red hands.

"Hi. I'm Alex. I'm the Hamiltons' handyman. What are you doing out here?"

"I'm Grace. I-I'm the new maid," I say, my teeth chattering. "Jack wants the yard cleared of pine cones."

His gaze darkens. "He asked you to do that?"

"Yes, and I'm doing my best, but it's a huge job." I clutch a stitch in my side, breathing deeply. "Filling four bags took me hours."

"I'll take over from here." Alex takes the bag and dumps everything on the grass. "These aren't the right bags for disposing of organic material."

I wipe my face. "Of course not."

"It's not your fault," he says, patting my back. "Jack is a character. He gets off on making our lives miserable. It's his calling in life."

I stick my freezing hands under my arms, blowing a puff of cold air. "Have you worked here long?"

"Yes," he sighs, resigned. "I did some handyman work for the former owners. Gardening, mostly, but also repairing the siding. Whoever built the house didn't install the flashing correctly, so it's prone to rot. I've mentioned it to Jack several times."

"Do they have any other staff?"

"No idea. I've never been inside." After he finishes filling the organic bag, he ties a knot and tosses it over his shoulder. "Not even to use the bathroom. I asked once. Jack didn't answer. He gave me a *look*. Like, 'how dare you?' I almost told him to eff off—pardon my French."

"I've seen that side of him."

"I bet."

I open the gate to their trash bins as Alex mumbles a thank-you. He groans, dumping the bag in the bin. He dusts his hands on his jeans before running them through his silvery hair.

"Do you remember the last maid?"

Sighing, he glances in the house's direction. "Oh yeah. Sure."

What happened? Was she fired? Did she die? I wait for him to elaborate, but he doesn't, and I bite my lip. Jack probably dismissed her for something stupid. Grilling him is pushing my luck.

"Anyway," he mutters, closed off. "You should get inside. It's freezing."

"If Jack sees you doing my job, he'll complain."

"I'll take the fall. Just go."

He wants me out of his hair. I'm too cold to argue. I

drag my feet into the house. Then I descend into the chilly basement. I pull a thick sweater over my uniform, and I'm still shivering. I turn on the space heater to maximum heat. It's almost noon. I have to prep for the party.

I peel myself off the bed and grab the new clothes Naomi bought me. I fling them over the table, along with an iron. As I'm filling it with water, my phone rings. Janice's name flashes across the screen. I answer the call.

"Hey, you."

"I've missed you," Janice exclaims. "How are you?"

"It's been a bit of a rollercoaster, to be honest. Living at the Hamiltons' isn't as great as I thought it'd be."

"Oh, no! Why? What's happened?"

I open and close my mouth, glancing around my depressing accommodations. I can't give her too many details. Jack made me sign an NDA. "Well, let's just say, Jack Hamilton is about as warm and fuzzy as a cactus in a snowstorm. He's got me running around picking up pine cones in the yard, of all things."

Janice laughs. "So he's turned you into Cinderella?"

"Just without the fancy ball and the glass slippers...or any slippers, for that matter. I'm stuck in ugly ballet flats."

"Don't worry. Just remember, every cactus has its bloom. Maybe Jack's is...well hidden."

"If it's hidden, it's buried deeper than Jimmy Hoffa. But thanks for the optimism."

"Have you made any progress with Blake?"

"No, but I'm seeing him soon. He's coming over for

dinner tonight." I chuckle, picturing his shock when he sees me at his brother's home. "I'll talk to him then."

She exhales a disapproving sigh. "He'll *kill* you."

I put the phone on speaker, scoffing.

"I'm serious. You'll be lucky if you walk out of that door in handcuffs."

I spread my blouse over the coffee table. "You're ridiculous."

"You seriously don't think there's anything wrong with what you're doing?"

"Not really, no. He got me pregnant." Steam hisses from the iron as I smooth out wrinkles from the fabric. "It's not like I'm *obsessed* with him. Sure, I've done my research on his family, but shouldn't I? We're having a baby together."

"By research, you mean spying on his brother and sister-in-law."

"I *applied* for a *job*. I'm not planning to steal, maim, or hurt. I just want to talk to Blake."

"And how do you imagine that will go?" she asks, her voice laden with sarcasm. "Do you think he'll thank you for bringing your pregnancy to his attention? Or will he freak out, call the police, and have you arrested for stalking?"

"I'm a maid, not a stalker."

"You applied to that job under false pretenses."

"Not true. I do need the money." I finish ironing the crisp white shirt and hang it, starting on the skinny black pants. "If he doesn't like it, he should've answered my calls. It's his fault."

"For God's sake. You can't keep blaming him for everything."

"Yes, I can. Blake is responsible for what happened to me." A twinge of pain digs into my chest as I replay my mother's condemnation of my soul before she kicked me out. "I shouldn't hold him accountable for what he did?"

"Sure, but the way you're doing it is creepy."

I bristle, glaring at the phone. "Why can't I scare him into behaving like a decent human being?"

"It won't work. He's not decent."

I shake my head. "Yes, he is."

She laughs. "He was trying to sleep with you. I'm sure he was the perfect gentleman. But this is different. You're coming after his wallet. He won't behave like your Prince Charming when you show up in his brother's house. I promise you."

My face screws up. I'm glad she can't see how little I care about her opinion. "Stalking" someone's relatives isn't crazy. The real insanity is how men get away with horrible situations *they've* caused.

"Blake's not an idiot. He knows he's done wrong. He just needs to be whacked on the nose with a rolled-up newspaper."

"He's ignoring you, babe. That should give you a clue to his intentions."

My chest tightens. "Once his family finds out, they'll convince him to act."

"No, what they'll do is pressure *you* into having an abortion. And when that doesn't work, they'll get him to sue for full custody. No offense, but they won't want a maid to co-parent their newest family member."

"What would you have me do? Where the hell am I supposed to go? I can't wait five months for him to sort himself out. I need help *now*."

"I understand. I do, but this is not the way to do it."

Janice launches into an eye-rolling speech about boundaries, consent, and how I'm playing with fire by messing with a powerful family. Blah, blah, *blah*. She can't fathom what I'm going through. I am protecting my unborn child. The Hamiltons don't scare me. What could they possibly do? I have nothing to lose.

"You're in too deep," Janice says. "You're doing it again. You overthink and build these fantasies, but real life doesn't play out like the scenes in your head. Just promise me you won't do anything rash—"

"I gotta go. Busy afternoon."

I disconnect, cutting her off. Then I pull on my freshly pressed uniform. The tight pants stretch, which is great because I'll need maternity clothes soon. I wear them under a pinstriped apron and a white long-sleeved blouse paired with a red tie. Naomi even got me comfortable black shoes. I slip my feet into them and pose in the bathroom's tiny mirror. I look good. I have that pregnant glow everyone talks about.

Sparks will fly. A baby isn't the greatest start to any relationship, but we had a connection, didn't we? I felt it while I lay in that hotel bed, wrapped in his arms. He whispered things in my hair. Things I can't forget, like, *I can be myself around you.*

Nerves flutter in my belly.

I can't wait to see him. The look on his face when he sees me in Jack's foyer, dressed in this ridiculous outfit, will be priceless. He'll be stunned. He'll *have* to take me seriously. It'll open a line of communication between us that will end with him whisking me away from this place. A prideful man like Blake won't be able to stand the mother of his child slaving after his brother.

He'll save me. I know he will.

SEVEN

"Grace, answer the door!" Jack's shout echoes from the family room.

I could scream. This is his third demand since I've started cooking. I turn up the fan so it drowns out his voice. Then I stir the port wine reduction that's for the steaks.

My wooden spoon clatters on the counter as I rip open the oven door. I pull out the baking tray with the sizzling filet mignon log. Grabbing the temperature fork, I stab it deep inside. According to the dial, it's so rare, it's practically mooing. How is that possible?

I shove it back in the oven, setting the timer for another twenty minutes, and then I stand in a daze. Steam rises from the multiple bubbling pots. I seize the pan of risotto, whisking it, cursing when it sticks. Damn. Why is this so difficult? It's just rice. I add more chicken stock, but that doesn't quite work. The rice is sticking. My steaks aren't done. This dinner will be a colossal failure, which sinks a heavy weight in my heart. I have to do a good job. I want to impress them. My position might as well be an audition to join his family, and I'm desperate to belong somewhere.

A hand rolls over my shoulder, squeezing hard.

I jump and whirl around.

Naomi stands behind me, beautiful in a long dress with a flared skirt. I helped her into it earlier, tying the intricate lace-up bodice over the embroidered corset. My favorite part was going through her jewelry to pick out the right accessories. She has so many wonderful things.

Naomi grins. "Oops. I think I startled you."

I realize I'm wielding the tongs like a weapon. I put them on the stove, pulse hammering.

"Is...everything okay?"

My throat tightens as I meet Naomi's anxious gaze. "I'll be fine. I mean, it's fine. The filet is taking longer than I expected. And I'll have to serve the scallops as soon as they're done. They'll get cold."

"Great. My in-laws should be here any minute."

I press my lips together, nodding.

"It's too bad you can't drink. You look like you could use a cocktail." She sips from the glass of white clutched in her bony fingers. "You worry too much."

"I don't know if it's seasoned properly."

She takes a spoon, dips it into the risotto, and slides it into her mouth. She stills. Softly, she exclaims, "My God. It's delicious."

She sets the spoon aside and grabs my hands. Then she looks at me. I want to glance away, but her liquid brown eyes drag me in, raising gooseflesh all over my arms. She's intense. Overwhelming, but in a *good* way, like an adrenaline rush from bungee jumping.

Her stare dives into me. "I appreciate you doing this. We won't ask you to cook like this too often. It's a lot of work."

"I don't mind. I'm just worried I messed it up."

"Don't worry. This will be the best dinner ever."

I smile. "Why's that?"

"Because you and I are deciding, right now, that it will be the best dinner ever. And if we do that, it doesn't matter what happens. Okay?"

I nod.

She pats my head, as though she's a goddess bestowing eternal wisdom. Then she giggles. She lets me go, laughing hard, and then it clicks.

So which drugs are you on, Naomi? Ketamine? LSD? I was hoping for a more dramatic reveal, some secret madness hidden under the thick paste of matte foundation. There's hope. Maybe I'll stumble upon a loose floorboard and find a dead body.

Jack walks by, glowering. "Am I paying you to stand there?"

Naomi scolds him, but then the doorbell chimes again. I turn to the stove, grabbing the tongs. One by one, I drop the scallops into the bubbling oil.

The door opens. Naomi's gasp fills the kitchen. "Look at you. Hello. It's been so long."

Heavy footsteps glide over the floor. Then a voice filters through, deep and smooth. The same one that whispered in my ear. It's *him*. He'll walk in here and recognize me. Any minute now. Then what? What's my plan?

I flip the scallops, the sear close to black. *Shoot.* These cook fast. I put a new bunch in the pan, listening to Naomi and Blake exchange kisses. They're warmer people than I imagined.

"What have you been up to?" she asks.

Blake's soft laugh tinkles into the kitchen. "Well, I hit the slopes the other weekend. Tried to do a back-lift, but I couldn't. Too much ice. A helmet wouldn't have saved me if I fell on that."

"How were the slopes?"

"Oh. Total shit show. Remember last year? How crowded it was? It's the same, only understaffed and dirty. It was fun, but I think I'll visit Crystal Mountain next time. We might go next week. You should come with us."

My stomach clenches as a breathy voice invades the room. Instantly, I loathe her. The hate is swift and hot, consuming me in a flash. She has this babyish whisper, and it grates on me.

I try to peek at the voice's owner, but I'm in the middle of plating my scallops. A generous helping of risotto. Two extra-crispy scallops for each plate. As I grate the parmesan, I try to follow their conversation, but the echo from Jack's harsh baritone crashes into their hushed murmurs, making it impossible. I recognize Blake whenever he speaks, though. That velvety purr. Tingles skate across my skin.

"Ashley, what do you want to drink?" Naomi's heels click-clack as she enters the family room, followed by a slender woman. "We have wine. Hard seltzer. Cocktails."

"Rosé?"

"Yes. Jack, can you—?"

Naomi beckons her to the bar cart, grasping the biggest wine glass I've ever seen. Jack pops the cork and pours. The bottle glugs out pink liquid. Then the girls clink their pint-sized glasses together.

My risotto is ready, so I slide bowls over the mats. Everybody takes their seats, chatting. Blake still hasn't caught on and I haven't dared to attract his attention. He looks incredible. A plain black button-up hugs his long torso, the ends tucked into dark blue denim. His jeans hang low on his waist. A layer of stubble clings to his powerful jaw, deepening the cleft in his chin. Thick eyebrows slant over blue eyes. Everything about Blake appeals to me, from his muscular body to the hollows in his cheeks, to the musical way he says *Grace*.

I hand him a plate. "Here you go."

He murmurs a thank-you without looking at me. Then I serve the girl sitting on his left.

"These scallops are *just* delicious." Naomi makes an appreciative sound, and the others—except Jack—follow suit with bobbing heads.

I beam at her. "Thank you."

The risotto came from a box. If Naomi got wind how much sodium was in this meal, she'd have a fit.

"Amazing," Ashley whispers, her pupils blown as she flashes me a vacant smile. "You're so talented."

Blake stiffens, slowly putting down his fork. Our gazes clash. My breathing hitches as he squeezes his eyes shut. Opens them. My skin tingles as he gapes at me, his surprise transforming into something dark. What did *I* do? I'm the one who should be mad. I have the raw end of the deal.

Maybe it's not about that. Perhaps he's annoyed because I'm in this girl's presence. Who is she, anyway? My mind does a quick inventory—pretty, tall, fake boobs, impeccably dressed, *a diamond ring*. A sudden chill envelops my stomach.

He's engaged.

EIGHT

My heart plummets through the floor and keeps falling. Did he get engaged while I hounded him to call me back? Or did he cheat on her with me? Both possibilities pit my stomach with dread. It's probably the latter. Blake wouldn't get engaged with a baby on the way. At least, not before I gave birth.

I'll kill him. The bastard had a million chances to bring up that he had a fiancée, but he didn't. Instead he dragged me to that hotel room. Didn't even consider how I'd feel about the situation. Then he ghosted me. I'm pregnant and homeless because of this worthless jerk.

My heart plummets through the floor and keeps falling. It takes strength not to throw the wine on Blake's head, but I spin around and go back to the kitchen.

A timer beeps.

I yank the filet mignon out of the oven and carve the steaks. Somehow, they're perfect. I drown his meal in the wine reduction sauce. I give him three less asparagus than everyone else. He's served last, and I practically drop the plate in front of him.

Choke on it.

I expect his eyes to light up with a plea for silence, but he smiles faintly. It's like he's daring me to pick a fight. He plucks his glass and holds it out.

"Could I have a refill?"

You can have my fist down your throat. I smile, wrenching the glass out of his grip. I pour water from the pitcher, wishing I could add a few gobs of spit.

"This is delicious," Naomi gushes as the others—except Jack—murmur agreement. "And I love the salad."

I put down Blake's drink so hard, water splashes onto his lap. I pretend not to notice, hitching on a big, fake grin. "I'm so glad you're enjoying it."

"What's in the dressing?" she asks.

"No idea. I bought it at the store."

"Oh. I thought it was homemade." Naomi bumps Jack's elbow, and he raises his head. "Aren't the scallops incredible?"

"Mine are burnt," he grunts.

That's on purpose. I shrug, feeling Blake's sharp gaze on me. He must be wondering what the hell I'm doing here, but he's showing remarkable restraint. "It was my first time cooking scallops. There are bound to be casualties."

Everyone smiles except for Jack, who frowns, poking at his meal. "The risotto is more like pudding."

Naomi rolls her eyes. "Jesus. Tell us how you really feel."

"Leave the girl alone." Blake cuts into a scallop and pops it into his mouth, catching my eye. "Everything is great."

Now I'm *the girl*? He's calm for someone who stumbled on a hookup at his brother's house. Isn't he worried I'll break up his engagement? I don't know what game he's playing.

I hold up a bottle of wine. "Would anyone like more?"

Blake's fiancée nods. As I stroll to her side, Blake digs into his food.

"That's a beautiful ring," I say as I pour wine.

She smiles. "Thank you."

"How long have you been together?"

She glances at Blake. "A few years, right, babe?"

He nods tightly.

I'm pushing my luck by engaging in conversation, but I'm in a reckless mood. "So when are you getting married?"

"June."

My chest blazes. "How nice."

"Yeah. It'll be modest. We booked Canlis for dinner. Then we're going on his father's yacht for drinks."

"Sounds incredible." I pull back the bottle before her glass overflows. I shouldn't be mad at her. I'm not. *He's* the jerk who knocked me up.

"What kinds of flowers are you going for?" asks Naomi.

"It'll be all roses, mostly white, but with a few shades of pink, too. We just visited a florist, and I love the

RACHEL HARGROVE

bouquets they're putting together. And we'll have a great band at the reception, some of our favorite songs in a jazz arrangement."

My heart breaks. This woman is so excited about her wedding. She adores Blake, and here I am, about to wreck everything with my pregnancy.

I glare at him. "Would you like more wine?"

Blake stares back, a challenge lighting up his gaze. "No, thank you."

"Are you sure? The bottle's almost..." I frown, trailing off as I pretend to unearth his identity. "Hang on. I *know* you."

"You do?"

"Yes, we've met before. Plenty of times. You were a regular at my old job. Canon."

His indulgent smile widens. "Right. That place. Every Thursday, me and my friends used to hit it. It's a cocktail bar in Capitol Hill."

"We loved it whenever Blake came in. Friendly. Not demanding. Always leaves with a high bill and a good tip. My manager would waive the corkage fee because he brought in so much business. Once, he showed up with a bachelor party and ordered two bottles of champagne. Top shelf, of course." I chuckle, my throat dry. "Oh man, that night was crazy. You guys got lit."

Jack leans forward, a sharklike gleam in his eyes as he addresses Blake. "I haven't seen you get drunk since college."

"He was a hoot," I say, embellishing the fake story. "He sang along to some oldies with the bartender. Even paid one of the waitress's medical bills. What a great guy."

Ashley frowns. "You did?"

Blake shrugs.

"Then you disappeared," I deadpan, smiling so hard my teeth ache. "And she's been wondering where you've been. Why you stopped coming to the restaurant. She wants to *thank* you."

Blake's mouth twitches. He says nothing, his stare drilling into me. "If I could send a message to her, I'd tell her I had a moment of weakness, and to not expect to see me again."

Jack's eyebrows shoot up. He exchanges a look with his wife, who drains her glass. Jack gapes at his brother as a brittle silence chokes the air. Then Naomi pipes up, shattering it. "More wine? I have a Chardonnay we could try, or perhaps a Pinot? Jack, be a dear and open the Pinot. It needs to breathe."

I take that as my cue to go. Throwing Blake one last withering glare, I retreat to the kitchen and start cleaning up. Once the pots are washed, I heat my cold dinner in the microwave. I chill for a few minutes, taking a few bites, before returning to the dining room to clear the table. I go back and forth, collecting plates and utensils, then I serve dessert. I feel Blake's eyes on me but don't look at him.

Back in the kitchen, my mood circles the drain. Once I collect their plates, I'll run the dishwasher and go to my room. I can't wait for them to finish. Today has been so disappointing. Naomi's drug problem is hardly shocking, but Blake is a cheating scumbag?

Once I'm in bed, a text blazes across the screen.

UNKNOWN

It's Blake.

We need to talk.

NINE

I ignore Blake's text.

I put him on Read and spend the rest of the evening curled up on my couch. Every time my phone chimes, I smile. The next morning, I wake to a barrage of demanding texts. It's unbecoming of such a powerful man. I carry on ignoring Blake as I clean his brother's house, who still has no idea who I am.

Jack's side of the bathroom is a disaster. Beard trimmings sprinkle the sink. Standing puddles. Blotches of shaving cream. Hardened toothpaste. Judging from his appearance, you'd never know he was such a slob. Jack routinely leaves the shower looking like a child had a water fight. What's wrong with these people?

I shake my head, mopping up his mess. My elbow hits a drawer left ajar, which rattles with a suspicious sound. I glance inside at the orange-tinted bottles. A thrill touches the base of my spine. Pills. I open the drawer, taking stock of the mismatched pills prescribed to Naomi

Hamilton: Lexapro. Wellbutrin. Vitamin D. Ativan. She probably keeps the hard drugs somewhere else.

I shut the drawer, deflated. My phone beeps, signaling my lunch break. Naomi scolds me when I work through my breaks, so I set a timer every day. I shuffle into the kitchen, where a puffy-eyed Naomi prepares a smoothie. She's not her normal, put-together self. A matching sweatshirt and pants dwarf her thin frame. Faint black smudges line her eyes.

"Hangover cure," she says with a rueful grin, patting her stomach. "Mixed with a little extra something. Would you like one?"

I wouldn't, but after last night's performance, I should do whatever she wants. I smile and nod. Beaming, Naomi grabs the blender and pours the green slop into a glass. I sip it and shudder. They keep getting worse.

"What's the secret ingredient?" I ask.

"Celery juice."

Gross. "Well, thank you."

Naomi clinks her nails on her glass, watching me instead of drinking her juice. "Dinner last night was wonderful. Blake and Ashley were so impressed. Where did you learn to cook like that?"

I shrug. "YouTube."

"I didn't realize you knew Blake."

My abdomen tightens. I slide onto a stool, gripping the glass. "I wouldn't say I *know* him. Quite the opposite." I drink the vile smoothie, trying not to gag. "He and I have crossed paths, but it's not like we're friends."

My answer seems to satisfy Naomi, and she sips her juice in silence.

I clear my throat. "He's a very interesting guy."

Naomi laughs. "That man is an enigma wrapped in a riddle. I never know what he's thinking. He's been ambitious since he and Jack were young. Sibling rivalry, I guess, but he has this strange...intense drive that allows him to focus on something endlessly. He's charming when he wants to be, like his father."

"Jack Sr.?"

Naomi nods slowly. "Blake isn't like he appears on the surface. Everyone sees him as this gentleman who always makes the right decisions, but there's much more beneath that polished exterior. He's a complicated person. He can be fiercely loyal, but distant and guarded with personal matters. Especially ones involving his feelings. He has an almost obsessive need for control over his life. He needs to be the best, just like Jack. He has a fear of failure and disappointment that often pushes him farther than he should go."

I lean forward, drinking in every word. "What does he want?"

Naomi smiles sadly. "I think his biggest motivation is proving himself to his dad. He's been trying to do that since he was a kid. I'm not sure he'll ever stop." She finishes her smoothie and sets down the glass.

Perfection is a heavy burden. He's had years of practice honing this façade. A pregnancy from a one-night stand is a hole in Blake's perfect image, made worse because I don't fit the trophy wife mold. But if he wanted that...why cheat on Ashley? Maybe he was on the verge of burnout and I was stress relief.

I swallow hard, breathless with rage. My pocket

vibrates with a call from Blake, but I'm as eager to talk to him as I am to drink another green smoothie. I take it out and glare at the screen. I mute the call and slam the phone on the counter, facedown.

"Sorry. My baby's father is blowing up my phone."

Her brows arch. "Shouldn't you see what he wants?"

I shrug, annoyed.

Janice was right. I built him up in my head. I cast him into a fantasy with a heroic role he'll never fulfill. In reality, he's a cheating coward who is only messaging me so that I don't wreck his flawless life.

Naomi shifts in her seat. "You don't have to answer him. You owe him nothing."

"I do want him involved." I play with my phone, spinning it in circles. "I'm just mad at him."

"Understandable. He hasn't been there for you." An uncharacteristic edge creeps into Naomi's voice. "You're doing this on your own, and you deserve more. He needs to understand that he can't walk in and out of your life as he pleases."

I sigh, resting my chin on my hand. "Yeah, I know. But it's hard to shake the feelings I have for him."

Naomi rubs my back. "Give yourself time. It's okay to be angry and hurt, but you'll see that you're better off without someone who only cares about himself."

As I finish my smoothie, I consider Naomi's words. Maybe I should let go of my expectations. I need to focus on myself and my baby.

Blake's texts continue to come in, but I feel stronger. I pick up the phone and unlock it, taking one last deep breath before responding to his last text.

BABY DADDY
Don't do anything rash.

Like what? Tell your fiancée the truth?

Would that be inconvenient for you?

BABY DADDY
Let's meet somewhere and talk.

Perhaps.

BABY DADDY
What does that mean?

I'm not sure I want to see you.

Plus, I'm busy. Your brother has me working round the clock.

I send him a picture of a framed photo in Jack's bedroom that I took earlier of Blake and Jack as teenagers.

BABY DADDY
Why are you working at my brother's house?

This doesn't have to escalate any further.

I'll let you know what I decide.

I put the phone away. "There. Done."

Naomi's lips whiten. "Did you find out what he wanted?"

"It's more like I'm discovering who he is. A coward. Someone who won't be there to welcome his child into the world."

"Men aren't wired the same way we are. A woman becomes a mother when she's pregnant, but a man doesn't become a father until he holds his baby for the first time."

"So he'll be useless until the baby comes?" I seethe.

Naomi shrugs. Her gaze flicks to my baby bump, her expression souring. "Decent men are hard to come by these days."

My throat tightens, her bitterness like a noose around my neck. I mumble an excuse and head downstairs, smoothie in hand. Tension loosens from my shoulders when I enter the basement without running into Jack. I haven't seen him since this morning.

I bolt to the bathroom, toss the rest of my drink down the toilet, and grab my phone. Blake needs to face the truth. My hands shake as I type out a message to him.

> Let's meet tomorrow at noon.

BABY DADDY
> Fine. Where?

> I'll text you the address.

I set the phone down, my heart racing. This will change everything. Tomorrow will reveal what kind of man Blake is—a good one, or something else entirely. The only certain thing is that I'll have an answer. I just have to be brave and accept it...or strong enough to protect the baby and me if there's another reason he doesn't want me. The Hamiltons are full of lies and deceit. I refuse to be his dirty secret. The only risk is what he'll do to silence me.

TEN

I exit my car, strolling over dark asphalt, passing well-maintained luxury vehicles, many with personalized license plates. Bellevue's upscale mall is an imposing building, made of gleaming glass and polished marble. People hurry to and from cars. It's gray and gloomy outside, with low-hanging clouds. The diffuse light casts everything in a hazy glow. The smell of damp concrete and exhaust fumes chokes the air.

I check my messages.

> **BABY DADDY**
> Here.
>
> I'm on the third floor. In the silver Tesla.
>
> On my way!

After a few minutes, I find his car beside a Range Rover.

He steps outside and waves, and I make a beeline for him. He opens the passenger door—*such a gentleman—*

and I slide in. He closes it for me. Then he rushes to the other side and joins me. It's intimate. I spread my palm over the luxurious seat, already warmed for my comfort. My phone fits into the hollow beside his. The glass cases kiss.

Physically, he looks amazing. As well-groomed as ever. Blake Hamilton never leaves the house without looking his finest, but he hunches. His shoulders slouch. He stares at me, his voice thunderous.

"So, what do you want from me?"

I return his burning stare. "I'm not sure I like the question. And I definitely don't appreciate your tone."

"What do you expect? You blindsided me at my family's home. You're sending photos of personal things in my brother's house. It feels like you're blackmailing me."

My ears burn. "That's not my intention."

His face is a glowering mask. "Really? Well, you're acting like it. I almost called the police."

"Why didn't you?"

He shakes his head. "I don't know. I'm hoping there's still time to control the situation."

"You're disgusting."

"You're *stalking* me," he says in a low voice, taut with anger.

I tug on my skirt's hem, my nerves fluttering. "Don't get excited. I'm not interested in you. You're not that great of a catch."

He laughs. Perhaps that is amusing to a man who has to fend off women everywhere he goes. His gaze slips down my body and back up. "You expect me to believe taking that job was coincidence?"

"No, I don't."

"Then *what*?"

My pride makes it difficult for me to respond, but I force out the words. "I had to get your attention somehow. You left me no choice. You stopped answering my calls."

"We had sex. *Once*. That doesn't mean you're entitled to see me again."

"I couldn't care less about you," I snarl, the lie burning my cheeks. "I only want what's best for our baby."

"How do I even know it's mine?"

"We both know what happened that night."

He shakes his head. "You're a stranger...this could be some other guy's kid."

"*Excuse* me?" I lean back, incredulous. "I don't know what kind of women you're used to dealing with, but I'm not looking for a sugar daddy. I'm here because you have the right to know about this, not because I want anything from you."

"That's not true."

"You think I'm after your money?"

He shrugs. "You pop up out of nowhere, claim you're carrying my child, and start hounding me for help. I'm entitled to be suspicious."

"We had a one-night stand."

"That's convenient."

I laugh bitterly, the sound echoing harshly. "Trust me, this pregnancy is about as convenient as a porcupine in a balloon factory. But believe what you want. It doesn't change the facts."

He narrows his eyes, as if searching for something in my face. "I don't know why I'm entertaining this."

I slap him, hard.

He jerks back. "What was that for?"

"Getting me pregnant. Turning your cheating fantasy into a reality by screwing me in a hotel room. Hinting that I'm trying to trap you. Why would I want to be with such a miserable jerk?"

He has the gall to look offended.

"You can be an ass or you can be a father, but you need to take some responsibility. We made this baby together. Own up to it."

He rubs his jaw and glares at me. "Fine. Let's say I have a baby coming. What's next? Are you expecting us to get married? That I'll dump my fiancée and skip off into the sunset...with you?"

My cheeks burn. "Once again, this is not about *you*. I'm only here for the baby. I thought you'd at least offer to help me."

He lets out a short laugh. "Help the woman who broke into my brother's home."

"I didn't break in."

"You violated every sane boundary."

I roll my eyes. "You're being dramatic."

"You're in Jack's house for God knows what. Why on earth would I trust you? I should call the police and report you."

"You should. But you won't," I rasp through gritted teeth. "Because you're too afraid of losing control."

"I'm not a coward."

"*You are*. If you don't do the right thing, I'll make sure

everyone knows it. You think your life sucks now? Wait until your parents find out you abandoned your kid before they were born."

He leans forward, growling. "Don't you dare."

"I will. And I'm telling your fiancée you cheated on her. I'll tell her you're a loser who dumped his baby on his brother and sister-and-law."

He pales.

I grab my purse and jump out of the car, slamming the door behind me. I face him through the window. "I won't let you manipulate this situation. You might be used to getting your way, but not this time."

He bristles. "You have no idea who you're dealing with."

"I'm doing this for our child. I won't back down. If you can't step up and be a responsible father, I will expose you for who you truly are. Your choice."

I march into the mall, pushing past a group of well-dressed women clutching designer bags. The place is dripping opulence, with giant chandeliers and marble pillars, filled with all the trappings I'll never own. But that doesn't matter. All that matters is fighting for the future of my child.

I pause, throat dry, heart thumping. Then I walk into the bathroom and lock myself in a stall. Tears burn my eyes as I slide to the edge of the seat and put my head in my hands. I spend too long in that bathroom, crying over that loser. Feeling sorry for myself. Cringing from what Mom and Dad would say.

We told you this would happen, Grace. We warned

you he wouldn't lift a finger for the baby. You didn't listen. You've ruined your life.

I take a deep breath. Echoes of their stern lectures flood my mind. They always had high expectations for me, hoping I'd achieve great things and lead a respectable life. They worked hard to provide me with opportunities, and my unexpected pregnancy shattered their dreams for me.

My parents are very traditional. Their beliefs about family, marriage, and societal norms are not flexible in the slightest. To them, an unplanned pregnancy outside of wedlock isn't just a mistake. It's a grave disappointment. They hoped I'd make choices that aligned with their vision of a perfect life, and my current situation was far from their expectations. Their disappointment cut me deep. I can still hear their judgment rolling off their tongue whenever my name was mentioned.

But as their voices fade, a fire ignites within me. I won't let their disappointment define me. I'll prove them wrong. I'll show them that despite the unexpected turns my life has taken, I will create a bright future for myself and my child.

I was going to do this differently. I would've compromised, but Blake doesn't deserve that. If he won't face his responsibilities, I will take him down. He wrecked my life. I will demolish his.

I want to go back there and throttle him, but my lunch break is just about over and Jack's dying to fire me. I blot my face and leave the mall, grimacing when I check the time. I'm cutting it fine. I get in the car, start it, and peel out of the parking garage. Ten minutes later, I'm winding dangerously over narrow roads. Then I pull into the Hamiltons' driveway next to an electric blue Lamborghini. It stands out among the dignified row of Mercedes Benz and Rolls Royce.

Shaking, I punch in the code to unlock the door. It yawns open. As I step inside, the air shifts. Gooseflesh erupts in rows down my arms. My boot slips on something hard, and I glance down, my heart sinking. Naomi's beloved antique vase, dating from the Han Dynasty, lies in pieces on the floor. I pick up the shard, my stomach caving in. My gaze flicks to the smashed fragments.

Who did this?

Not Jack. He's more anal about the house than Naomi. Something's wrong.

A sound echoes down the hall.

I freeze, holding back a scream.

Someone else is here.

ELEVEN

Distant voices boom down the hall. A woman and a man, arguing passionately. I grab my phone, thumb hovering over the keys. Should I call the police? Is this a break-in? Whoever it is left a trail of destruction in their wake. Overturned chairs. The kitchen floor glitters with shattered wine glasses. I take it all in, my throat tightening.

Get the hell out of here.

I should. I'm not winning any fights with a ceramic shard clutched in my shaking hand, but I ignore the warning in my head. A terrible feeling beckons me forward, swimming through murky waters. Are they fighting? As I approach the open door of the master bedroom, a woman moans.

She's not unhappy, though. She utters a keening whine, then switches to begging. *Please, Jack. Harder.* Nausea roils through my stomach. A deep male groan punctuates the rhythmic sound of flesh slapping on flesh. A woman's pleasured sigh follows his loud curse.

"Baby, that was so good. I love you."

Oh my God. I slap my mouth to stifle my gasp, but it cuts through their post-coital bliss. Jack shushes the girl's babbling. "Is someone there? Naomi?"

Run. My limbs freeze as adrenaline scorches my veins. The hand gripping the fragment trembles violently. *Run, you idiot.* But I can't. Some glitch in my fight-or-flight system has me rooted to the spot. A cheerful female voice breaks the silence.

"Come out, Naomi! Let's chat."

"Shut up," growls Jack, his blistering tone followed by ripping sheets and a heavy thump. "I don't want to hear my wife's name in your mouth."

The girl purrs, unfazed. "And if I don't listen? What'll you do to me?"

"Make you wish you kept your lips closed."

His low growl is threatening, but that only seems to excite her. "Don't threaten me with a good time."

I've had enough of this. I turn and rush down the hall.

"*Jack,*" she hisses. "Someone's out there."

Jack appears in the hall, his chest bare and his glare trained on me. "Oh. It's you."

"Well, who the hell is it?" the woman roars.

"Nobody," he mutters, turning away from me. "Get dressed."

A girl emerges from the bedroom, wrapped in a bed sheet that barely covers her naked body. She's about my age, tall, with shining ebony hair draping her shoulders. Her intense gaze sweeps over me like a hawk searching for prey. Her eyes dart between Jack and me as though deciding which one of us will suffer.

The tension is palpable as we all stand there in silence, the air thick with anger and uncertainty.

"Who is she?" she demands.

"Just the cleaning lady, Brandi. Leave her alone." Jack grabs her by the bicep, pulling her into the bedroom.

Sensation creeps into my limbs. I stiffly head toward the foyer and disappear in the upstairs stairwell. My mind is blank as I peek from the wall, watching the front door.

They emerge a short while later, Brandi in a leather skirt that ends high above her knees. A mini red jacket wraps her tiny waist. Her Chelsea boots stomp the floor, announcing her presence before she makes it known with her pleading whine.

"I need to see you more."

Jack sighs. "I told you. I can't."

She flips in an instant, hardening. "That won't work for me."

Jack lets out another sigh, sounding aggrieved. "You should find someone else."

"Are you breaking up with me?"

"No...I'm suggesting you move on. You're a wonderful girl. You deserve a guy who will give you his full attention."

"If that's true, why haven't you left your wife?"

He grimaces. "It's complicated."

"That's not an answer. Either you want me or you *don't*."

"Right now, I don't," he blurts, making her flinch. "You show up at my house unannounced one more time, and it's over."

"You'll break up with me just like that?"

"Without a second's hesitation."

Her brow lifts. "I don't think so. It takes two to end a relationship, and frankly, I'm sick of you calling all the shots."

"Brandi, don't you think this has gone on long enough?"

"Don't start with that." She leans forward, her palm splayed on his chest. "I'm done talking about splitting up. You love me, don't you?"

"Yes," he deadpans.

"Then act like it. If you ignore my calls again, I'll lose it. I swear to God, I'll tell your wife about us."

He pulls her into his embrace, kissing the top of her head. "I won't. Promise."

She sniffs, her arms encircling his waist. "There is nobody else in my world. There's only you."

"I'm married. My wife—"

"'My *wife*,'" she explodes, shoving him back. "'My wife,' 'my wife.' Every week, it's the same crap."

"Brandi, please. We can't keep doing this."

She scoffs. "You never seem to mind when we're in bed together."

He clenches his fists, his growl deepening. "I'm asking you, as someone who cares about me, to give me space. Please."

"I won't be your little secret forever."

Jack exhales deeply. "Give me time to sort things out. But for now, you need to go."

She wipes her cheeks and nods. "I love you."

"I love you, too."

I crane my neck around the wall, watching them kiss. They're perfectly visible to anyone in the driveway. Naomi could roll up any second, climb the patio stairs, and catch them. They're so brazen.

Jack disengages from her first. He opens the door, beaming, but his smile is brittle. He runs his hand down her arm and takes her palm, kissing her knuckles.

She grabs the bulge between his legs and leans in, pressing her mouth to his ear. She utters something that makes him cringe. When she pulls away, he's smiling again.

"Bye, baby."

She steps out. "Will you call me soon?"

"Absolutely," he says, closing the door.

When it shuts, he moves to the window. He waves at the girl. The Lamborghini makes a sound like a jungle cat as it backs out of the driveway. He waits, his body language tense. Once she's gone, the act drops.

He turns around, scowling. He pours himself amber liquid from the bar cart in the living room and returns. Staring at the ruined ceramic, he drinks. It's evidence. Proof that his perfect life is in shambles. Clearly, Jack's had issues with Naomi for a while. He's cheating on her. He's probably done this with multiple women. Only, this one isn't so keen on being discarded.

And I thought I couldn't loathe this man any more than I already did.

Jack wheels toward me. Apparently I didn't do as good a job of hiding as I thought. "So, did you enjoy that?"

"No," I say, stepping out of the stairwell. "As melodramas go, it wasn't worth watching."

He approaches me, his broad shirtless torso still dewy from having sex with his mistress. The brazenness of his cheating sickens me. What should I do? I don't want to be involved in this.

To his credit, Jack doesn't make excuses or beg me for my silence. His steady gaze impales me as he speaks.

"Tell her nothing, or I'll fire you."

I hate him. "And how are you going to explain the state of the house?"

"You'll clean everything up, and I'll buy new glasses."

"And the smashed vase?"

Jack stands there, boldly intimidating. "Easy. I'll say you broke it."

My stomach drops. "You're blaming it on me?"

"Well, I can't confess that my psycho girlfriend threw it on the floor after I told her I couldn't go to the movies because my wife and I have plans."

My throat aches with a pulsing knot. "She destroyed a valuable piece of art because you wouldn't take her to the movies?"

He shrugs. "I'll buy another one."

"You can't. It was priceless."

"You're not mad about the vase," he taunts, cocking his head. "You're upset that I'm cheating on my wife."

"You think you can get away with this forever?" The house echoes with my shrill voice as Jack stares at me, unblinking. "Eventually, you'll run out of things to blame on me."

"That's my problem."

His dead-eyed expression fills me with revulsion.

"It's not enough that your mistress shows up? That you have sex with her in the same place Naomi sleeps? You're a monster. You need help."

"Tell Naomi you broke it," he deadpans. "Or I will."

"No. I'm not lying for you."

He grabs my shirt and jerks me toward him. "If I don't get what I want, you don't get what *you* want. My money. So be a good little maid and clean up my mess."

I yank away from him, breathing hard.

A smirk flashes on his broad face. Then he swaggers into the living room, calling over his shoulder, "Oh, and I'll need fresh sheets for the bed."

I swallow tightly as I glance at the shattered vase. This isn't just about a broken vase, it's about a broken life, and Jack is one shard in a giant disaster.

TWELVE

I clean up the evidence, but I feel dirty.

Stuffing Jack's filthy sheets in the washing machine makes me complicit in his crime. It's like a dagger to my soul. I never signed up for this. I'm here to wipe floors, fluff pillows, and cook meals. What will he ask me to do next—get rid of a dead body?

As I stuff the bag of broken glass in their garbage bin outside, Naomi's car rolls into the driveway. My ears ring with Jack's threats as she gets out, swinging a purse over her shoulder. She catches my gaze and waves me over, her pale face shining.

I dust my palms and join her. "Hey."

"Hi. I got you a present," she chirps, reaching into her car to pull out a bulky object. "It's way too soon, but I couldn't resist. I saw it while I was shopping."

It's a pregnancy pillow. I take it, my throat tightening. "Thank you. That's so thoughtful."

Too thoughtful. Naomi buys me gifts while I help

cover up her husband's affair. I don't deserve her kindness.

Smiling, she closes the car door and fishes a key from her camel overcoat. Her forehead wrinkles. "Are you doing okay?"

No. I nod, my lips pulled into a wide grin.

Naomi opens the front door and we stroll inside. "You sure? You look tired."

"Well, I-I am a bit upset."

"What's wrong, honey?"

My stomach clenches tight. "Um...I was vacuuming and I bumped into the console table. Your vase fell before I could catch it. It was an accident."

I picture Naomi sliding her hands on her hips and screaming, but she merely takes out her phone and dumps her purse on the floor.

"Something broke?"

"Yes. I tried to salvage it, but there were too many little pieces. I'm sorry. I know you were very fond of it."

Naomi swipes a notification on her phone. "Sorry, I have a million things going on. You said it was a vase?"

"The one that used to be right here." I tap the space under the gilded mirror, incredulous. "It was green."

Her expression clouds over as she removes her coat, hanging it in the closet. "*Oh.* Don't worry about it. I'll find another one just like it."

"But—"

"Jack, honey?" Naomi calls out, removing the scarf from her neck. "We have a problem. We need to finalize the details of my party, but your father hasn't RSVP'd."

She joins Jack in the kitchen, who is in the middle of

unboxing a crate of new wine glasses. Flustered, I hang back and watch them. Jack hangs them by the stems, frowning. "That's because he's upset with me."

"Why?" she asks.

He waves a hand. "He's pissed that we didn't go to his dog's birthday party."

Naomi gapes at him. "Are you kidding me?"

"I wish I were," he mutters.

"But he knows I'm *allergic* to dogs." Naomi crosses her arms, leaning over the counter where Jack works. "I can't be around them without sneezing every five seconds."

"I know."

"Are you certain that's why he's mad?"

"Dad never explains himself. He...expects you to read his mind. I don't know. He's probably annoyed that I don't invite as many VIP guests as Blake to our events." Jack grabs a glass, setting it down hard. "As if it's my fault that the Seahawks quarterback doesn't care for luxury cruises."

Naomi sighs. "Do you think he'll come?"

"Not until I apologize."

"Well, *can* you?"

Jack stops his movements, glowering at her. "I've been apologizing to that man my whole life."

"Baby, my birthday's in a few days." Naomi slides to Jack, hugging him. "Can you suck it up for me? Please? He's an important part of this family."

Jack breaks down the cardboard box, relenting. "Fine."

She presses her lips to his face. "I love you."

That almost makes that miserable man smile. His mouth spreads in a thin-lipped grin. "What's one more apology in thirty-six years of being humiliated by my father?"

She nudges his side. "Don't be so grumpy."

"Can't help it," he mutters.

They kiss, arms wrapped around each other. I can't keep this secret any longer. It's eating me up inside, and Naomi deserves better. I'll come clean to her as soon as possible, even if it costs me my job.

I retreat to the basement, trying to push away the guilt and anxiety threatening to consume me.

◆

I NEED a break from their dysfunctional marriage.

So on my lunch break the next day, I drive to a nearby café, where I like to go to unwind. It's a beautiful day. I sit outside, absorbing the sun's rays. I eat, washing down my sandwich with an overpriced decaf latte. My heart weighs me down like stones tied to my feet. My thoughts wander to Jack and what he's done: cheated on his wife with a mistress who seems to have no idea how disposable she is, who destroyed a priceless piece of art without batting an eye, and threatened a pregnant woman who only wants to do her job.

I force down another bite as the timer on my phone beeps. Then I groan, catching Steve's eye. He's a chatty, twenty-something barista who works at the café. He has a sharp jawline and a well-groomed, angular face with a hint of stubble. Steve has a way of speaking that's animated with lots of hand gestures.

His warm smile widens. "Back to work?"

I nod, already depressed.

"What do you do?"

"I'm a maid for the Hamiltons."

He lights up like the bulbs on Broadway. "No kidding?"

"You know them?"

"Somewhat," he says, his gaze raking me head to toe. "You must have stories."

I inhale deeply and exhale. "I signed an NDA."

He blows a whistle as he wipes a table. "My cousin renovated a bathroom for them. He said it was a nightmare. The wife, Naomi, seemed out of it. She kept changing her mind, so he had to take out a bunch of tiles."

Unfortunately, I've seen that scatterbrained side of her. It's not easy to stay even-keeled when you're popping pills to escape your domestic hell.

Poor Naomi. "Did he say anything about Jack?"

"Oh yeah. He's a world-class jerk. Gave my cousin a hard time. He didn't want to pay the bill. Tried to argue that there were issues with the grouting. You'd think a guy like that wouldn't be so stingy with money. He could paper the walls of his mansion with hundred-dollar bills and still have plenty to spare." He makes a disgusted sound, irritation flickering over his thick brows. "He comes in here sometimes. Always the same order. An Americano with no sugar."

"What about Naomi?"

Steve tucks the rag in the pocket of his black apron. "I

don't see her much. She's made herself scarce since her medical license was suspended."

My back stiffens. *"Suspended?"*

"You didn't know?"

"When did this happen?"

"Years ago," he says, flooring me. "It was a huge deal. She was caught prescribing pain meds to herself."

There's no way that's true. Every day, Naomi leaves the house for work. Unless she got it back? This seems so unlikely. I shake my head. "I don't believe you."

"I'm not making it up."

"Then why haven't I heard anything about it?"

Steve grins, clearly pleased that he has a captive audience. "That's because only one person blogged about it. I'm guessing Jack or his father paid off local stations to kill the story."

"Then how did *you* find out?"

"My sister was a patient at her clinic. They sent out an email canceling everyone's appointments, saying that Naomi had left the practice. Nobody would say why. Then I found a blog post."

"A blog post? That's your proof?" I roll my eyes and crumple up the plastic wrapper of the sandwich. This gossip queen is inventing stories. "You shouldn't spread rumors about people."

"It's not a rumor."

"It *is*. She left this morning for work."

"Do you know that for sure?" he asks, his tone belligerent. "Did you follow her?"

"No. I'm not a stalker."

Irritation heats my skin like a rash. I slide my straw

up and down the cup. Why would Steve lie about something I can easily confirm? What happens when a doctor's license is suspended? If Naomi isn't working, where the hell does she go all day? I'm suspicious, but I need to hear more.

"Why would they kill the story?"

A smug grin tiptoes across his face. "Jack Sr. is retiring soon. He's in charge of that luxury cruise line. They've spent a lot of time and money building that brand. A drug-addicted wife getting her license revoked is not quite the polished reputation they've cultivated for Luxe Pacifica Cruises."

I look them up on my phone, clicking through the company's social media. No wonder Jack is so bitter these days. His younger brother is the icon of Luxe Pacifica Cruises. In between gorgeous snapshots of Rome, Strasbourg, and Seattle, there's a shot of Blake standing on a yacht in white linen pants, celebrating the naming of a new ship. There's another of him speaking at a podium at said event. Jack is off by the side, clapping. He looks uncomfortable, like he'd rather be the guy diving off a board into the ocean.

I show Steve the photo, pointing at Blake. "What have you heard about him?"

He leans over, peering at the image. "Not much. Other than he's the hot sibling. I've seen him once. Seemed like a nice man."

Time to cut this chat short. "Thanks for the gossip, but I think I'll stick to facts," I say as I head for the door.

My thoughts swirl with the possibility of Naomi's medical license being suspended. I pull up a website that verifies doctors' licenses. Heart pounding, I search for Naomi's name. She's not in the results. Does that mean Steve's crazy story is true?

I'm stunned. How could someone with a bright future make such a mistake? But she's not anywhere on this website. Unease settles on my shoulders like a weighted blanket, but I push it aside. This is none of my business. Poking around in Naomi's past won't help me with my situation, and frankly, I need to stay out of other people's drama. She's been more generous to me than members of my family.

Everything will be fine.

THIRTEEN

"Where have you been?"

Jack stands in the doorway, holding a coffee mug that stinks of bourbon. He smells like he fell into a vat of alcohol. His glazed eyes center on me, radiating distrust.

What are you, my dad? I push aside my annoyance and nudge the door. He tightens his grip, preventing me from squeezing past him.

"I asked you a question."

I sigh, loudly. "I went to lunch."

"You're late."

"You're in the way."

He peers at me, his frown deepening. "That's not how you talk to your employer."

"It is when he's blocking me from my home."

Jack looks like he'd rather slam the door in my face, but he steps back. I slip inside the entry, straining my ears for Naomi's cheerful hum. Nothing. I'm alone with Jack, again.

My stomach clenches. "Where's Naomi?"

"Off somewhere," he mutters with a flip of his hand. "Planning God-knows-what for her birthday party."

"You seem aggravated."

"I didn't hire you to show up twenty minutes past your break."

Great. Now I have to deal with a drunk man-child.

"I'm so sorry," I say, not sorry in the least. "It wasn't on purpose. I had a nasty bout of nausea."

"Aren't you in your second trimester?"

"Yes, but some women are sick during their entire pregnancy." And if Jack keeps acting like an unbelievable jerk, I'll milk that until the baby comes out. "It's not something I can control."

"That's convenient."

"Take it up with Naomi if it bothers you so much." I flash him a smile, knowing he wouldn't dare.

He follows me into the kitchen as I prepare a kettle, taking out the pregnancy tea sachets Naomi encouraged me to try. "So where did you get lunch?"

"You sound like my dad."

He flinches. "I'm not your dad."

No kidding. "Then what's with the inquisition?"

"I don't want you running amok in this town. If you go out, it's to run errands, and that's it. No hanging out with friends and no chatting with the locals."

This guy is ballsy if he thinks he can control me. A couple days ago, I might've indulged him, but that was before I walked in on him screwing Brandi. Immunity is my one silver lining in this big mess. Jack can't fire me without blowing up his marriage. If he gets rid of me, I'll tell Naomi about his affair, and he knows it. He'll avoid

THE MAID

that at all costs. Maintaining his picture-perfect image is more important than his happiness.

"You can't order me around when I'm off the clock," I say, facing the cupboard to grab a mug. "If I want to chat with a barista at a café, I will."

Jack grabs my wrist, seething. "I mean it. You work for the Hamiltons. That means you represent us when you're outside this house. Understand?"

I'm dying to spill everything Steve mentioned, including the bit about Naomi losing her medical license, just to show Jack that everybody already assumes the worst about his family. But a cold thrill touches my spine as I imagine his violent reaction.

"I'll keep my mouth shut." *For now.*

"Good. This could go well for you if you play your cards right. You just might get an introduction to a fine jewelry designer I'm friends with. *Or,*" he adds, applying pressure to my arm, "you could screw me over and spend the rest of your life regretting that."

What is he talking about? I stare at the fingers encircling my wrist, my throat tightening. The words Naomi uttered weeks ago flare in my head: *You won't scare off another maid.* Did he hurt her? Maybe she stumbled on his affair and threatened to tell Naomi.

"What happened to the last maid?"

Regret for that question sinks in too late. A smirk flickers across Jack's broad face. Without releasing me, he leans in close. His black eyes threaten to swallow me whole. "She crossed me, so I ruined her."

"How?"

"Trust me. You don't want to know."

My mind flies in many directions. There are many ways to ruin a person. Jack is well-connected. It's within his power to wreck my future. He isn't just a bully. He's a *sociopath*.

The electric kettle beeps. He relinquishes me, and it's like air returning to my lungs. My relief is short-lived, a cool wind over a blazing furnace. Turning away, he switches off the kettle and pours into my cup.

"Why were you late?"

Ice stabs into my stomach. "I-I did nothing *wrong*. I drove to a cafe. I had lunch."

"What did you have?" he barks.

"A sandwich."

"It took an hour and twenty minutes for you to eat a sandwich? Where did you go?"

"It's that place beside Trader Joe's. And I wasn't in a hurry to get back."

"Don't be coy with me. Remember who I am."

A bitter taste rolls over my tongue. *"I'm telling the truth."*

His eyebrow lifts. "I didn't see a transaction on my credit card."

"I paid with cash."

"You're supposed to use the card for that. Your meals are covered in your compensation."

"Well, I'm not a fan of my employer tracking my every move." My head pounds as I grab the mug, sipping the piping hot tea. "The guy who worked there was chatty, and I lost track of time."

"What did you talk about?"

I swallow tightly. "Nothing important."

Jack's burning gaze drills into me. "I hope you didn't violate our nondisclosure agreement."

No, but I came close. "We didn't discuss you."

"Glad to hear that." He pulls out his wallet, slipping out a folded bill. He tucks it in my apron's front pocket before I can stop him. "Keep your mouth shut, and you'll get more."

Then he pats my shoulder like I'm a Golden Retriever who fetched the ball. He couldn't make this situation more slimy if he tried. I fantasize about balling the twenty-dollar bill and throwing it at his face. I lock eyes with him, my lips pinched tight.

"Never do that again."

He laughs. "Give you money?"

"I don't take bribes. It's insulting."

"Feel free to leave anytime. Say the word, and I'll even help you pack." Jack flicks his wrist, and the numbers on his watch glow. "Now you're twenty-*five* minutes late to work. Dump your drink and come with me."

Holding up two fingers, he beckons me like a master summoning his dog. The gesture strikes me with a lightning bolt of fury. I want to sever his hand, but I can't because he's Jack Hamilton and he'll ruin my life. Gritting my teeth, I shove the mug into the sink. Then I trot after him, starting to feel like a helpless, beaten creature. But it's not about me. Protecting my unborn child supersedes my pride.

I halt behind him when we've entered a guest bedroom with draped furniture. Jack points to a bucket on the floor, painter's tape, a shallow pan, and a paint roller.

"I need you to paint this room."

I gape at him. "But I've never done that before."

"It's not quantum physics. Pour some paint into the pan. Dip the roller in the paint. Put it on the wall, and roll."

"I'll leave streaks."

He rolls his eyes. "It's white paint in a bright room. Nobody will notice."

"It doesn't need a fresh coat."

"I don't care what you think. This is what I'm asking you to do." Jack crosses his arms, nodding toward the roller. "Naomi wants everything perfect for her birthday, and there are fingerprints on these walls. We have guests coming in a few days. We need this house sparkling before they arrive."

"Can't I get on a ladder and wipe off the fingerprints?"

"*No.*"

I run my hand over my face. "This is not part of my job."

"Your job is whatever I need at the moment. Right now, that's repainting this room."

"Why can't you hire a painter?"

"Because I have *you*. You're perfectly capable of rolling paint up and down a wall. Aren't you?" He pockets his hands and regards me with a small curl of his lips. "Be sure to tape the baseboards."

"Great," I say through gritted teeth. "This is such a ridiculous request."

THE MAID

Cruel levity shimmers in his eyes before the light flickers out in them once more. "One more thing," he says, holding up his pointer finger. "Friday is Naomi's birthday. If you ruin my wife's special day, you'll regret ever crossing me."

He sweeps out of the room, his threat like a coil around my throat. I exhale, but it's hard to breathe. Ignoring my budding panic, I tape along the baseboards, lay down plastic drop cloths, and fill up the tray. The roller trembles as I strive to keep the monster happy, but every stroke of paint is a reminder of Jack's iron grip on me.

FOURTEEN

I brace myself for the chaos upstairs.

It's Friday. Naomi's big day. I have the day off and stay in the basement for as long as I can, but eventually my insides ache with hunger. So I climb the staircase and push through the door.

The house is like a Francophile's wet dream. Purple and pink hydrangeas, roses, and peonies spill from pots on linen. A man on a ladder hangs a crystal chandelier in the foyer. Vintage French posters with brass frames adorn the walls. Tiny red, white, and blue flags stick from food splayed on ceramic plates. Parisian cafe music plays from overhead speakers. A frantic Naomi directs a stream of traffic into the house in a little black dress, rollers in her hair.

"Where am I supposed to put that?" she says sharply, gesturing at the three-tiered cake propelled into the kitchen by two men. "Our fridge isn't large enough—Jack, did you order this? *Jack.*"

He breezes to her side in navy slacks and a white button-up shirt, his polished appearance so magnetic that everybody seems to defer to him.

"Marty's outdone himself," he deadpans, grabbing Naomi's waist. "The house looks amazing."

"Yes, it's nice. But did you see the cake?"

Jack shrugs. "What about it?"

"It's huge. It'll never fit in our fridge."

"Should be okay to sit out for a bit."

Her cherry lips pull into a strained grin. "Honey, our guests won't be arriving for four hours. We won't have cake for another hour and a half after that. It'll melt."

Jack's brows furrow. "I'll buy one from the store."

"With your father coming? He'll notice."

"So what? He's never happy with us anyway."

Naomi's thin arm flails. "You promised you'd take care of this."

"I will, baby. I swear. Everything's fine. Look at this place. It's going to be a great party, with or without cake." He heaves a sigh, rubbing Naomi's back. "It's just dessert, for Christ's sake."

A scarlet flush blooms over Naomi's pearl-strung neck. She says nothing, staring daggers at Jack, who seems to realize he screwed up. His voice lowers as he pleads her to *chill, baby. I'll figure it out.*

I approach Naomi with a wavering smile. "Hey. I couldn't help but overhear your conversation...why not put it downstairs? The basement is cool enough."

"Fantastic idea," says Jack, stepping from Naomi. "I'll tell them to move it."

"You're sure it'll keep?" she asks.

"Yes. But I'll call the baker to make sure." Jack slips his phone from his pocket and swipes through screens. He disappears into the kitchen.

She faces me, smiling. Jesus, her pupils are *huge*. "I'm sorry for being such a nut. You must think I'm ridiculous."

No, I think you're high. "Not at all."

"I know it's a silly thing to be worried about, but his family is all about appearances." Naomi glances behind her before leaning closer, whispering. "I *love* Jack's father, but he can be very harsh. I don't want to give him any excuse to criticize us."

"He sounds like my mom and dad. He'll find something to pick at no matter how perfect you are. My advice is, don't seek approval from someone who'll never give it to you."

It's a little presumptuous for me to hand out advice to Naomi, but honestly, she could use it. She's on drugs and it's barely eleven in the morning.

Naomi's fragile smile trembles. "Do you ever hear from them?"

I shake my head.

"I'm so sorry." She palms my shoulder and strokes my arm, the warm gesture forming a knot in my throat. "I can't imagine how painful that must be."

I shrug. I have more pressing issues than my terrible parents, like Naomi's evil husband. I catch his eye as he leaves the kitchen, arms crossed. Heart hammering, I plaster on a fake grin. "Do you need help with anything?"

"You're off today."

"Are you sure? I don't mind."

Naomi shoots me down, her voice kind but firm. "No work. I insist. I want you to enjoy yourself."

I beam at Naomi, pretending to be overjoyed that I'll be sipping mocktails and eating macarons like everyone else. It'll be nice when I'm not tiptoeing around Jack. And I'm nervous about running into Blake or his fiancée. A confrontation would be disastrous.

I slip to the basement and change into something appropriate for the party. My dress isn't as luxurious as Naomi's, and all I have are black ballet flats, but at least it matches her party's theme. Then I make myself scarce until the late afternoon. Guests slowly arrive, dressed in cocktail dresses with full skirts and cinched waists. Naomi gives them *la bise*, welcomes them into her home, and they totter inside, looking like groomed Labradoodles. They compliment her taste in decorations—"Such gorgeous hydrangeas"—and the food—"Where did you get those croissants?"

"Seawolf," she boasts in a commanding voice reminiscent of her husband. "They're the most authentic. Too many bakeries don't bake them long enough. My pastry chef told me it's done on purpose to appeal to the American palate. Apparently, we have soft mouths and can't handle crunchy baguettes."

This sparks a fierce debate about which country has more elevated tastes. Naomi pours everyone wine. She makes sure everybody has a drink before turning to me, her hand on my shoulder.

"Can I make you anything?" she asks.

She's so nice. It kills me that she's stuck with Jack. "I'm good, Naomi. Thanks."

"Have you tried these yet? They're incredible." She grabs a plate of prosciutto-wrapped goat cheese. "Give it a try."

"That's okay. I'm not hungry."

"Go on. Eat."

Fine. I take one, popping it in my mouth. As it melts over my tongue, Naomi flutters to another guest. I pick at the food as the house fills with people. I sample the croissants, unleashing a flurry of buttery flakes. I keep to myself and avoid Jack, whose eyes flash with icy contempt whenever he spots me eating. My head whips to the door every time it opens, but it's always someone else.

A car honks outside.

I yank open the door as the headlights of a BMW turn off. Two men of similar statures in sharp black tuxedos exit the vehicle. They make their way up the driveway. Their heads are bent together in conversation. My heart races as the men climb the staircase, familiar male laughter rippling the air.

Blake enters, followed by a handsome older man, Jack Hamilton, Sr., the patriarch of the Hamilton family. He's tall and broad-shouldered, with a full head of silver hair. His jawline could cut steel, and his piercing blue gaze twinkles with shrewd intelligence. Despite his age, he carries himself like a younger man. He's the epitome of old money. Sophistication comes naturally to him.

Standing beside him, Blake is a striking contrast to his father. Where Jack Sr. is distinguished, Blake is carefree youth. Same chiseled jaw, but his wayward brown curls fall into his eyes with effortless beauty. His tuxedo is also tailored to perfection, but his stance is relaxed. He greets Naomi with a hug and a kiss on the cheek. Where is his fiancée?

"You look fantastic, sweetheart. Happy birthday."

Jack Sr. slips out a thin package from his jacket, sliding it into Naomi's hands. She tugs off the ribbon and opens the Cartier box, gasping.

"Oh, Jack. You shouldn't have." Naomi's gaze widens as the gold chain spills into her palm. "This is...*wow*."

I cringe. It's a double-row necklace probably worth over twenty thousand dollars, and it would've been fine if it was from her husband, but her father-in-law?

Jack Sr. smirks. "I figured you'd like it."

"I do. It's beautiful. I-I didn't expect anything, to be honest." She pulls him into a hug, her smile on the verge of collapsing. "You're too generous."

He pats her on the back. "I saw it on display and thought, my God, that'd look incredible on my daughter-in-law." Jack Sr. plucks the delicate chain from her grip, his lips curving. "May I?"

"Of course."

She turns, and Jack Sr. fastens it around her throat as his son watches, glowering. At least I'm not the only one weirded out by her father-in-law's wildly inappropriate gift.

"You're stunning." Jack Sr.'s fingers linger on her skin for a second too long. "If only I were a few decades younger."

Naomi's awkward chuckle bleeds into the tense

silence, which Blake shatters with his ringing baritone. "You wouldn't know what to do with her if you had her, old man."

"Maybe not. But I'd sure try."

Jack Sr. laughs, looping his arm in hers. She gives the box and its ribbon to Jack, who stuffs the garbage in my hands like I'm a trash bin.

Heat claims my body as they walk away. I'm invisible. A prop in their world of yachts, multimillion-dollar homes, and opulence. Blake is just as bad as his brother. He doesn't acknowledge me—the mother of his child—but he greets everybody else. I retreat to the kitchen.

Jack made it clear I'd pay if I ruined Naomi's birthday, but he should've been more worried about his dad. What a weirdo. Who does that to their son? And why doesn't anyone call him out?

I wander back to the party. People move toward Jack Sr., drawn to his gravitational pull. Then Jack taps him on the shoulder and jerks his head. They break from the crowd to a less-populated corner with the grand piano. I grab a glass of sparkling apple juice and hang nearby, pretending to admire a bouquet of hydrangeas. Through the purple blooms, I watch them.

Jack Sr. sits on the leather bench as his namesake hovers over him like a dark cloud. He plays a chord, wincing. "You're supposed to tune these things once in a while. It's a Steinway, like the ones on my ships."

"I'm thinking of donating it to UW," Jack deadpans.

His father grimaces. "Why would you do that?"

Jack shrugs. "It takes up a lot of room."

"You have no sense of value. A Steinway is a masterpiece, unlike you."

Ouch.

Jack flinches. I don't know why. The comment is nasty, but it can't be the first time he's heard it. A short ditty chimes from the piano, the notes jarring but still precise. Glowering, Jack drinks his cocktail.

"Dad, you never emailed back about my proposal."

Jack Sr. scales up and down the keys before answering. "No, I didn't."

"Why not?"

"Because it's the stupidest idea I've ever heard of."

A red flush claims Jack's neck. "Can't be dumber than eco-friendly yachts."

"Nobody wants to travel to Antarctica, believe me."

"That's not true. There's been an explosion of interest since a video on social media went viral. There are about a half-dozen ships that sail through the Drake Passage. Most of them are small expeditions, but—"

"You want me to create a cruise through one of the most challenging stretches of water based on one video? You must be joking."

"It's not one video, Dad. There are several with millions of views. This will appeal to travelers who are looking for off the beaten path vacations."

"*Luxury* is the brand. Not expeditions through thirty-foot waves."

"I'm not suggesting a bunch of drunken twenty-somethings cram into a tiny boat. We can retrofit a larger ship and provide high-end accommodations. It's an opportunity for Luxe Pacifica to attract a new customer base."

"You don't understand our clientele. They want indulgence, relaxation, and sun-soaked destinations. Antarctica is frigid, inhospitable, and isolated. It's a niche market."

Frustration flickers across Jack's face, but he stands his ground. "It's not just about expanding our audience, Dad. It's about being pioneers in the industry, offering something nobody else does. This could be our chance to reshape how people perceive luxury travel."

Jack Sr. smirks. "Such an idealist. I admire your enthusiasm, son, but you're misguided. Our clients are content with what we offer. There's no reason to gamble with our reputation."

Jack clenches his fists. "Reputations evolve. Just because we've always done things one way doesn't mean it's the *only* way. We can't afford to be complacent. We need to grow and innovate, or we'll be left behind."

"I built this company, and I know what works. Your idea is too farfetched."

"You could've told me that days ago."

"I'm a very busy man," he says dismissively, staring at the black-and-white keys. "I have a life outside of you and your problems."

"But I'm the chief operations officer."

His father nods. "For now."

Jack's voice is tight. "What's that supposed to mean?"

"Your girlfriend showed up at the country club on Saturday, looking for you," he murmurs, his gaze wandering over the guests. "Very sloppy. I thought you had more sense than that."

Jack runs a hand through his hair, growling. "I tried breaking it off."

"Well, the longer you keep gallivanting around town with that lowlife, the more I lose faith in your decision-making. She's not even attractive. She's a five out of ten, at best." Jack Sr. grabs his cocktail and sips before setting it back on the piano. "The Hamilton name stands for excellence and class, and an affair tarnishes that."

"My personal life is none of your business."

"You've made it my business. It takes a lot of money and effort to maintain my brand, and you're wrecking it."

"Dad, that's ridiculous."

"Your actions reflect on the family. You represent us. It's not about you. It's the Hamilton legacy." Jack Sr. gives his son a pointed look, swiveling on the bench to face him fully. "Which I'm not sure you appreciate."

I bite the inside of my cheek. This conversation has taken a turn I wasn't expecting. I knew his father was tough, but this feels...like a threat.

"Of course I do," Jack deadpans.

"Then get rid of her. And while you're at it, start a family."

"We're not ready."

"You've been saying that for years. You're not getting any younger."

"I'm only thirty-six."

"And your wife is thirty-five. Tick-tock." Jack Sr. punctuates his statement with a few discordant notes on the piano. "I suggest you get your priorities straight. And if you can't, maybe it's time for you to step down as COO."

Jack blanches. "You can't be serious."

"If you're unable to handle the responsibilities of being a Hamilton, you're not fit to be COO."

"You're willing to fire me over this?"

"It's not just the affair," his father says, his voice dripping with disdain. "It's everything. Your lack of ambition, your careless attitude, your poor judgment. You're a liability, and we can't afford to have that kind of weakness in our family." Jack Sr. finishes his drink and sets the glass down with a hard clink. "Now if you'll excuse me, I have guests to entertain."

"This is my house. They're *my* guests."

Jack Sr. snorts. "They're my friends. And unlike you, I actually know how to hold a conversation that doesn't involve scandal or financial ruin. Try to behave yourself for once. Oh, and son? The piano stays. You have no respect for the things that truly matter. It's high time you learned."

The men stare each other down, the tension thick and suffocating. Finally, Jack breaks eye contact and slumps off. Shame radiates off him. His father's comments must cut right to the bone. As he slinks off, Jack Sr. turns to the piano and launches into a ragtime tune.

People gather around him, drawn by the joyful music. When he's commanded everybody's attention, he switches to a Billy Joel song. Everybody sings along. Laughter fills the house, but it feels artificial. They don't know the truth. The Hamiltons might have prestige, but they're not a family. Nobody realizes the damage Jack Sr.

will cause to maintain this gilded lifestyle. What else is he capable of?

I shudder, hands clasped over the growing life in my belly. My heart pounds recklessly. I head out of the living room. As I round the corner, I collide with a solid wall of muscle. I back away, but two strong arms lock me in place. I glance up, meeting his intense gaze. A horrifying current runs through me.

FIFTEEN

Blake yanks me into Jack's study, and a primitive alarm sounds in my brain. He slams the door, no longer the poised gentleman who kissed the air over Naomi's cheek. His sparkling charisma is dialed into something more primal. He grabs me by the arms, not hard, but enough for me to flinch.

"Why haven't you returned my calls?"

Between fulfilling Jack's bizarre demands and my guilt over keeping the truth from Naomi, I completely forgot about him. "I've been busy."

"Cleaning my brother's house?" he deadpans. "Scrubbing his toilets. Wiping his floors. Changing his sheets. You couldn't manage a text through all that?"

I shrug. "Your feelings are dead last on my list of priorities."

Shock widens his gaze before it narrows. "Look, all I can do is explain my side. You're a girl I met at a bar. You were claiming you got pregnant after one night together. You sent me a barrage of messages when I didn't immediately reply. Then you turn up at Jack's house without warning. I thought you were crazy." Blake yanks at his collar, glaring at me as though the jury's still out.

"Dial back the insults. You have no right to drag me in here and scold me like *I* wronged *you* when it's the other way around."

"Ignoring me isn't helping."

"So? You've made it very clear you want nothing to do with the baby."

"I never said that."

I click my tongue, fuming. "You didn't have to. You implied it by ignoring me for weeks."

Cursing, he runs a hand through his hair. His handsome face is a portrait of vulnerability. He's scared. He tries to hide it, but he can't. He blows a stream of air and massages his temples, speaking slowly.

"I'm sorry. How I treated you is not who I am. When you cornered me, I was nervous and upset. I didn't mean half the things I said." Blake clenches his fists over his thighs. "My lawyer kept hissing in my ear. He wanted me to keep my distance, but I can't twiddle my thumbs for months while you're in this situation. I have to help you."

I cross my arms. "Do you?"

"Yes."

His gaze bores into mine. Tingling pits my stomach. I fiddle with my dress, the room suddenly too warm.

"What do you want?"

"I'd like copies of all your medical bills. Going forward, I'll pay for them. Send me invoices for supplements. Anything you need, but I want full transparency. Dates of ultrasounds. Blood tests. Everything."

My heart jolts and my pulse pounds. "Fine."

"And I can make an appointment for the best OB/GYN in the area."

"No need. I'm already seeing a great one in Bellevue. I switched doctors the second I moved here. I'll text you her details. I...I noticed that your fiancée isn't here."

"Yeah, I broke up with her. It wasn't pleasant, but it had to be done." His lips twist into a cynical smile. "Turns out she was cheating on me."

"Sounds like you two deserved each other."

Blake bows his head, silky brown strands clinging to his smooth jaw. He pushes hair behind his ear, the movement stirring something in my chest. When he glances up, pain flickers in his eyes.

I will not feel bad for this guy. "I'm guessing you spared her the worst part?"

Blake crosses the room and collapses on the tufted couch. "No. I told her everything."

"Do I need to worry about her keying my car?"

"No."

A strained silence swallows the gap in between us. I stare him down, but Blake seems immune to intimidation. He drums his fingertips on the leather arm of the couch, watching me calmly.

"We should think about our next steps. You could live in one of my apartments. They're full, but I'll evict someone and move you in."

Alarm bells ring in my head. "*Absolutely not.*"

Blake's face clouds over with confusion. "Why?"

I gape at him. "Because that's terrible karma."

He makes a flippant gesture. "The people I rent to are rich. They'll cope."

"I don't care. You're not kicking out a family to give me a home, especially when I have a place to stay."

"Well, you can't go on living here at Jack's." Blake takes out his phone, scrolling through an app. "I just need to check with my real estate lawyer. I'm sure we can offer someone a buyout or refuse to renew their lease."

"You're not evicting anyone."

He sighs, heavily. "Fine. I'll rent something."

Bad idea. My scalp prickles with a needling sensation. Weeks ago, I was desperate for his help. That was before I found out Hamiltons could compete for gold in the Crazy Family Olympics. Living on his dime puts me deeper in his pocket. I've always prided myself on my independence, even when life threw its worst at me. Becoming dependent on Blake would be like relinquishing that part of me that's gotten me through so much. This is about setting an example for my child, showing them that even when life gets tough, you don't take the easy way out. You stand your ground and fight, even if you're fighting alone.

"I'm not okay with that." My temples pound with a headache. "Moving will be an enormous hassle. I think I want to stay here."

He shoots me a twisted smile.

"I'm not joking."

"Seriously? Why?"

I don't know. I'm scared. Maybe he's planning to sue for full custody. He might be already drawing up the paperwork. He could convince the court that it's in the

THE MAID

baby's best interest. He'll claim that I can't look after my child. He could ask Jack to testify as a character witness that I'm a violent employee who shouldn't be trusted with children. I can't believe anything he says. He's not trustworthy.

I swallow thickly. "I'd rather keep things as normal as possible for now."

"Living with my brother is far from that."

"It's convenient for me."

"Not as much as having your own place." A suspicious edge creeps into his voice. "Why the sudden change of heart?"

"I wanted my baby to know their father. But now that I've found you, I regret coming here. I'd rather my baby not have a dad than realize he's a heartless person who cheats on women and evicts a family from their home so he can stash us away, guilt free, to hide his shame."

His expression darkens. "Don't make this personal. This is about the baby."

"You're still doubting it's yours."

"I'm not. Again, I apologize for what I said. There's no excuse for it, but try to put yourself in my shoes. I haven't had enough time to come to terms with this."

"I can't just forget all the hurt you caused me."

"And you shouldn't." Blake takes my wrist, the sensation burning through my skin. "But we're in this together, aren't we?"

"I-I guess."

"I'd like us to start over. Can we do that?"

My cheeks flush. I want to believe his earnest plea. Tingles skate across my body as his touch moves up my arm to clasp my shoulder. The faintest smile curls his lip. I can't tell if it's a sneer or something genuine, but my heart wants me to give in. Doing this alone is so difficult. It'd be nice to have the support of someone other than Naomi.

Her comments about Blake flicker in my head. His about-face makes me feel like I'm being set up. How do I know this isn't a calculated move to fulfill his "obsessive need for control"? Naomi wouldn't mention that unless Blake had massive issues. I won't be in a position where I rely on him for anything.

Blake's hand slips on my shoulder, stopping short of a caress. Cheeks flushing, I brush his hand off me.

"You don't get off that easy. I've been through hell the past few months. You haven't been there. You didn't even pick up the phone to hear me out."

"I'm not asking you to forgive me."

"I don't care. You can't just walk into my life, say you're sorry, and expect me to trust you."

He steps closer, his breath fanning my face. "What will you do when my brother kicks you out of his house?"

I swallow hard. "I'll provide for my child."

"*Our* child. And what if you can't?" Blake asks, the question cutting into me. "What if you need help?"

"Then I'll ask for it, but not from you."

"What the hell does that mean?"

I almost flinch from the harsh response. Narcissism clearly runs in the family. "I've changed my mind about wanting you in my life."

Blake takes a step back, a gallery of emotions flickering on his face—confusion, hurt, anger. He looks like he wants to say something, but he doesn't. He nods and turns to leave, his gaze burning more than his touch. "I want you to get a good lawyer, Grace. Because if you think my kid is growing up without a father, you're mistaken."

He leaves.

Wild music from the party floats inside. People laugh and chatter in a happy din as my stomach tightens. He's setting himself up for success by laying out the legal groundwork for later battles about residency or custody rights or whatever else might come up. He's going to fight for his child.

Well, so am I.

Blake will never take away my baby.

SIXTEEN

The next morning, I wake to thundering footsteps.

I close my eyes and try to drift off, but the stampede keeps me awake. Groaning, I force myself upright and rub my temples. I stayed up until three writing emails to attorneys. My throat constricts as I imagine Janice's response: *You'll win a custody battle against Blake when hell freezes over. He'll drown you in legal fees until you declare bankruptcy.*

Besides working for the Hamiltons, my only job is growing a healthy baby. Staying employed is more important than ever. I can't screw this up.

After a scant breakfast, I dress in my uniform. Then I climb the stairs, finding a team of maids picking up after last night's party. I jump in to help, but I don't know where to begin. The whole place is a mess. Nobody bothered to box up the food. They left it out overnight. Someone empties an untouched pan of scalloped potatoes into the trash. I pick up its corresponding white card

—Gruyère potatoes au gratin. A woman grabs a basket filled with pastries and heads toward the bin.

I move in front of her. "Don't. They're still good."

She hesitates. "Mr. Hamilton wants them thrown out."

Mr. Hamilton is an idiot. I pry the basket from her grip and wedge it between my hip and arm. "I'll take care of it. I'll make bread pudding or something."

"Who are you?"

"I'm the live-in maid."

She peers at my outfit, her gaze centering on my belly bump, but wisely keeps her mouth shut. Then she resumes trashing every single food item.

I carry the croissants to the kitchen and set them on the counter, shaking my head at the rows of lipstick-smudged wine glasses and the pile of dishes by the sink. They couldn't load the dishwasher? Outside, a cleaning lady fills a composting bin with hydrangeas. For God's sake, they're not even wilting. Why not donate them to a nursing home? Again, what is *wrong* with these people?

Jack's baritone floats down the hall. In the guise of sweeping, I grab a broom and follow the sound. Jack stands outside their bedroom with a mug, fully dressed, his expression pained. Muffled crying escapes from the gap in the door. He raps his knuckles against the wood.

"Baby, please come out."

His soft plea lingers in the air before Naomi's firm, *"No."*

"Don't you want breakfast?" he asks.

She sniffles. "I feel sick."

Jack slides a hand over his hip, still speaking to the door. "You caught a cold?"

"Maybe," she mutters. "I don't know."

"Okay, baby. Stay in bed." Jack kneels, sliding the mug over the floor. "I made you a latte. It's outside."

Naomi doesn't respond.

Sighing, Jack turns around. The exhaustion pinching his face vanishes when he notices me. "Shouldn't you be mopping up something?"

"Sure thing. Which mess do you want me to clean up? The one in the house, or the one waiting for you when Naomi realizes you're a philandering drunk?"

His laser-like stare pierces me. His shoulder brushes mine as he storms off, disappearing downstairs. Moments later, the front door slams. As I glance outside, a champagne-colored car peels out of the driveway.

Dick.

Since the cleaning crew is taking care of the mess and the weather is nice, I spend the day in the yard. The surrounding trees dumped more pine cones onto the lawn, so I grab an organic trash bag and get to work. Bright skies are rare in March. Like every Washington native, I soak up the rays when I can. Within a few minutes, I feel better.

By noon, I've filled three giant bags and my sweat-soaked blouse clings to my body. I take a break, sitting on the patio steps with a bottle of water as Alex, the silver-haired handyman, prunes and shapes the hedges.

He catches my eye and waves with the shears. "How's it going?"

"Fine."

"You shouldn't be working so hard in your condition."

I hate how old men believe that pregnancy is a disease, but I smile and say nothing. Maybe I can squeeze more information out of him. I have questions about the Hamiltons. What's behind the locked door upstairs? I shrug, wiping my brow. "You did an amazing job on the garden. It really is beautiful."

"Thanks." Alex snips another branch from the evergreen bush. "Someone's got to keep this place looking good."

"Did you tell Jack about the rotten siding?"

"I did. Again. He doesn't think it's a big problem and wants to wait until next year, which is just...*stupid*. I've fixed so many homes over the years. He'll regret waiting for so long, I'll tell you that, 'cause all that rotting wood attracts pests. Woodpeckers. Ants. This one home I worked on had an infestation. It was gnarly." He abandons all pretense of work and sighs, loudly. "If it were my house. I would get on that quick."

"Jack doesn't seem to care about a lot of things."

"How is he treating you?"

I suck in my lip, averting my gaze downward. "He's all right...just high-maintenance."

Alex fiddles with his gardening tool. "Be careful around him."

"What do you mean?"

He returns to his work, tension flicking in his jaw. "He's not the most stable of individuals."

Putting it lightly. Jack's been waving red flags since I moved in. "Yeah. I've seen that part of him."

"I doubt it. If you had, you would've already quit your job."

A chill black silence follows that alarming statement. Alex faces me, his grim expression throttling my nerves. Does he know what's behind the locked door? Is there a severed head? A row of heads? Perhaps the other maid died in that room.

Alex offers me no explanation. His pained sigh cuts through the brittle quiet as he squats down beside me, whispering. "I need to tell you something."

"Okay."

He hesitates, glancing around. "It's about Jack."

"What about him?" I ask, my heart rate picking up.

Alex leans in closer. "A few years ago, there was an incident between Jack and his brother, Blake. It was bad. Real bad. I don't know what happened. I wasn't there, but I heard about it from Sharon, the last maid. She said that during Thanksgiving dinner, there was a fight between the brothers. And I don't mean the typical sibling rivalry crap—it was vicious. As in, Jack nearly killed Blake."

My throat tightens.

"She was shaken. She couldn't talk about what she'd seen. After that, Jack Sr. ordered her to mop the floors. She told me there was so much blood, it soaked through a bath towel. I used to be a medic in the navy. That's a lot of blood." Alex glances over his shoulder before continuing. "Blake was taken to the hospital."

"Was a police report filed?"

He laughs, bitterly. "Are you kidding? This is the Hamilton family we're talking about. They've got the money and influence to make problems disappear. Like *that*. No, there was no report. Only a few of us who've been working here for years know about it."

A wave of nausea washes over me. I knew Jack could be volatile, but this is...wow. "Why are you telling me this?"

Alex sighs, his gaze fixed on the ground. "Jack treats people like they're beneath him. He's dangerous, and he won't hesitate to hurt anyone who gets in his way. I want you to be careful, that's all."

I swallow hard. "Thank you. I will."

He nods, his expression somber.

Alex returns to work and I'm left in the garden, its tranquil beauty now dark and sinister. My mind races with thoughts of Jack, Blake, and the horrifying secret binding them together. The Hamilton family is known for their wealth, but covering up attempted murder? Having a baby with Blake was going to come with its share of drama, but this is a whole new level.

How could Jack do something like that? And how do I protect myself? I take a deep breath, tamping down on the growing hysteria. I need to stay focused and keep my wits about me. If I play my cards right, I can use this information to my advantage.

SEVENTEEN

Today is the day. The eighteen-week ultrasound will tell me the baby's gender, whether the baby is growing normally, and its due date. The stakes couldn't be higher. I'm nervous. I almost called Janice for backup, but Blake insisted we do this on our own.

After a restless sleep, I drag my feet upstairs and shuffle into the kitchen. A bright-eyed Naomi sits at the kitchen island in a light purple yukata, her face caked with matte foundation, her hair brushed to a pale gold bob.

"Morning. Sleep well?"

"Yeah," I lie, rifling through the cupboard for a mug.

It's been a stressful few days. The knowledge of Jack's violent past with Blake gnaws at me. A dark cloud looms over the entire mansion, casting its shadow on everyone within it. I do my best to avoid Jack, but it's difficult when he's constantly in my space, watching my every move.

And it doesn't help that his brother has been blowing

up my phone with demands. We've exchanged a few terse messages since our last meeting.

I open my mouth and close it. I need to ask Naomi about Jack's fight with Blake, but I can't get the words out. Doubt clogs my thoughts. What if I accept Blake's offer, only to land myself in a worse situation?

"Can I fix you something to eat?" she offers, striding to the fridge. "It won't take long. I cooked most of it already."

"Um, okay. Thanks."

"You're very welcome." Naomi drizzles a nonstick pan with olive oil. Then she unwraps a salmon filet from butcher paper. She seasons it with a spice blend.

"I'm supposed to do that," I mumble, fiddling through the drawer of tea.

"You have the day off."

"I know, but I feel bad for relying on you."

"You're not." Naomi lays the salmon over the pan, the flesh sizzling. "Accepting help doesn't mean you failed. It just means you're not alone."

"But...I'm your employee. You owe me nothing."

"I don't think of you that way," she whispers, pressing the spatula into the filet. "You're a friend. Or at least, I'd like us to be friends."

"Really?"

She shrugs, flipping the salmon. "I have a lot of friends, but almost no genuine relationships since I married into Jack's family. I'm surrounded by social climbers. I never know if someone is around me because they want to be, or if they want something from my husband. I can't trust anyone, but I trust you. You're nothing like them."

I'm flattered by her words, even as they twist my insides with guilt. Will she feel the same after finding out why I took this job? After she discovers I helped Jack hide his affair? Heat scorches my cheeks.

"I shouldn't take advantage of your kindness."

"It's just breakfast," she says, her mild tone disarming me. "Sometimes asking for help is the bravest thing you can do. You don't have to do this by yourself."

I lower my gaze to the marble counter, torn by conflicting emotions. I don't deserve her friendship, but I crave it. A longing for family stabs inside me like physical pain.

A timer on the oven beeps.

Naomi pulls out a baking sheet of roasted Brussels sprouts. She slides it over the stove. She scoops a handful of the blackened sprouts onto a small plate, along with a filet of pan-fried salmon. Then she drops the meal in front of me.

"Here you go. Breakfast of champions." Smiling, she folds her hands like an aspiring chef waiting for my verdict.

I'm too shocked to object, but I can't think of a more disgusting breakfast than Brussels sprouts. I don't want to hurt her feelings. Grimacing, I pick up the fork and flake off the salmon. I stab through a shriveled green lump, lifting it to my lips. The foul stench turns my stomach, but I shove it into my mouth. The bitterness of the leaves cuts through the savory fish.

"I just love cruciferous vegetables," Naomi chirps as I try not to gag. "Whenever I make a salad, I always include at least one. Don't ever give me iceberg lettuce with those horrible, dry carrot sticks. I need broccoli. Brussels sprouts. Kale."

I nod, trying to hide my disgust.

Naomi's smile widens. "I'm so glad you agree. It's important to eat healthy when you're pregnant. I mean, you're eating for two now."

I force down another bite. "Right."

I chew in silence as Naomi drinks her coffee, the only sound the scrape of the fork against the plate. It's not terrible, but my mind is elsewhere, my anxiety growing by the minute.

"How is it? Do you need more salt?"

I grin. "Everything's perfect."

Truth is, nothing makes Brussels sprouts taste good. They're tiny balls of bitterness, lingering in my mouth long after I swallow. But I can't say that to Naomi. Not after she called me her only friend.

I chew a forkful of the greens, washing them down with water. "So, about the ultrasound—"

"I'm so excited for you. Have you thought of names yet?"

"Not really. I'm waiting to find out the sex first. And I wanted to make sure nothing's wrong with the baby."

Naomi sobers, lowering her mug from her lips. "It'll be fine."

I suck in a lungful of air. "I hope so."

Naomi's watery gaze hardens as she reaches over, gripping my hand. "I'm here for you."

A lump forms in my throat, choking off my gratitude.

All I can do is take another bite of the Brussels sprouts, the bitterness a reminder of the looming meeting with Blake.

Heavy footsteps approach, announcing Jack's presence. He's like a draft of icy wind, and his voice is a full-on blizzard.

"What's going on?" he demands.

Naomi releases me, wiping her face. "Nothing."

Jack looks like he wants to press the issue, but my phone chimes, giving me the perfect escape route.

"Time to go?" she asks.

I nod, slipping off the stool.

Jack's expression darkens. He's silent, but his wrathful glance communicates his displeasure.

My heart pounds. The uncertainty swells to a crescendo as I squeeze past him on my way to meet his brother. Soon, he'll find out the truth.

EIGHTEEN

I speed to the doctor's office. Then I wait outside, my anxiety over Blake's presence burning through the forty-degree chill. His Tesla rumbles to a stop in the parking lot. Blake exits the car with the grim attitude of a soldier preparing for battle.

He looks great, and I hate myself for noticing. A crisp white shirt hugs his torso, covered by a dark gray sports jacket. His jeans look indecent on him, hanging low on his tapered waist. My gaze skips up his athletic body, my breath hitching. A familiar spiced scent clinging to his shirt taunts me with a steamy memory of us stumbling into a hotel room.

Blake approaches me, his expression blank. "You're early."

"I wanted to make sure I was here on time. How've you been?"

"Good. How about yourself?"

I nod, swallowing hard. I'd planned on playing it cool,

but I don't think I can. This is a big deal. I'm allowed to be a little on edge.

"I'm doing my best." I inhale a deep breath and exhale, the sound ragged. "The eighteen-week ultrasound is typically when you find out if the baby has major health defects. I never asked about your health history."

"You don't need to worry about that."

"No genetic issues?"

"None that I'm aware of." Blake's frosty demeanor warms from subzero to a spring thaw. "My dad's prediabetic and he has high blood pressure. What about you?"

"Nothing crazy. The older generations had cancer, but they were smokers." I force a smile and quip, "Well, as long as our baby doesn't inherit a stubborn streak from both of us, we should be fine, right?"

Blake smirks. "That would be one incredibly determined kid."

We chuckle, and the tension in the air dissipates. Still smiling, Blake nudges my arm. "Shall we?"

I follow him into the OB/GYN office. It's filled with expensive-looking, stiff armchairs made of white leather. An indoor waterfall trickles down a wall into some shrubs. Tasteful art fills the walls.

As always, I feel out of place here. I try to relax in an uncomfortable chair, but it's fruitless. I can't find a position that doesn't hurt my back. A pregnant woman across the room fidgets with her expensive-looking bag. A woman in her thirties wearing a stunning suit swipes through her phone, her manicured nails stabbing the screen. How is she comfortable in those heels? I imagine her stepping into the bathroom, gathering her blow-dried hair in a fist, and gracefully vomiting into a toilet.

Will Blake pressure me to be perfect, like everyone here? I study him as he checks his phone for the millionth time. Blake fires off an email with a flick of his thumb, oblivious to my inner turmoil. He obviously regrets what happened between us. He's playing nice now, but as soon as this is over, he'll sue for full custody and shove me out of his life.

Blake's heavy gaze swings to me. "You okay?"

I shrug, twisting my hands in my lap.

He leans over, whispering. "There are four million births every year in the States, and a majority of them have normal results. It'll be fine."

An overwhelming sense of inadequacy suffocates me. I'm not like these women, with their designer bags, manicured nails, and supportive husbands. They're happy to be here. I'm just a maid who's in over her head.

A cheerful greeting cuts across the room. "Grace?"

My heart races as a nurse holding a clipboard motions for us. I stand, smoothing down my jeans, and follow her into the ultrasound room. She asks how I'm feeling, records my vitals, weighs me, and leaves. I sit on the exam table as Blake takes a chair next to me.

"Relax," he murmurs. "You look like death warmed up."

"Careful. I might swoon."

He rubs my knuckles with his thumb, showering my skin with sparks. "Breathe. You're getting worked up over nothing."

I wipe my palms over my maternity jeans, willing

myself to calm down, but approaching footsteps kick my heart rate into the nth gear. A knock hits the door, then a thirtysomething woman in pink scrubs enters. She introduces herself as Melissa, the ultrasound technician.

She sits on a stool next to the exam table, bursting with positive energy. "Ready to see your baby?"

She's waiting for an enthusiastic *yes*, but tension keeps my jaw wired shut.

"Okay. Let's get started. Roll down your jeans. Then I'll apply some gel to your belly, and we'll take a look."

I push my jeans past my bump and lie back. Cool moisture spreads over my belly before Melissa slides the wand over my bump, the monitor flickering with a gray landscape. I hold my breath as she moves it around. Blake leans in, watching intently. An amorphous blob blooms onto the screen.

The technician pauses her movements. "Here's the baby's head."

I gasp as the profile swims into view—a nose, forehead, and chin. Excitement bubbles in my chest. Even Blake utters a hushed "wow," as the shape morphs again into a human hand.

"There's a hand..."

I count the fingers—five. So far, so good. Melissa rotates the wand, and a rapid *dub-dub* fills the room. She smiles. "That's the baby's heartbeat. Sounds normal."

Blake grabs my wrist, squeezing it tight. His smile broadens. "See? Everything's fine."

Melissa continues the scan, pointing out various parts of the body—the spine, arms, legs, and abdomen—all coming together to form a precious life inside me. Tears sting my eyes.

"Do you want to know the sex?"

I glance at Blake, who nods. "Yeah."

The technician beams. "You're having a girl."

A girl. I picture her with a head of dark hair, her tiny fingers curling around mine. Emotion constricts my throat. This is real. I'm having a baby girl.

Blake's thumb rubs circles across my skin. The intimacy is a shot of adrenaline to my chest. He's right. Everything's fine. This will be a breeze.

The technician tells me Dr. Lin will be in shortly, then leaves. After what seems like an eternity Dr. Lin enters, wearing a crisp white lab coat over slacks and a blouse. She greets us and asks how I'm feeling.

"I'm good."

"Tell me, have you had any bleeding?"

It's a casual question, but it sends a jolt of fear through me. "No."

I try to keep my heart cold and still, but my pulse beats erratically. I meet Blake's eyes. "Is something wrong with the baby?" he asks, his grip on me tightening.

She shakes her head, her eyes focused on the monitor. "Your baby is fine. The growth is on track for your due date, but it looks like you have placenta previa. That means your placenta is partially covering the cervix. It usually isn't a problem. Most cases resolve on their own, but if it doesn't it can cause bleeding and serious complications."

My stomach drops.

"Is there anything we can do?" Blake asks.

"We'll have to monitor the situation. The placenta may move as the uterus grows, but if it doesn't, we might have to consider a C-section."

The room falls silent as we absorb the news.

My mind whirls with everything that could go wrong. I can't fathom having a C-section. What if something happens to me during the delivery?

I'm too stunned to ask for more information. Luckily, Blake takes over. He fires question after question at the doctor. When he seems satisfied, she leaves with strict instructions to repeat the ultrasound in a couple of weeks.

I bury my face in my hands, trying to process what happened. One of Blake's hands rests on my back, rubbing circles. His other hand gently wipes off the gel from my belly with a towel.

"You okay?"

I shake my head, overwhelmed. "I don't know. Everything is happening so fast. A baby girl...placenta previa."

"It's a lot to take in, but the baby is healthy, and the condition will most likely disappear on its own. All things considered, I think this went pretty well."

"This is not what I thought would happen." I press my palms into my eyes, struggling to inhale even breaths. "How will I get through this?"

"Look at me." His thumb sweeps over my hand. "You're not alone."

I burst into tears. He pulls me into his arms and holds me. It's the closest we've been since...that night. He smells nice. Just like he did in the hotel room, like spice and citrus. My body melts into his, and I cling to his back.

It's been too long. I'm starved of human touch.

Dangerously vulnerable. He tucks a strand of hair behind my ear, the gentleness shattering my defenses.

His hands slide to my cheeks, cradling me like glass. "You have to move out of my brother's house. You can't continue to work there."

"What do you mean?"

"You have a high-risk pregnancy." Blake wipes a tear from my cheek, his voice lowering. "You'll have to significantly reduce your activity levels. That means you won't be able to do your job."

"I don't have any symptoms. She said I could keep working as long as it stays that way."

"I don't want to pressure you, but this arrangement with Naomi and Jack won't last. You'll have more doctor visits. It'll be stressful. The last thing you need is my brother breathing down your neck."

I take a steadying breath. Blake's right. I can't stay with them forever. The thought of giving up my job and relying on Blake is terrifying, but delivering a healthy baby is more important.

"Look," he says earnestly. "I know you hate me, and I don't blame you. I'm sure I seem like a selfish, self-absorbed asshole to you. I might be all those things, but I'm not ashamed of you."

I pull away from him, wiping my face. "I'll figure something out."

Blake's scowl darkens. "I'll drive you."

"My car is parked here."

"Give me the keys. I'll have someone drop it off." Blake reaches into my purse, pocketing them before I can protest. "You're in no state to drive. Come."

He escorts me out with a hand pressing into my lower back. I'm not aware of my feet taking me anywhere, and suddenly, we're at his car. He tucks me inside the passenger seat and slips behind the wheel. We drive to Jack and Naomi's in total silence. I feel his eyes on me, studying, *assessing*.

Once we're at Jack's front gate, Blake parks the Tesla. I unbuckle the seatbelt and grab the gate, but his gentle baritone stops me.

"Hold on. You forgot this."

I turn around, glancing at the black-and-white photo clutched in Blake's fingers. He hands me the sonograph, and I slip it into my bag.

"Thanks. See you soon."

"Take care."

He grasps my shoulder. Then in a swift moment that leaves me breathless, his lips press into my cheek. The warmth from his kiss lingers like a patch of glowing sunlight. The dizzying current throws me off kilter. Blake pulls away, his smile sending a shiver down my spine.

What the hell just happened?

I fumble with the door latch and stumble outside. Blake's arresting gaze follows me as I punch in the code and head through the gate. With one last lingering look, he drives off.

Disoriented, I stroll down the driveway. I grip the sonograph. Despite my desperate hope that he's on my side, a warning blazes through me: *Don't let him fool you.*

NINETEEN

A heavy knock resonates through the house, a prelude to the storm brewing within its walls. I ignore the persistent visitor. Let Naomi extricate herself from her ten-thousand-thread count Egyptian cotton sheets, put on her Versace slippers, and greet her visitor.

As I'm wiping the kitchen window, the door opens. Footsteps tap the marble. A male voice rings out. "Hello?"

My heart thunders as I hurtle around the corner, assuming that my brooding employer is back, but it's Blake.

He stands at the entrance, breathtakingly handsome in jeans and a sports jacket. Blake has been on my mind since the ultrasound appointment a few days ago. I've been obsessing over the results and avoiding Naomi, who has barricaded herself in her room again, but he's never far from my thoughts.

As I watch him, my stomach flutters with the wingbeats of a hundred butterflies. I didn't expect to see him so soon. Part of me wants to throw him out. His forehead knits as he faces the direction of Naomi's faint crying.

I clear my throat. "How did you get in here?"

His head whips toward me, his expression unapologetic. "I know the code."

"So you just let yourself into their home?"

Blake snorts. "You're a fine one to bring up boundaries."

I cross my arms, ignoring my burning cheeks. Jack's cameras probably caught him approaching the house. "You can't just show up. They'll figure it out."

He shrugs. "Wouldn't be the worst thing in the world."

I grit my teeth. "What are you doing here?"

"Looking for you. We should talk."

I press my lips together. "Talk to my lawyer."

"You can't afford one, Grace."

The confidence in his tone grates on me. "You don't know that. Maybe I'm sitting on a fat trust fund like you."

Blake rolls his eyes.

"I'm serious."

"Okay. Then what are you doing here?"

"I got bored of being rich and wanted to live a more authentic life."

Blake smiles, and my insides jangle with excitement. I like his smile. It's effortless, warm, and puts me at ease. "Come with me for a couple hours."

"Why?"

"We're having a baby. Don't you want to get to know me?"

He takes my arm, and the warmth from his touch

travels to my face. This man shouldn't still affect me after everything he's done.

"I-I can't. I'm on the clock."

Blake gazes in Naomi's direction. "She sounds busy."

"She'll notice I'm gone."

"Tell her you went to lunch," he murmurs, sliding his grip around my elbow and pulling me along. "We won't be long. Promise."

I'm torn between anger, fear, and an undeniable longing. I let him drag me out of the house, even though it's a bad idea. When he opens the passenger-side door and places his hand on my upper back, my breathing shallows. I glimpse my reflection in the darkened glass. I imagine sunglasses perched on my head, our toddler fast asleep in a car seat, and a pang hits my chest.

Blake's car automatically drives us. He glances at the windshield, shooting off emails and texts on his smartphone. Then we pull into the cafe I frequent. I hold my breath as we walk inside, hoping the gossip queen isn't here. He'll lose his marbles if he sees me walking in with Blake Hamilton.

Judging from the hostess's megawatt smile, Blake is a local celebrity. She grabs two menus and takes us to a secluded table near the windows. He pulls out a chair for me. My mind buzzes as I sit down, and then he follows suit.

He picks up the menu. "Pellegrino."

I grin at the waitress. "And I'll have a double vodka on the rocks with lime and a shot of tequila."

Blake sets the menu down slowly. I savor Blake's

wide-eyed alarm, chuckling. "Just kidding. I'll have water. From the tap."

Relief smooths Blake's forehead.

"Of course," the waitress says, hands clasped behind her back. "Can I get you any appetizers?"

"Tuna tartar." Blake turns toward me. "Do you like raw fish?"

"I'm pregnant."

He shakes his head. "Right. Chips and guac?"

When the waitress zooms away with our order, there's an awkward silence. It's midday and busy. A family sits beside us, their toddler babbling on his father's lap. A troubling thought trickles into my brain. *We'll never be like that.*

Hurt squeezes, deep inside me.

"So how are you?" he asks. "Are you getting enough to eat?"

Instantly, I'm on guard. "Why?"

His smile tightens with strain. "You kept blowing up my phone with demands for money. I assume you need cash for the basics. Food. Clothes."

"I did, weeks ago, when I was newly pregnant, homeless, and desperate." I cock my head, staring at him. "If only someone had messaged me back."

He grimaces. He's so tense. I expected him to be smug and confident, but he's a bundle of nerves. Blake seizes his drink the moment the waitress slides it over the table. He waves her off when she asks for entree orders, and she trots off.

"I'm sorry for abandoning you. That's not who I am."

"I guess you're the guy who cheats."

The grip around his glass whitens. "It's not that simple."

"Spare me the violin solo."

He takes a swig of his sparkling water as though it's alcohol. "I wasn't in love with her, and I could tell she felt the same."

"Why didn't you break up with her until now?"

"Every time I tried to end it, she'd call my dad, cry to him, and I'd get a visit from him pressuring me to take her back. He'd give me a speech about the Hamilton legacy, how the match was perfect because her father owns a luxury hotel chain, and for some stupid reason, it'd work."

"Is that what you want? A business partner for a wife?"

"It's what I believed I wanted. But living with her was a nightmare. Within a few months of her moving in, I realized we weren't compatible. I stayed with her because I thought that was normal." Blake glances at me and lets out a bitter laugh. "Everybody I know is unhappy in their marriage."

"So your father guilted you into getting engaged."

He hardens. "He can be very convincing."

He ends that sentence in a tone so dark it seems to throw a shade over the lights in the room. So what if his father's a domineering jerk? He's a big boy. He could've ended things. Instead he sulked in a bar, drank his feelings away, and spent the night with me. Now he's saddled with *another* woman he doesn't want.

He rubs his forehead, raking his messy brown waves. "Enough about me. How have you been?"

"Fine. I'm still processing the news."

"Do you need anything?"

"I told you, no. My salary covers everything." *Almost.* "I'm content at Jack and Naomi's place."

His stare drills into me, but I glare back.

"I'm not leaving my full-time job that pays my bills and has the best health insurance."

"Find another one."

I snort. "Like what? A crummy retail job where I'm forced to stand for eight hours a day? No thanks."

"I'll pay your expenses."

"I'm not comfortable with that."

"You'll be forced to leave anyway." Blake leans forward, looming over me like a storm cloud. "I know Jack. He won't tolerate a screaming infant in his house. He'll kick you out. Then you'll call me for help. What's the point of delaying the inevitable?"

"I need you to respect my decision."

He scrapes a hand over his face. "Has anyone ever mentioned that you're incredibly stubborn?"

"My parents, many times."

"Wouldn't you rather have a place that's yours?"

I scramble to put my erratic thoughts together. He sounds sincere, but he could be lying. "What happens when you stop paying my rent?"

"I wouldn't do that."

I force my lips to curve. "Women are stiffed by deadbeat dads all the time."

"You could sue me for child support."

"Sure. But litigation takes weeks. Meanwhile, I'm stuck in a women's shelter with a baby, fending off drug addicts and God knows what else. No. I can't do that to my kid. I'm far better off at Jack and Naomi's house."

Blake looks like he's close to banging his forehead on the table. "They have no idea whose kid you're carrying. You can't do this to them."

"*I* did this? You pulled me into that hotel. You got me pregnant. And then *you* ignored me when I begged for help."

He gives me a black look layered with annoyance, his long fingers tapping a beat. "You're not exactly being consistent here."

I blink, taken aback. "What?"

He leans forward, placing his forearms on the table, his words punctuating the air with their truth. "One minute, you're ringing my phone off the hook, begging me to help you. The next, you've got a roof over your head and suddenly, my involvement is too much of a hassle?"

His accusation stings, but I don't interrupt him. I can't. He's...right.

"And now you're painting me as the bad guy," he continues, his voice hard. "As if I forced you into this situation. As if you bear no responsibility whatsoever for what happened."

His icy stare pins me to my seat. "But we know that's not true, don't we? We both got drunk that night, Grace. We made a mutual decision to sleep together. You act like I've trapped you in this situation. You willingly walked into that hotel room with me. You could have said no. You could have walked away, but you didn't."

His eyes soften. "I'm not saying I handled the aftermath correctly, because I didn't. But you're not entirely innocent in this either. So before you start preaching about karma, maybe you should take a long hard look in the mirror."

His words hang heavy in the air between us, and for the first time since this conversation began, I'm speechless. Because as much as I hate to admit it, Blake's right. I'm just as culpable in this situation as he is.

The waitress returns with our appetizer, oblivious to the tension gripping our table. She beams at me. "Any questions about the menu?"

"Nope. I'll get the surf and turf plate, a side of french fries, and I've changed my mind about the water. I'll have a strawberry lemonade." I hand her the menu, expecting Blake to be annoyed that I've ordered the most expensive thing on the menu, but he doesn't bat an eyelash.

"And I'll have the club sandwich. Thank you."

The waitress takes his menu and whisks away, but the reprimand I'm waiting for never comes. He merely watches me with his lightning-rod stare.

"I'll pay you to leave my brother's house."

"Why do you want me out of there so badly?"

"Because," he says, his curt voice lashing at me. "It's not safe. You should be in a place you'll be taken care of. If you're in a crisis, you have nobody to turn to."

"I have Jack and Naomi."

"Who will evict you as soon as the baby starts wailing at three a.m. They won't put up with a crying infant keeping them up all night. Even if they did, my brother and his wife deserve their space."

His words make sense. Too much sense. Blake's gaze bores into me, willing me to say yes.

"I'll think about it," I say finally. "But I can't promise anything."

He nods, and the tension melts from his face.

We sit in silence, our appetizers forgotten. The family beside us leaves, and the restaurant has quieted down. Blake reaches across the table, taking my hand. "I'm committed to looking after you and the baby. I want to be involved in her life."

I glance at our interlinked fingers, the warmth of his skin seeping into mine. What are his real motives? Is he trying to make things right, or is he manipulating me?

He pulls out his wallet and takes out a credit card. "This is for you."

My face flushes. "No."

"I insist."

"I'm not comfortable—"

"I don't care," he growls. "It's non-negotiable."

"You don't decide that."

"You'll accept the damn thing. I'll feel better knowing you have a lifeline if there's an emergency. Consider it a peace offering."

The gesture is nice, but something beneath his generosity is left unspoken. I grasp the card, battling relief and guilt. Accepting his money comes with an agreement. He's attempting to buy my silence, but...this will make life easier for me.

Our food arrives. We quietly eat our meals while stealing glances at each other. When we're finished, Blake stands up and throws cash on the table before turning to leave. I follow him outside, stuffed to the gills with lobster and steak. We climb into the car and Blake zooms back to Jack and Naomi's house.

He drops me off in front of the gate. His strong fingers curl around my wrist before I get out, dragging my attention to him. "Call me if anything changes."

"With the baby?"

His gaze flicks to the house. "With them."

"Like with Jack?"

"Or Naomi."

"What's wrong with her?"

His face closes, as though guarding a secret. "Just promise me you'll call."

Fine, don't tell me. I grab my purse. "Whatever."

"Not *whatever*. Promise. Me."

"*Okay*. God. I promise. But you shouldn't worry. I like living with them."

He raises a brow. "You do?"

"Yeah. Naomi cares about me. She's not some frigid, rich jerk...she's nice. She makes me feel welcome. Treats me like family." A blush creeps onto my cheeks. "I'm not ready to lose that."

A shadow of alarm touches Blake's expression. He squeezes my wrist, and a shiver dances across my skin. "I'll pick you up for the next doctor's appointment."

A warning erupts inside me, but I smile, playing dumb. My mind whirls. What does he really want? The questions spin in my head as I unbuckle myself, feeling more lost than ever.

I slide from the seat, but he catches my arm, stopping me. "I'm sorry for what I said earlier. Your life is your own. It's not my place to judge what you do with it."

"Thanks. I appreciate that."

"No hard feelings, all right? I'd like us to be friends."

I look at him for a long moment and nod. If the Blake from the bar was here, I would've jumped at his offer of friendship, but the man in front of me? I don't trust him.

He lets me go, and I step out of the car.

Blake's apology rings hollowly in my chest, and so does his extension of an olive branch. It reeks of desperation. Underneath his charming smile, there is a restless undercurrent of *something*.

My throat tightens as I stroll the driveway. This home is less welcoming by the day, courtesy of Jack. His Darth Vadar–like presence sucks the joy from the air. I breathe easier when he's not in the room. If he weren't here, living here would be such a treat.

I climb the staircase to the door. Instead of going inside, I admire the view of Lake Washington. A hazy gray sky floats above the water, silhouettes of boats bobbing on the waves. A ferry horn echoes. I breathe in deeply, enjoying the peacefulness. It sits in my lungs, warming me from the inside out. Then a loud creak breaks the serenity.

God, what now?

I spin around as the front door slowly opens.

TWENTY

Naomi shuffles outside in a lavender robe, puffy-eyed and pale. She blinks, almost wincing, then seems to notice me. "There you are. I've been looking for you."

"Hey. Sorry, I was out."

"Out *where?*"

"At a café for an early lunch."

She ushers me inside and shuts the door, her cheeks blooming with pink. Is she mad? She tucks a wayward blond curl behind her ear, her fine brows knitting.

"I know it's before my scheduled time. I should've told you, but it was last-minute. I needed to see someone. Yeah...I had to go to Shoreline to this place off Aurora, so that's why it took long."

"You went to Aurora Avenue *alone?*"

"The restaurant was a couple blocks away."

Naomi gapes at me like I've lost my mind, but I can't blame her. Aurora Avenue is one of Seattle's worst streets, famous for its crime, scantily clad women in thigh-high heels, and drug addicts. I used to live near the street. It was a horrible experience. Lying to Naomi doesn't feel good, but I can't tell her that my baby's father bought me lunch at a Bellevue café without it ringing alarm bells. It's better if everyone believes he's dirt poor.

"My baby's father works in the area."

Naomi rubs the back of her neck, revealing long red lines. She flips her hair, covering the marks. "You should've asked. I could've dropped you off."

"I'm fine with driving."

She gnaws on her lip, gazing outside where my car is parked. "If it were me, I'd feel more comfortable in a safer vehicle. That Toyota is, what, seventeen years old?"

"Twenty."

Naomi blinks. "Do you have a death wish?"

"It's fine. They build cars to last forever."

Naomi crosses her arms. "You can't run around in that part of town. It's unsafe. You should've asked him to meet you *here*. I could've ordered food. You wouldn't have had to walk down Aurora in your condition."

"I'm fine."

After a beat, she lets out a tiny sigh. "You're right. I'm being ridiculous. I get so anxious when I think about your pregnancy."

A question lingers in her tone. I chew on my lip. I never got the chance to discuss the ultrasound results, and truthfully, I'm dying to confide in someone. "There was a minor problem. I have placenta previa. It means my placenta is partially covering my cervix."

"Oh God. I'm so sorry."

"It's not as serious as it sounds. I'll just have to be monitored closely."

My stomach flips as Naomi ushers me into the family room, where Jack is settled in his recliner, iPad in his lap. "Do you need a second opinion? I'm friends with the head of the OG/GYN department at Swedish. I don't mind making some calls."

I smile. "That's okay. I'm happy with my doctor."

She clutches my shoulder. "It breaks my heart that you're going through this alone."

"Well, my baby's father has been involved."

Her hand slips from me. "*Oh.* I didn't know he was in the picture."

"He took me out to lunch today, but I'm not getting my hopes up. I don't want to be disappointed."

"That's...good."

"Yeah. It's a tremendous relief. It's dawning on me how hard this will be without him..." I trail off, distracted by the glaze spreading over Naomi's eyes. "Are you okay?"

She blinks, and the strange look disappears. "If you'll excuse me, I need to get changed. I'm late for my Pilates class."

Then she rushes to the bedroom, leaving me with Jack. He sets down the iPad, his lightning-rod stare striking me across the room. "You're lying."

My throat tightens. "I'm sorry?"

"You didn't drive *anywhere*. My camera feed caught you walking down the driveway." He swivels the screen around, which blazes with an image of my retreating back. "A man picked you up in his car."

I lick my lips, my heart hammering.

"You gave your baby daddy our address after I forbid

him from coming here." He makes a faint noise, gesturing toward the entry. "Practically invited him through the front door."

I gape at him, refusing to believe anyone could be so ridiculous. "Are you pitching a fit because someone drove past your house?"

He stands, the iPad dangling from his grip, his smooth baritone infecting me with anxiety. "I thought I made myself clear about my expectations. I don't tolerate liars."

"For God's sake, I didn't lie. When I said I drove, I meant *him*. Besides, why does it even matter? What, you can't stand that a stranger's vehicle was too close to your home? Are you that conceited?"

He erases the distance between us with a long stride, slamming the iPad on the counter. The harsh *slap* sends a current down my spine, making me jump. Jack points at the iPad's screen. It's grainy and blurry, but the sleek silhouette of the Tesla is prominent.

"That's not a cheap car."

Heat steals into my face. "Seriously, Jack? You're cross-examining me over this?"

"I told you," he snaps, tapping the screen for emphasis, "that I don't tolerate liars."

A harsh laugh escapes my lips. "Oh, I see. You're not upset because I lied. You're upset because the car he picked me up in is nicer than yours."

Jack stares at me. "That's not true."

"It is. This is a male ego thing. You see a fancy car and instantly make assumptions. You can't stand the idea that the father of my baby might be wealthier than you thought. It threatens your little power dynamic, doesn't it?"

His jaw clenches, and I know I've hit a nerve. But I don't care. This whole situation is ridiculous.

"Who is this man?"

I hold his gaze, my eyes burning from not blinking. "Some guy."

"What are you hiding from us?"

"I'm not hiding anything."

"You are. In the middle of your shift, you decide to meet with your baby daddy. But not before instructing him to pick you up outside the gate. Why?"

I shrug. "You told me he wasn't allowed on your property."

"Who is he? I want his name."

I'm done being polite with this ogre. "Well, you can want that until you pass out. It still won't happen."

"You're blunt for someone with no options."

"And you're a disgusting creep, but I guess we'll have to learn to tolerate each other."

He takes a swig of his coffee. He swallows. His shining lips yank into a malicious smile. "I'm guessing you slept with a techbro and got knocked up, but he won't give you a second glance until there's a paternity test. Is that about right?"

A dark, ugly feeling wells inside me as the awful echo of Blake's hurtful words replays in my head.

My throat aches. "No."

"What do you mean, no?"

I swallow tightly. "No is a complete sentence."

"Yes, but it sounded like a very loaded no. Like there's more to the story than you're letting on."

I cross my arms, shrugging. "It's a tale as old as time."

"Why are you carrying the baby to term?"

"Why don't you and Naomi have children?" I fire back.

He drains his cup and sets it on the kitchen counter, breaking his gaze from mine. "We're not ready."

"That's what all men say when they're stalling."

He gives me a black look. "Don't presume to know what I want."

"You're not that hard to read, Jack. You have all the money in the world, but you're miserable. Hence the existential crisis with the college girl whose name doubles as an alcohol."

I expect him to blow up, but he barely reacts. His face hardens but he speaks softly, like an orderly in a hospital waiting room. "I'm no saint, but you're in no position to judge me. If you had any brain cells, you'd get an abortion and move on with your life. Instead you're cleaning my toilets and living in a basement."

My hand aches with the urge to slap him. "That's my decision."

"Right. But it's stupid."

He moves closer, towering over me like a redwood. Jack scans me as though he's searching for something. He's close enough that I can see the red veins in his brown eyes and the way they're not quite focused. I want to run, but I can't let him win.

"Why are you looking at me like that?"

"You're what, twenty-one?" he says, his voice hoarse. "You should be in school."

My chest tightens. "I was."

"And you dropped out to take a minimum wage job?"

"I'm not a kid anymore. Where I choose to work is no one's business but my own."

He returns his mug to the sink. "Seems a little odd, that's all."

"Oh, it seems odd to you?" I retort, my voice laced with snark. "I forgot you were the expert in making life-altering decisions over a cup of coffee in the morning."

His eyes narrow at me. "I'm just trying to understand why—"

"*Sometimes*, life doesn't hand you a neat little trust fund and an all-expenses-paid education at an Ivy League. Sometimes, you have to make decisions that are best for you, not what others expect from you."

He stares at me. "I see."

"Do you? Because I'm not some victim for you to save. I've got this."

He scoffs, a smirk playing on his lips. "You're living in a basement, working as a maid, pregnant by a man who can't be bothered to be seen with you in public, and you've got this?"

He's baiting me. "I didn't ask for your judgment. I can handle my own life."

"That's clear," he replies dryly. "But just so you know, life is a series of choices. You've made yours."

"And you've made yours." I raise my brow. "Seems like we're both just trying to make the best of our own messes."

"Except mine doesn't involve a *child*."

"And mine doesn't involve hiding behind a wall of money and bitterness," I shoot back. "So I guess we're even."

"Half of my poker buddies are cheating on their wives." His body leans over the kitchen island as he faces me, his expression pinched with fatigue. "You're young. You've got your whole life ahead of you. Why are you ruining it?"

I grind my jaw. "I'm not. I'm taking charge."

His gentle laugh ripples through the air as he takes an apple from the fruit bowl. "No, you're not. You're resigning yourself to hell. You'll never finish college or be able to advance in any career. You'll be stuck in a dead-end job you hate. All your aspirations…your goals…*poof*. How is that not giving up?"

I ball my hands into fists, wishing I could punch his annoying face. Perhaps that's his goal. He'll provoke me, make me lose it, and then he'll have a cast-iron excuse to fire me. Jack bites into the apple, talking with his mouth full. "Do the smart thing now so you can have a better future."

"I'm not accepting life lessons from you," I say, rinsing out his cup and slamming it on the drying rack. "Especially when you're only saying it to intimidate me out of your house."

"If that's what you think, you really are in trouble."

"What about *you*? What'll happen when Naomi finds out what you're doing? Think she'll sweep it under the rug and pretend it never happened?" My shout bounces off the ceiling but he says nothing, his obstinate glare raking my skin.

"Staying here won't do you any good."

"Maybe it would if you got off my back."

Jack's grip on his coffee mug whitens. He puts it down, spreading his fingers on the counter. "Your presence is bad for my wife."

Unbelievable. I had him pegged as a raging narcissist after watching him with his father, but this is proof. "Because I'm poor? Or because your wife is my friend?"

"Both. I don't give a damn how much she spends on charity, but my tolerance ends when she brings it home."

"I'm not a charity case," I snarl, not bothering to keep my voice down. "I didn't beg anyone for money. She hired me. Your wife wants me here. I don't know why you're giving me such a hard time."

I turn around and walk out of the kitchen. We're two powder kegs, and the tension between us is a live wire. I head toward the butler's pantry, but Jack stops me with a hand on my shoulder.

He steps closer, his breath hot on my face. Suddenly, we're both locked into each other's gaze. There's something dangerous in his eyes, like he's dying to smack me. A knotted muscle flexes in his neck as he leans over me.

"I pay the bills. I can get rid of you at a moment's notice."

Empty threats. "If you coulda, you woulda. But I guess you like to move at your own pace."

"I'll throw you out."

"Not before I tell Naomi I saw you and Brandi in bed together."

His mouth pulls into a sour grin. "If I want her to believe you're stealing our prescription medications, I can do that. Or I can make her think you're endangering our lives."

"Then I'll sue you for a hostile work environment."

"With what money?"

"I'll ask my baby daddy."

His jaw works. "If you're hoping to rope my wife into a scam, I'll hit you where it hurts. I'll find out who the father of your baby is, and then I'll do everything in my power to give *him* full custody."

A sheer black fright sweeps through me.

I hurtle toward the basement, slamming the door. Jack can't fire me without risking his marriage, but he can threaten me, withhold my pay, or do many horrible things to make me miserable enough to quit. And once I cave, I'll be at Blake's mercy. God knows what *he'll* do to me.

The only thing I have is my baby girl, but even her presence feels tenuous, like a fragile thread on the verge of snapping. The air is thick with danger, like a storm cloud about to unleash its wrath on the world. If I don't get out of this house soon, something terrible will happen.

TWENTY-ONE

I don't sleep. I can't. I'm going crazy. It's this basement. The low ceilings and lack of windows trigger my claustrophobia, and the cold doesn't help me relax.

Jack's latest threat has me rattled, which is the point. The Neanderthal *wants* to get rid of me. Unfortunately for him, I don't respond well to threats. My gut reaction is to dig in my heels and fight. Why should *I* leave? He's the unreasonable one. He's a controlling, abusive monster who deserves to be punished. If I don't stand up to him, it'll embolden his behavior. He'll abuse the next maid.

I spend the evening fantasizing about life without Jack. No more living in a dank cave with spotty Wi-Fi that never works. I envision breaking the news to Naomi about Blake, her excitement, followed by a tearful embrace and a promise that I'll always have a family. This could work—if Jack is out of the picture. I'll think of a plan.

I get out of bed, shoving my feet into slippers. Then I climb the staircase, opening the door to a swell of warmth. I wander out of the butler's pantry, following the blue light flickering over tiles. I peek inside the family room.

Naomi sits on the chaise lounge, curled up in a throw beside Jack, who types on his laptop. She picks baby carrots from a bowl and dips them in hummus. Bites. Sips her white wine.

Hidden in the corridor, I watch them.

"Jack, can you get me a refill?"

He stops typing. "Of course."

"Thank you."

Naomi holds out her empty glass as Jack slides the computer onto the coffee table. He plucks the glass from her grip and stands, the delicate stem dainty in his massive fist. He peels himself from the couch and strides into the kitchen. As he grabs the opened bottle, Naomi bursts with another request. "Actually, can you make me a martini? With a bunch of olives?"

"Sure," he grumbles, retrieving a coupe glass from the fridge. "Want a lemon garnish?"

"Yes, please."

He prepares the drink with laser-focused precision. All it takes is one whine from Naomi's lips, and he's making her a cocktail, grabbing her a snack, whatever she wants. Who *is* this man? It's hard to reconcile this simp with the monster who cheats on his wife and threatens me.

When did their relationship become so toxic? The framed photos touching every wall illustrate such an innocent portrait of their love. Sweet hugs. Tender kisses. Matching tattoos. In person, they are insufferable lovebirds. After handing his wife her martini, Jack sits through an episode of *The Kardashians* with Naomi in his arms. After it ends, Naomi cups Jack's cheek and strokes his beard.

"By the way, did you paint the guest room? It smelled strange in there the other day."

"I did," he says, infuriating me. "You said it was dirty."

She clicks her tongue. "You didn't have to do that."

"Anything for my baby."

Are you kidding me? He's taking credit for *my* work. I can't believe this guy. I gape at Naomi, begging her to see through this act, but she swallows it. Hook. Line. The whole darn rod. She leans into his arms.

"I love you." She gives him a peck on his lips and then slides out of his embrace. "I think I'll go to bed. My stomach hurts."

"Should I call the doctor?"

"No, I'm okay. I just need rest."

"All right."

When Naomi disappears into their bedroom, Jack changes channels to the Seahawks game. It's like a switch flips in his brain. He bellows profanity. Slaps the couch. Yells abuse at the players when the opposing team scores.

A pulse throbs at the base of my throat. I fight the impulse to dump the tub of olives over his head. I picture him jumping up, his black hair plastered to his skull like a drowned rat. How satisfying would that be? At the very least, I should call him out for being so pathetic, but what's the point? The crazy jerk won't care. He's so far gone that he takes credit for the maid's work.

I stomp upstairs, itching to retaliate. The air vanishes from my lungs as I rush past the locked door. I stare at the golden doorknob, seized by a desire to do something reckless. Jack warned me from opening it on my first day. He'll freak if he finds me here. Maybe I want that. I hate him. He's an abusive, philandering, drunken pig who needs to be taken down fifty pegs. I can start by uncovering the secrets behind this door.

I seize a hairpin from my bun, jiggling it in the lock. It springs open, and I step into a dark room.

TWENTY-TWO

The room isn't a torture chamber. It's a nursery.

A single window overlooking the backyard lets in little light, casting long shadows across the floorboards. The bookshelf on the left wall is covered with rows of dusty board books. A porcelain doll stares at me, its frozen smile twisting my stomach.

Honestly, I'm let down. I expected to find a room filled with taxidermied heads. Jack's behavior hinted at a horror behind this door, but this isn't scary. What's in this room that he didn't want me to see? The changing station stocked with diapers? The neatly folded onesies...or the crib?

An icy finger trails my spine.

A bundle lies under a thin blanket. The sight twists my guts. I step closer to the crib, studying the small body underneath the knitted fabric. Reaching inside, I grab the blanket and pull, revealing a teddy bear. Its eyes stare at the ceiling, sightless and black, arms splayed to the sides.

My heart pounds as I study the monogrammed initials stitched onto its chest.

O. H.

What do they stand for? Something Hamilton? I inhale sharply, the musty air settling in my lungs like lead. They must've had a baby, but where is it—or what happened to them?

Nothing good.

A dark suspicion rears its head, tearing at my insides. Was it a miscarriage? Did their baby die? Is that why Jack said this room was off-limits? My mind races with awful questions, but the answers don't matter to me.

This is none of my business.

I'm intruding on a sacred place. Hallowed ground. Breaking in here was a mistake. I need to leave. I stride for the door, but it swings toward me.

Naomi bursts inside, her skin flushed. She's still wearing her silk robe, the belt untied and hanging loose. She clutches the door frame. Her widened eyes dart everywhere before finding me. A thread of panic shakes her voice. "What are you doing in here? Didn't Jack tell you this room is off-limits?"

"He did. I'm sorry."

"Then why are you in here?"

"Well, I mean, I've been living here for weeks and *only* this room was locked. Sometimes I get too curious for my own good...sorry."

I shift from foot to foot, eager to return to the basement. I would if she weren't glowering at me like I set the rug on fire. How could I've screwed up so badly?

"I don't believe you'd intentionally invade my privacy, but this room holds a lot of pain for me." She speaks calmly, but I wince at every word. "I can't bear anyone else seeing it. Please don't come in here again."

I swallow hard. "Okay. I won't."

"It's not just any room," she murmurs, sliding her arms around herself. "It was meant for my baby, but he's gone."

Ice spreads through my stomach. "He died?"

Naomi nods, her lips trembling. "It happened very fast. I went into labor at thirty-nine weeks and pushed for two agonizing hours. Then he was out and I couldn't wait to hold him, feel his tiny fingers, and look into his eyes. But instead, the doctor whisked him away to the other side of the room. I watched as she performed chest compressions. She told me his heart had stopped. She did everything she could to bring him back, but he...he didn't make it."

Her voice cracks, but she holds herself together, reciting the story like a well-worn tale etched onto her soul. Perhaps her grief runs too deep for tears. My world shifts, the pieces falling into place. All the times I heard her crying, her distant stares—this is the center of her trauma. Her baby. Her precious little boy.

A raw anguish washes over me, its weight crushing and unfathomable.

Naomi presses a hand to her belly. Her misery is a physical pain, throbbing inside me. She limps to the rocking chair, collapsing in the seat. "I wanted an autopsy, but Jack didn't, so I'll never know why. All the scans were perfect."

"Oh my God. I'm so sorry."

"It was years ago," she murmurs, wiping her glistening eyes. "It's so hard. Nobody understands the pain. How it never, ever leaves you." She fingers the crib, leaving a streak in the dust. "I thought if I kept the room ready, maybe one day we'd have another baby. Now it's a reminder of what we lost."

I don't know what to say. I stand there, mouth open like a dead fish, guilt eating me alive. "I'm sorry. You must be furious with me."

She smiles sadly. "It's perfectly normal to be curious about a fully stocked nursery behind a locked door."

"We don't have to talk about it."

"I want to, though. I can't pretend like he never existed." Naomi works her jaw. She says nothing for the longest time, then gets up, fingering the changing station, the crib, and then she takes the stuffed bear with monogrammed initials. She holds it to her chest and sinks into the rocking chair. "I can't bring myself to clear out all this stuff. Part of me wants to move on, but that feels like a betrayal. Like I owe it to him to sit in my grief forever."

A knife twists in my heart. I'm uncomfortable, but she obviously needs this. Jack probably hates whenever she brings it up. I want to hug Naomi, to ease her suffering, but that's not my place. I'm just a maid.

Tears streak down her cheeks. "When my feelings get…too much, I come here. Sometimes I hold his toys, or I sit here and imagine what he'd be like. Is that weird?"

"No. Not at all."

"I'm sorry. I don't mean to make things awkward." Naomi wipes her face, a smile trembling on her lips. "This must be overwhelming."

It is. This isn't a subject I'm equipped for, considering my fears about my pregnancy, but I have to help her. I take her shoulder, squeezing it.

"You're doing the best you can."

She shakes her head, her wide eyes streaming. "It was my fault. Instead of embracing my pregnancy, I was at war with myself. Trying to stay fit. I pushed too hard and lost the baby. That's why I worry when I see you around the house working yourself to the bone."

A dull ache pounds in my belly. "Have you and Jack tried for another baby?"

Naomi sets the bear down and strokes his fur. "No. It's causing tension between us. I'm sorry. I shouldn't unload all of this on you. You must feel so uncomfortable."

"Don't apologize. I'm glad you told me."

She takes my hand, her gaze swimming with emotion. "You're not alone. I care about you."

The way she says that slices my chest open. I feel laid bare. I need support. Raising this baby without that will be incredibly difficult. She knows that. She's telling me that I can rely on her.

I blink away tears. "I care about you, too."

"You're a good person." She gives my wrist a final squeeze and stands, heaving a great breath. "Well, I think I'm going to go to bed. Thanks for listening."

She sweeps out of the room, and a hollowness gapes inside me. I'm *not* a good person. I barged in here without regard to Naomi's feelings. All I cared about was revenge.

I follow Naomi outside. The dark hallways are empty as I wander to the basement. As I clutch the railing and descend the steps, my mind drifts to Blake's offer. I should leave, but how can I do that now? Naomi needs me. I can't abandon her. But if I stay, this becomes my life...forever comforting a woman who has lost so much. The weight of Naomi's sorrow suffocates me. I reach the bottom of the stairs and stand in the basement's darkness. Apprehension creeps up my spine.

I can't take it anymore.

I dial Blake's number.

TWENTY-THREE

I need a break from the Hamiltons.

Blake picks me up the next morning. At my suggestion, he drives us into Seattle. It's cherry blossom season, my favorite time of the year, and the quad at UW is the best place to enjoy them. Pink blossoms blush against dark branches. Clouds float over a misty blue sky. Couples in smart clothing pose for photographers. Petals lazily drift in the air. It's perfect for a date—not that this is one. I'm not expecting another kiss on the cheek. That was a one-off.

Blake spreads a checkered blanket on the lawn, pulling out two sandwiches from an insulated bag, chips, fruit, and cans of seltzer. When he catches my questioning gaze, he shrugs. "You said you hadn't eaten yet."

"That's thoughtful of you. Thanks."

He hands me a sandwich. My tongue waters at the thick slices of pastrami and pickled vegetables. I'm glad Blake doesn't share Naomi's mania for healthy food. I rip open a kettle chip bag and pop one in my mouth. I groan, savoring the grease and salt.

He frowns. "Do they feed you all right?"

My forehead pinches. "I'm not a toddler."

"Naomi's very maternal. I assumed she'd try."

I sigh heavily. "She's constantly making me smoothies and meals. It's sweet. She'd give me so much crap if she saw me scarfing this down."

"She controls what you eat?" he asks, frowning.

"No, she offers until I cave." I laugh, but Blake doesn't look pleased. "I thought you'd be the same. I figured you'd want me to be the perfect pregnant woman."

He shakes his head. "I'm no health nut."

"How would you describe yourself?"

"I'm more of a live and let live kind of guy. I believe in balance and enjoying life. You should be able to savor those chips without guilt." He leans back on the blanket, his eyes sparkling. "Besides, I'd be a hypocrite if I expected you to be flawless when I'm far from the perfect brother or father-to-be."

I smile, more at ease in his company. It's refreshing to be around someone who doesn't have unrealistic expectations of me. "What do you like to do for fun?"

"I love hiking and exploring new places. Capturing their beauty with my camera. It helps me unwind." He opens his phone and flips through an album of stunning landscapes.

"Wow. These are great."

He makes a flippant motion. "It's a hobby."

"All that traveling must make you appreciate the

world more. No wonder you're obsessed with retrofitting yachts for green emissions."

"You heard about that?"

"Jack's mentioned it once or twice."

Blake's mouth pulls into a wry grin. "Yeah, he hates the idea. He doesn't think it's possible to pull it off. Cruises aren't eco-friendly in the slightest. They're one of the biggest polluters. One ship has roughly the same emissions as twelve thousand cars, which is insane. Cruise ships devastate oceans, coastal communities, reefs, the list goes on and on."

I nod, biting into my sandwich. "What's your plan for these eco-yachts?"

"Well, it's a work in progress." Blake shifts a hand behind his head. "We're researching hybrid engines, solar power integration, and even experimenting with advanced wastewater treatment systems. It's challenging, but it's the right thing to do."

"That's cool."

He snorts. "Uh-huh."

"No, I'm serious. It's fantastic. It shows you care about the environment and your business."

His burning stare holds me still. "Thanks. It's not easy going against my brother and father. They're more focused on short-term profits."

I wink. "And it doesn't hurt that customers are looking for more sustainable options."

"Maybe."

"Trust me, I know. I'm a master at spotting trends, and I'm telling you, green is the new black."

His grin broadens into a full-blown smile. "Perhaps I should hire you as a consultant."

"Sure, but only if I get paid in chips and pastrami."

"*Deal.*"

After I finish my lunch, I lay down beside him. My gaze travels up and down his body. His broad shoulders, toned arms, tanned skin, and inviting lips fill me with steam. I ache to touch him, to feel the warmth radiating from him. I'm dying to run my fingers through his hair. He looks perfect against the sun-drenched grass.

"I'm glad you suggested this," he says with a happy sigh. "I can't remember the last time I stopped and stared at the sky. It's calming, isn't it? Makes you feel small in the best way possible."

"I guess so, but sometimes feeling small sucks." I glance at a patch of blue between the swaying cherry blossoms as Blake's gentle baritone floats over me.

"What's bothering you?"

"Nothing."

He props himself up on an elbow, his brows furrowed. "I can tell something's wrong. Just talk to me."

My throat tightens. "Naomi told me about the loss of her baby. It's messing with my head. All I want is for our baby to be healthy."

He sighs, lying back down. "She will be. What happened to Naomi and Jack won't happen to us."

"But how can you be so sure? Naomi said everything seemed fine until the baby was born. That freaks me out."

He gently touches my wrist, sending shivers down my spine. "If you need some space, you can leave for a while."

I shake my head. "I can't do that to her."

"Naomi's emotions aren't your responsibility."

"But she's become like a sister to me. I have to be there for her."

"You can't fix this for her," he says, his expression darkening. "The only person who can help her move forward is my brother."

"Why doesn't he?"

He shrugs. "Jack cares more about proving himself to our father."

Funny. Naomi said the same about him.

"Has either of you ever stood up to your dad?"

"Jack has. It never ends well for him."

He makes it sound so dire. "And what about you?"

"I'm not stupid enough to mouth off to the man dangling an inheritance in my face." He slides an arm over his eyes, blocking the sunshine. "You've got to play the game and appease the old fart."

"You're happy doing that? Jumping through his ridiculous hoops like a trick pony?"

"Everybody plays tricks," he murmurs in a suggestive tone, moving his arm to bump into mine. "The difference is, I get what I want. Always."

Goosebumps spread across my skin. "Wouldn't it be nice to be free, though?"

"I will be when he's gone."

I catch my breath. He's so intense. It's a little frightening.

His attention drifts back to me. "You could cause me a lot of trouble if you repeated anything I said."

"No worries. We're in a standoff, like the Cuban Missile Crisis. You know, I nuke you, you nuke me."

He chuckles, the tension in the air easing. "Sounds like a fair deal. We'll keep each other's secrets safe."

The warmth in his voice heats my skin. My heart pounds. I can't get carried away again. I need to stay focused on the bigger picture—the future of our child.

"It's funny how something so small can bring so much joy."

He picks up a fallen cherry blossom. "Yeah, they're pretty."

"I meant the baby."

His smile is alive with affection. Our gazes lock, and the air between us crackles with electricity. For a moment, he seems to lean in for a kiss. Then he pulls out his phone, snapping a photo of me.

My cheeks flush. "What'd you do that for?"

"I want to remember today. It's a beautiful day, and we both needed this."

As we stand, I'm bombarded with confusing feelings. Hanging out with Blake was so easy, but it was like walking on a tightrope. I'm trying to maintain a balance between enjoying myself and not getting too invested. He's not just my baby's father, he's a Hamilton. They're a family with secrets and expectations I don't understand.

As we walk through the quad, I study him. He's smiling, his eyes dancing with happiness, his magnetism dragging me toward him. I'm well aware of where this is headed, but I can't tell my beating heart to shut up. I want—I'm not sure *what*—but I need more.

Blake drives me to our meeting spot, the local café's parking lot. When he cuts the engine, he unbuckles his seatbelt and turns at the waist, his attention riveted on my face.

Tingling pits my stomach. I try to throttle the current racing through me. I'm wrapped in warmth, but my attraction to him is dangerous. We'll never be together.

"We should do this more often," he says, one hand on the steering wheel. "Once in a while, get away and hang out. No pressure."

I swallow hard. "Okay."

He leans over and presses his lips to my cheek. A bolt of electricity zings through me at his touch. My mouth yanks into a foolish grin.

"I'll call you," he whispers. "Take care, Grace."

I fumble with the seatbelt before it slides free. I leave his Tesla, as breathless as a teenage girl. Then he drives off. I watch until he disappears. I can't stop grinning. I'm excited. I don't know why, but it's a pleasant change from the constant anxiety.

Time to go home. I stroll to my parking spot, but it's empty. What the hell? Was my car towed? I take out my phone, searching for the tow company. My hands tremble as I dial their number. How much will it cost? What if they hauled it to the other side of town?

As I make the call, a figure catches my attention. It's Jack, leaning against a BMW. He strides toward me with a glint in his eye. My pulse spikes. He looks like he caught me in the middle of something. I gape at him, more and more alert.

He knows.

A lead weight drops in my stomach.

I freeze, my heart racing. This is it. The moment I've been dreading...when everything falls apart.

TWENTY-FOUR

"Get in."

Jack yanks open the car door, his venomous tone slapping my cheek. Instantly, I'm on alert. I square my shoulders and glare at him.

"Why are you here? Did you follow me?"

"I'll take you home," he says, blowing past my question.

I stuff my phone in my purse. "I can't. My car got towed."

"Who do you think called the tow truck?" he growls.

A groan escapes my lips. "You did that? Why?"

"Take a wild guess."

I chew on my lip. He saw Blake and me together. That's why he looks like he's itching to put his hands around my neck. Maybe I can salvage this.

"Get in the car," he barks.

"I'd rather stick my arm in a blender."

Jack mutters under his breath and guides me toward his car, pushing me inside like a cop making an arrest. I flinch when he slams the door. Then he gets into the driver's seat and starts the car, peeling out of the parking lot.

"Is something wrong?" I ask, trying to sound calm.

He wrenches the steering wheel, and I collide with the door. "Do you have any idea what you've done?"

"I-I don't know what you're talking about."

"My brother is the father," he barks, disgust lacing his words. "Isn't he?"

We blaze through a yellow light. I picture a car T-boning us, my motionless form on a stretcher. God, what if I lose the baby?

"I'm pregnant. Could you slow down?"

"Don't tell me how to drive," he snaps, gunning the motor. *"Answer the question."*

"Fine. *Yes.*"

"How did it happen?"

"You want a blow-by-blow of our one-night stand?" I clutch the door handle, my chest pulsing as he races around another bend. "Jack, please slow down. The baby—"

"Unbelievable. You're living in my house, eating my food, treating us like fools. You must think you're so damned slick."

"Stop the car!"

"You're fired," he snarls. "You're out. Once we're home, you'll pack your things. I don't give a crap if my brother's a cheapskate. You are *out of here.*"

Jack slams the brakes to avoid clipping an oncoming car. My heart lodges in my throat as we clear it by inches. Then he accelerates.

THE MAID

"*Jesus*. Are you trying to kill us?"

Sneering, he jerks the wheel. We make a hard right down another road. He finally slows when we reach his street, punching in the code that opens the gate. As it swings open, his hostile glare burns through my skin.

"Go straight to the basement. If you see Naomi, don't say a word. Never speak to my wife again. If I catch you sending a text, I'll file a restraining order."

"Fine," I choke out, my heart still pounding. "Just let me out."

The BMW lurches into the driveway and stops right beside my car. He must've towed it straight home. He yanks on the parking brake before shutting the engine. "And don't for one second believe that sharing his DNA makes you a Hamilton. You're a *maid*. It's an embarrassment to this family."

You're not welcome here.

My father's parting words eat at me like acid. Tears fill my eyes, but I swallow my despair. I attempt to unbuckle my seatbelt three times before I succeed, stumbling upright on shaky legs.

"Trust me. I'm doing you a favor." Jack walks around the car, glowering. "You don't belong in this family."

"If joining a family means I have to make peace with pigs like you, I don't want to belong."

"I'm glad we understand each other."

His sneer rakes me like a knife. I slam the door, storming toward the house. Jack follows, hissing in my ear. "You'll pack and be gone in an hour. And if I hear so much as a peep from you, I'll make sure you regret it. Understood?"

"*Fine.*"

"Good." Jack races up the staircase to the porch, opening the door. "And don't bother harassing my brother. He wants nothing to do with you or the baby."

I burst inside the house.

"Jack, is that you? I can't find—*oh.*" Naomi pops out of the kitchen, wearing yellow dish gloves. Her eyes widen as they center on my face. "Are you okay?"

I shake my head. "Y-your husband fired me."

"What?" she gasps. "What is she talking about?"

Jack steps into the house and slams the front door, his attention riveted on me. "Get your things and leave."

"*Jack.* What's going on?"

I swallow hard. "He saw me and Blake—"

"*Shut up.* Naomi doesn't want to hear any more lies from you."

Naomi grasps her husband's arm. "Tell me what happened."

"She's done," he thunders, the veins standing out on his neck. "And you're not to speak to her again."

Naomi slides her gloved hands to her hips. "I'm not a child. I'll talk to whomever I please. And you can't fire her without reason."

"She's pregnant with my brother's kid," he bellows, gesturing toward me. "That's reason enough."

"*Blake?*" Naomi's widened gaze flickers to me, then Jack. "But...how? How long have you known?"

"I just found out," Jack says smoothly. "She deleted footage from the camera a few days ago. I got curious, so I put a tracker in her car. Followed her to a cafe where

Blake picked her up. They've been seeing each other in secret."

Naomi's forehead wrinkles. "But that doesn't mean—"

"She admitted it. Baby, they've made us a laughingstock."

"What do you mean, *they*?"

"Blake knew she was living here. He knew and said nothing. I have no idea why he let her stay or what the hell's going on, but she's no longer welcome here. I'm sorry, but I've had it." Jack grabs me and pushes me in the basement's direction. "You have an hour to get out of my sight."

I nod again, my eyes stinging with tears. I make my way to the stairs, still trying to reconcile the fact that I've lost my job and home in one fell swoop. How will I support myself? Where will I go? Back to my parents, who I'd have to beg to take me in? No. It has to be Blake.

Naomi rushes to my side and stops me from leaving with a firm hand on my shoulder. "*Wait*. Let's talk about this calmly."

"There's nothing to discuss," Jack snarls, his face beet-red.

Naomi glowers at him, her voice shaking. "Grace is carrying your brother's baby."

"*So?*"

Naomi puts her hands on her hips. "We can't throw her out on the street! Grace has been a part of this family for weeks. She's a kind, hardworking person, and she's giving birth to your niece. We can't turn our backs on her."

Jack scoffs.

"This is your niece we're talking about," she says.

"Don't care," he bursts. "This is my house. I make the decisions."

I walk away, unable to bear the tension and hostility in the room. "It's okay, Naomi. I'll leave."

Her tearful gaze lands on me before snapping at Jack. "Why are you doing this?"

"Because she's *Blake's* problem. Not mine."

"But she's family."

"Give me a break." He makes a violent motion with his arm. "Just because my brother knocked up some girl doesn't mean we're obligated to her."

"Stop it. You're being awful!"

"Yeah? Well, I don't give a damn. I will not be made a fool of by my brother. He's making us look like a joke."

Naomi lets out a tense breath. "There must be some explanation. Maybe he can't help her."

"Of course he can. He could buy an apartment through one of his LLCs, and my father would *never* find out. Instead he humiliates me by hiding his mistress in *our home*. No, I can't let this go. I'm sorry Naomi, but I'm done."

"I'll go," I whisper. "It's fine."

Naomi comes to where I stand and grips my arm. "Don't you dare."

I hesitate. "But I can't mess up your marriage."

"Marriage is built on trust, love, and understanding. We'll work through this. But right now, it's important to focus on you and the baby. You are family. We take care of our own."

Tears spill down my cheeks. "But it's causing too much trouble."

"That's my husband's fault." Naomi slides a protective arm around me, facing Jack. "And I won't put up with his behavior."

Jack's brows furrow. "Baby, think about what you're suggesting. She's just a maid."

"And wasn't your grandfather a carpenter?" she fires back. "Shame on you. I never took you to be such a snob."

"Oh, for Christ's sake. This isn't about that."

Naomi steps away from me, bellowing. "Then *what*?"

"He's my brother. We've never gotten along. You're out of your mind if you think I'll tolerate her presence."

"That sounds like a *you* problem," she says coldly, crossing her arms. "I am not throwing her out."

"Fine. I'll leave." Jack saunters to the door. "Screw this."

Naomi stiffens. "Don't be dramatic."

Jack's lip curls into a sneer. "If you want me to stick around, she has to go."

"Well, that makes things easy. I pick her."

I blink rapidly, stunned.

Jack's neck flushes. He seems unable to believe that Naomi chose me over him. He stares at her like he's never seen her before, then swings his gaze to me. His piercing stare stabs into me.

"You should have never let her into our lives. She'll ruin everything."

"She's carrying our niece."

"*Our* niece? That's a sick joke. You're not my wife anymore. You're nothing but a psycho that destroyed our family. I can't even look at you."

Jack looks like he'll say something else, but he storms out of the house, slamming the door behind him.

I exhale, releasing the stress from that intense fight. Gratitude for Naomi hits me hard. She didn't just have my back, she went full-on mother bear against her husband. She's as much of a mother figure to me as I hope to be to my unborn child. She looks past our social status and sees the connection between us.

My body sags with relief. Naomi's unwavering support is so important to me. What we have is way beyond employer and employee. We're more like sisters. With her, I can take on whatever the world throws at me. And I won't have to tackle this crazy rollercoaster alone.

Naomi faces me, her expression kind. "I'm sorry. I didn't know he'd react like that."

"That's all right. I'm sorry I didn't tell you about Blake."

"Oh. Don't worry about that."

I wipe my eyes. "I can't thank you enough for standing up for me."

She smiles. "Of course. You're like a sister to me."

I return the smile. "I'm sorry he left."

She pats my hand. "He'll be back. But when he does, you won't be in that basement. Now that he's gone, you don't have to stay down there."

I glance up at her, stunned. "For real?"

"We have plenty of guest rooms. Pick one."

"But...what if that makes him even more pissed?"

"Jack's feelings are not my priority. Yours are." Naomi nods, squeezing my shoulder. "I want you to be comfortable until this mess is sorted out."

I turn away, blinking back tears. I never expected that I would find a family with Naomi. Sighing, I set down my purse and head for the basement. Naomi follows. As I walk, I can't help but imagine sprawling on one of the luxurious beds upstairs. I open the door to a pitch-black void. I flip the switch, illuminating the carpeted, narrow stairs. Halfway down the steps, I pause and face her.

"Are you sure about this?"

I study Naomi, trying to make sense of the odd vibe I'm getting. She steps backward, leaving the door threshold. Her mouth twists into a weird half-smile, and her eyes glimmer.

"Oh absolutely," she murmurs. "I'm positive."

An electric charge fills the air and my heart pounds. *Something's wrong. Get out of here.* Panicking, I rush toward the door, but she slams it, cutting off my escape. A click echoes as the deadbolt slides into place.

I'm trapped.

TWENTY-FIVE
NAOMI
FOUR YEARS AGO

"Naomi, you have a visitor."

An orderly stands with his hands folded above a table scattered with puzzle pieces. He's a fit black man named Kyle, who always wears a white polo tucked into tanned khakis. He's nice, but I've seen him restrain too many patients to relax around him. My muscles tense as I meet his gaze.

"A visitor?"

A smile spreads under Kyle's trimmed mustache. "Yeah, how about that?"

I shrug. I can't get excited about anything, but that could be due to the drugs they have me on. There's not much to do in a psych ward except play board games while fighting a stupor of trazodone, lithium, or whatever antidepressant they have me on, so I spend a lot of time pushing around flimsy bits of cardboard.

"Would you like to see them?" he prompts.

"Not really."

"You sure? It could be fun."

I return to my unfinished puzzle, bristling at his infantile tone. "Send them away."

After a beat of silence, Kyle sits beside me. "You've refused to see everyone since you've been here."

"I saw my husband."

Once, about thirteen days ago. He was out of it and high, but I'm not judging. After my son died, I stopped eating, so Jack got a 5150 hold and put me here. Then he talked me into signing a waiver for a longer stay. I've been here three weeks. Maybe more. It's hard to keep track.

"You don't even know who it is."

It's probably my mother, father, or my husband's assistant. I continue assembling the puzzle. "My son is dead, and when it gets out that I'm in a psychiatric facility, my career in medicine is over. So no, Kyle, I don't care who visits me."

"You know that's not true. It's illegal for an employer to discriminate based on mental illness. Your job is still waiting for you," he says, an edge creeping into his solemn voice. "You don't want to spend the rest of your life here, do you?"

Of course I'd rather be at home. If only to escape mind-numbing boredom at this place, but they won't let me out until I show progress. That means participating in group therapy, talking about my trauma, and eating. The last one is difficult for me.

I sigh. "Fine. Lead the way."

Kyle and I stand, heading toward the communal room. It's hectic. Julia, my least favorite patient, sits in a corner and bawls. Standing in the middle of the chaos is my brother-in-law, who watches the spectacle with a locked jaw. When he spots me, he moves quickly forward.

"Hi, Blake."

A fake smile flashes on his handsome face. "Hey. How are you?"

"Doing okay."

Blake grabs me in a tight hug, compressing my postpartum belly. "It's so good to see you. Jack's sorry he couldn't make it. He has a work conference this weekend." Blake pulls away, his soft gaze gliding down my clothes. "Did you get that care package I sent?"

"They confiscated most of it."

I'm not allowed a phone. Keys. Belts. Stuffed animals. No snaps or buttons. The list goes on and on.

Blake makes a troubled sound. "I'll talk to them."

"Don't bother. I'm fine."

"That's great. I'm happy to hear that."

But his deadpan delivery implies he doesn't believe me. With a hand pressed to my back, he leads me to a secluded area. We sit in the plastic chairs around a square table. Julia faces off Kyle, screaming. Blake beams at me, ignoring Julia's meltdown across the room.

"So why are you here?" I ask.

"For a couple reasons," he murmurs, brushing off nonexistent dust from the table. "My father wishes to convey his sympathies. You and Baby Oliver are in his heart."

There's no way Jack Sr. said those things, but I smile and nod. "Thank you."

"He also is wondering when you're coming home."

I shrug. "When the doctors say I can."

"When do you think that would be?"

"*I don't know.*"

Flames heat my chest. This family is obsessed with keeping up appearances, but I can't pretend to care about the Hamilton legacy. Grief has hollowed me out.

"Is there anything you need?" he asks, sounding like my mother. "Is the food to your liking?"

"Why are you asking?"

His probing stare flicks to my wrist. "Well...I heard you weren't eating, and I'm concerned. The whole family is."

More like they're worried about bad PR.

I shake my head. "I can't eat."

"Why not?"

There's no point in answering. Blake can't handle my dark thoughts. He won't understand what it's like to fail at the *one* thing you're meant for. This stupid, *perfect*, model-thin body failed me. I can't bring myself to feed it.

"You're angry with yourself," he states, as though reading my mind. "But you shouldn't be."

"I'm not angry."

Blake's hand snakes across the table and grasps mine. "You are. You're punishing yourself for what happened, but it wasn't your fault."

Hearing that out loud stabs pain into my gut, the agony reaching inside me like a curved blade. I ache everywhere. I bite my lip until it throbs. "All I want is my baby, but he's gone, and there's nobody to blame but myself."

"You have nothing to feel guilty about. This wasn't your fault. Did Jack say it was?"

"He doesn't have to. He can't stand to be in the same room as me. He only visited me once, and all he did was talk about the Seahawks' new quarterback."

Blake squeezes his eyes shut, sighing. "He probably had no idea what to say."

"I get that. But how is talking about football helping?"

"You know how he is. Opening up is not his strong suit." Blake pats my hand and sighs. "Neither are emotional heart-to-hearts."

I stew on that for a moment, the ice in my chest thawing. Maybe he's right. "How is he doing?"

Blake hesitates. "He's...okay."

My stomach clenches tight. "Should I call him?"

"No, no. He's totally fine."

"That totally sounds like a lie."

He laughs, pulling at his collar, but it's short-lived. Blake's gaze fractures before his smile.

"I'm worried about Jack. He's been acting strange since it happened. At first, I assumed it was a defense mechanism, but now I'm not sure what to believe."

I lean in. "What do you mean?"

"Well, he's distant. More than usual. He's distracted and irritable. He's just...different."

A cold sensation grips my abdomen. "Is it because of me? Because I couldn't give him a healthy child?"

"No, it's not that. He's struggling to process everything, and he can't communicate his feelings. But he's also been with someone else." Blake pauses before continuing. "He's hanging around with a coworker of his. A woman. They seem...close."

Breath leaves my lungs. My voice trembles. "He's cheating on me?"

"I'm not sure," he murmurs. "I hate making assumptions, but it looks suspicious. I figured you should know."

And I thought my heart was too broken to break again. I stare at Blake, eaten alive by the image of Jack and another woman. I feel like I'm being twisted in a vise, a mixture of pain, anger, and disbelief surging through me.

"How could he? We just buried our son and he-he's screwing ar*ound*?"

Blake's sad eyes lock onto mine. "I can't say for certain."

Bitterness stirs inside me. I clench my fists under the table. I wipe my face as tears slide down my cheek. "What am I supposed to do with this information?"

"You get better," he says, squeezing my hand. "I know it's hard, but you need to make yourself the priority. Focus on healing, and then you can confront Jack. You're an incredible woman, and you deserve to be happy."

"Fat chance that'll happen."

"It will. It might be a while, but you'll learn to live with the pain and find joy. You don't have to do it alone, either. We're all here for you."

"Even you?"

"Especially me. If there's anything I can do to help you through this, I'll be there."

His words fill me with relief, releasing the tension in my neck until I sag into my chair. He hands me a tissue, and I dab at my cheeks. "Thank you. That means a lot."

"No thanks necessary, Naomi. You would do the

same for me." His words echo the warmth in his smile. "It just...makes me sad. My brother is such an idiot. I can't force him to change, but I promise I'll be there for you, as much as you'll let me."

My chest aches.

Blake releases me. Then he reaches into his pocket and pulls out a bar of Theo's dark chocolate, handing it to me. "Brought this for you. I can't imagine they have the good stuff."

My mouth waters as I unwrap a piece. "Thank you."

"Of course."

I bite into it. The rich, bittersweet flavor floods my senses. I close my eyes and savor it. It's the first thing I've enjoyed eating in weeks. As sugary decadence melts on my tongue, Blake gives my shoulder a reassuring squeeze.

"You'll get through this."

TWENTY-SIX
NAOMI

Grace puts up quite a fight. Her fists batter the door. She bashes into the frame like a wild animal. Screams like I'm putting a knife to her flesh. I tell her I mean her no harm, but it's no use.

I spend an hour calmly explaining myself, reasoning with her. She won't let me speak. She's hysterical. At one point, she begs me not to kill her baby. Kill her baby! Where does she get these fantasies? She's forgotten everything I've sacrificed. For God's sake, I threw out my husband for her.

What I say doesn't seem to matter. Grace throws a tantrum that's worthy of record books. She screams and *screams*. Sitting outside the door, I plug my ears and wait it out. I'm a patient woman. I've had years of practice enduring Jack Sr.'s snide comments. Compared to that, this is nothing. When my eardrums stop throbbing, I remove my fingers.

"You need to talk slowly. I can't understand you."

Her fist hammers the door. "Let me out!"

Sighing, I shake my head. "Sorry. I can't do that."

"Naomi, open the door. Please."

"I would if I trusted you to do the right thing."

"What the hell are you talking about?"

Her rapid mood swings are giving me whiplash. Is this pregnancy hormones or undiagnosed bipolar disorder? Another loud bang interrupts my thoughts.

"Hey!"

"Yes, I'm still here."

"Then answer me."

She won't like this. I lick my dry lips, heart hammering. "Okay, well...I'm worried about the baby. No offense, but it's obvious that you're out of your depth, and if I let it continue, you'll hurt the baby."

"What? There is nobody more invested in her health than me."

"I strongly disagree." I clear my throat, imagining shock twisting her features. "You might *believe* you're doing a great job. Maybe you are, according to your standards. But according to mine, you're falling very short."

"Who the hell do you think you are?"

"A doctor. A concerned friend."

"Friend? You don't get to use that word."

I twist the pendant at the base of my neck. "I'm sorry you feel that way."

"Screw your sorry. You're keeping me hostage in your basement."

"You gave me no choice," I shout back, my hands trembling. "You stuff your face with candy. I found the wrappers and the snacks you're hoarding in the chest.

You treat your body like a trash can. I'm sorry if that's harsh, but hearing the truth hurts. I only want to help."

"Then let me. The hell. *Go.*"

"It's too dangerous." My eyes mist over, and I palm the door. "But don't worry. I'll help you through this."

"You can't take care of anybody. You're crazy."

"I know you're lashing out, but you need to wake up. You're in denial. You have a serious complication, and you're engaging in all kinds of risky behavior. I warned you—if you don't slow down, you'll lose the baby—but you didn't listen. Instead you're endangering your baby's life, and I can't allow it anymore."

"What does that mean?"

"You're staying here for a while. Now, I understand that's not ideal, but this way, you're safe." I wince as her body collides with the door. "This door is very sturdy. You can't knock it down. All you're doing is hurting yourself."

"Help!"

"Enough," I growl. "You'll tear a blood vessel in your throat and—"

She screams so loud, my ears pulse.

I stand, sighing. "Okay, I'm leaving. It's impossible to have a dialogue when you're interrupting me. I'll be back later."

I close the door to the butler's pantry to muffle her protests, but my God, she has a pair of lungs. Vicious insults pour from her mouth. They needle my skin. Grace is downright hateful when she's cornered.

Things will improve. We'll have another chat. She'll see how reckless she's been with the baby's health. Grace is a reasonable girl. She'll come to her senses and agree that this arrangement is for the best.

In the meantime, I tie up loose ends. I park her car in the garage. I shut off Internet access to the guest network. She doesn't have her phone, but better safe than sorry. Fortunately, Grace doesn't have much of a social life, so I don't have to worry about people dropping by. Her parents haven't kept in touch since they abandoned her. Nobody will miss her...except Blake.

Several hours later, I decompress with a glass of rosé in the family room. Grace has stopped screaming, but thumps echo from downstairs. I don't know what's going on, but it can't be good. I'm too tired to confront her.

The doorbell rings.

Grace starts shouting. It's muffled, but easily identified. I'll have to start leaving the TV on. I put my drink down and sprint toward the front door. I can't risk anyone else finding out about her. I unlock it and wrench it open. Quickly, I step outside and close the door.

My brother-in-law stands on my porch, rubbing his brow as though warding off a headache.

I smile weakly. "Hey, Blake. How are you?"

"All right...Jack called."

I bet. "Look, he's really upset. He took off a few hours ago."

"Did he say where?"

"No, but you can't be here when he returns. To be frank, it's probably best you don't come around for a while."

"Not a problem. I'll collect Grace and be on my way."

I frown. "She's gone."

Blake stiffens. "She left?"

"Yeah." I shrug, gesturing to the road. "She packed her belongings and drove off. After Jack's reaction, I can't say I blame her."

A dark cloud settles on his face. "What did he do?"

"Oh. Yelled lots of horrible things. 'You don't belong in the family.' 'We'll never accept you.' I tried to intervene, but you know how he gets. I couldn't control him."

Blake steps backward, swearing. He takes out his cell and swipes through screens, presumably to dial her number. Holding the phone to his ear, he waits. Then he grimaces.

"Straight to voicemail."

I blow out my cheeks. "Try again."

He complies, no doubt waiting for a ringtone. Too bad Grace's phone is turned off and in my purse. After he leaves her a tense message, he shoves the phone in his slacks, his neck flushing.

"I'm sorry, Blake. I wish I could help."

He leans on the railing, drumming his fingers on the steel. His hostile glare burns right through me. "Did she say when she'd return?"

"She's not coming back."

"I can't believe you let her go without *calling* me."

I cross my arms. "She's a big girl, not some invalid."

"You could've put up a goddamn fight and convinced her to stay."

"Why would I do that?" I ask, swallowing bile. "You didn't make her happy."

Blake lets loose another volley of swear words. I

watch his tantrum, amused. It's not often that a woman refuses his advances. It must aggravate him endlessly.

I raise my hands. "Don't get mad at me for taking her side. She lived here for weeks. I care about her."

"So where did she go?"

I shrug. "Check the homeless shelter."

To his credit, he looks devastated. His posture droops. He runs a jerky hand through his hair. Maybe he feels something for Grace, but if he truly cared, he would've rescued her by now. Instead he dumped his problem on me.

"Okay. I'm going to look for her." He jogs down the staircase, yelling. "Call me if she returns."

I won't. "I will."

Blake dashes into his Tesla. As he drives away, I feel zero remorse. He had his chance to be a decent human being, but he was selfish. He never gave a damn about the baby or the dangers Grace put herself into. It was all about him—his desires, his expectations, his image. But I can't dwell on that.

Grace is still in the basement. She needs me.

TWENTY-SEVEN
GRACE

She won't let me out. I've tried everything—screaming, pleading, banging the door until my knuckles bleed. I don't get it. One minute, Naomi and I are getting along fine. The next, she's locking me up and lecturing me about the baby. I thought she was screwing with me, but no, she's dead serious. *Stay calm. Stress is bad for the baby.*

I sit on the staircase, hands twisting in my lap. I think I've been here the whole day. Without my phone, my only sense of time is the TV. How long does she plan to keep me? What if she does something batshit insane while I'm *trapped*? What if I give birth down here? Is that what she *wants*? She must've had a mental breakdown. That's the only explanation for her turning into a monster. The Naomi I know is harmless...but maybe she only showed me her best side in the same way that Jack is only ever sweet to Naomi. The darkness inside her was buried so deep. I have no idea who I'm dealing with.

My throat aches. I've ruined my voice yelling.

Nobody can hear me, and their closest neighbor is too far away. The only window in the room doesn't open, and breaking it won't help because I can't fit through. I should do it anyway, stick my arm out, and get *someone's* attention.

Whose?

The handyman rarely comes, and his schedule is too unpredictable. Jack's gone. He may never come back. I study my surroundings. Surely there's *something* to work with here. I have access to the gas furnace, but messing with it is a terrible idea. Setting things on fire won't end well for me. I could flood the basement, but again, not a smart move.

All Naomi has to do is unlock the door. I have to talk to her. I'll convince her it's the right thing to do. My legs cramp as I kneel, ready to pounce, but after a while, I have to use the bathroom. Just as I'm washing my hands, a creak echoes downstairs.

I sprint to the staircase. The sliver of light peeking from the gap in the door closes as I scramble up the steps. The lock strikes home before I'm halfway there. Irritation heats my skin like a rash as my gaze falls on a silver tray balanced on the stairs.

"I left you a snack," Naomi chimes from the other side. "Dig in."

I glare at the apple slices, celery, cucumber, and mounds of almond butter. She knows I can barely choke down raw vegetables. There's a glass with a foul-smelling green sludge that I'm not brave enough to try.

"I won't eat this," I mutter, heart throbbing in my throat. "Open the door and take it back."

"Grace, you need your nutrients."

"I hate celery. It's stringy and hard on my stomach. I can't stand almond butter. It sticks to my teeth. And I'd rather stick a knife in my eye than drink another revolting shake."

Naomi sighs. "You're fussy today."

"As long as I'm down here, I'll be insufferable. Why are you doing this? Is this punishment?"

"No," she says, sounding appalled. "Why would you think that?"

A muscle tics in my jaw. "Um—because you've locked me in a basement?"

"To take care of you, not to punish you."

I stare at the door, disoriented by her logic. "You're not helping me. You're holding me hostage."

"You had your chance. If you wanted your freedom, you shouldn't have been so careless with the baby. It's not your fault," she quickly adds. "You don't know any better. That's not a crime."

"Then why are you keeping me locked up like I committed one?"

"To protect you. Why else would I do this?"

"You're not in your right mind. I have no idea what your plan is." My stomach lurches as I grab an apple slice, inspecting it. "You could've poisoned the food."

"I would *never*." Naomi's weight creaks against the door, as if she's slumped against it. Her soft weeping filters through. "It hurts my feelings that you'd assume I'd poison you. After everything I've done for you. I didn't have to let you in my home, but I did. I welcomed you in my life like a sister."

I wrench at my hair to stop myself from screaming, gritting my teeth to stay silent.

"You're my only friend."

My neck burns. "You're my *jailor*."

"I'm sorry you feel that way. But you've given me no choice."

"You're keeping me away from my real doctor, and risking this baby's life."

"That's absurd. I would never." Naomi blows her nose and sniffs. "Do you know how hard it is, watching you? You're so cavalier with your health. You don't understand the miracle growing inside you. Some women would do anything for a baby. You walk in some restaurant drunk—and *bam*."

"I was working. I wasn't drunk." *You judgmental bitch.*

"You're still a lucky girl. It takes serious skill to trap the wealthiest and most handsome bachelor in Seattle."

Now she's implying I trapped him.

"It was an accident," I hiss.

"Sure, okay. An *accident*."

"Well, it freaking was."

"So...let me get this straight. You just happened to sleep with Blake Hamilton on a day you were the most fertile? You didn't plan that at all, did you? Didn't track your fertility? Or ply him with free drinks and suggest a hotel?"

My mouth gapes. Naomi must take my silence as a confession because she laughs. Her soft chuckle rakes my face with hot coals.

"It wasn't planned."

"I don't believe you, but it doesn't matter. I'm not judging. I'm in awe of your raw talent. Not any girl could pull that off with one of the Hamiltons." She lets out a rough sigh, mumbling. "You've no idea how hard it was for me, and that was with Jack being head over heels in love with me. I constantly have to bow and scrape to his dad, like a *peasant*, because my family wasn't rich enough to appease him. Can you imagine what he'll do to you?"

"Blake doesn't care what his father thinks."

"Is that what he told you?" Her harsh laughter pounds a nail through my temple. "Blake is a liar."

I bite the inside of my cheek. "He cares about me. He'll come looking for me."

"I can't deny that he likes you, but your baby is a threat to Blake's dream of inheriting Luxe Pacifica." Naomi's voice softens, but her words still sting. "I know you believe in the best of people, but you have to understand the stakes. The Hamiltons are powerful. They'll do anything to maintain that. A baby born outside of marriage, especially with someone like you...it's a scandal. It could tarnish their reputation, and it could jeopardize Blake's position in the company."

"But he wouldn't abandon his child."

"He won't have a choice once his dad gets involved. Jack Sr. is ruthless with protecting the family's image. He'll do everything in his power to ensure this baby remains a secret."

My heart sinks, the weight of Naomi's warning pressing down on me. What if she's right? The Hamiltons are known for their high standards and relentless ambition. How could I have been so naive to think that Blake would put his child before his legacy? If Blake doesn't come looking for me, I might never leave this basement.

"But what about Jack? You said he loves you, that he fought for you despite his father's disapproval. Maybe Blake would do the same for me."

Naomi's silence stretches out, heavy and uncomfortable. "Jack and Blake are different. Jack had already proven himself in the business world when we met. He had more leverage. Blake was still establishing himself, and this baby could undo what he's been working toward."

Tears prick at the corners of my eyes, a knot forming in my throat. As much as I want to fight for Blake, for our baby, I can't ignore my situation. If Naomi is telling the truth, our child endangers Blake's future, and there's nothing I can do to change that.

Naomi's apologetic murmur echoes from the other side of the door. "I know this is hard for you, and it's a lot to take in, but there might be another option. One that could work for everyone involved."

"What do you mean?"

"Jack and I have wanted a baby for years, but it hasn't been easy for us. I'm too traumatized by the stillbirth. We've considered adoption, but it's a long process. And, well..." She takes a deep breath, as though gathering her courage. "What if you let us adopt your baby?"

Shock flies through me. I can't believe what I'm hearing. "You...you want my baby?"

"Oh yes," she says in a rush of bubbling joy. "I'd give your child a stable, loving home free from the scrutiny of being a Hamilton out of wedlock. That would help you avoid conflicts with Blake and his father. You could go back to school without worrying about childcare."

"Are you insane? You can't kidnap me, lock me up, and then ask for my baby! Who do you think you are?"

"I'm helping you," she replies, her voice thick with emotion. "You don't understand the reality of your situation. This is your child's future we're talking about."

I slam my fist against the door. "You have no right to steal my freedom and make decisions for me!"

"I just want what's best for you, your baby, and our family."

"You don't get to decide that," I yell, hot tears streaming down my face. "You have no idea what I'm capable of. I'll fight for my baby, and I won't let *anyone*— no matter how rich they are—take her from me."

A heavy pause fills the space between my panicked breathing. I can almost feel Naomi's heartache. She weeps for a few moments, her sobs wracked with grief. The sound dives into me, wrecking me.

"I-I'm only offering a solution that could help everyone."

"Help everyone? Or just you and Jack? I'm not some pawn in your twisted game, and neither is my baby. So take your manipulative bullshit and shove it up your ass." My pulse races, throttling me with adrenaline. "I'm keeping my baby."

"Are you?" she says in a frosty tone. "I figured you'd give her up for adoption. Blake would trade full custody for a couple hundred grand."

"I'm not selling my child."

"That's not...you'd be providing her with a nice home."

I snort. "Like a pet."

"Please don't mock me."

I seize the little glass filled with her kale concoction and hurl it at the door, screaming. "Let me out of here! I'm not giving away my baby!"

Green juice flies everywhere, splashing the door and walls, where it drips down like molasses. Her stony silence pits my stomach with dread.

"Sure. You're entitled to want that."

I bristle. "Open the fucking door."

"I can't," she snaps. "I've told you why, but you refuse to listen. It's good I stepped in before you did actual damage to the baby."

I rattle the doorknob.

"I accept who you are," she says in a steely tone. "I just can't allow it to injure an unborn life."

She whisks away, her footsteps fading into a dim echo. All that stuff about Blake was a manipulation, right? Then again, she could be telling the truth. Blake never fully embraced the idea of having a baby with me. I might be stuck here for a while.

My body grows cold as I consider the possibility. I'm fine for now. But in a few months, I'll have the one thing Naomi wants most in the world—a Hamilton baby. And then I'll *cease* being valuable and become a problem.

Will I ever leave this basement? And when I do, will it be in a coffin?

TWENTY-EIGHT
NAOMI
TWO YEARS AGO

"You're leaving?"

The maid we hired a few months ago, a twitchy girl named Sharon, jumps at my question. Her wide gaze meets mine and then flicks to the floor. She nods, head bowed like a dog drowning in guilt. She's strange but very sweet. She does everything she's supposed to and never complains. I never considered us close, but my chest caves in at the sight of the open suitcase on the bed.

"Why?" I ask, trying to keep the tremor from my voice. "Sharon, what's going on?"

She chews on her lip, her eyes dancing around the room as though searching for an escape. "I can't stay here anymore. I just don't feel safe."

"We live in Bellevue. This city is one of the safest in the country. What could possibly make you feel unsafe?"

"It's not about the city or the neighborhood."

"Then what?"

Sharon sighs. "Does it matter?"

"Hold on. Did you stop taking your anxiety medication?"

"Yes."

I bite my lip, fighting the urge to scream. "Sharon, you can't quit those meds cold turkey. You have to taper down the dose. It can be dangerous."

"I couldn't handle the side effects."

"Then you need a different med. I'll prescribe you something else."

"No. I'm good." Flushing, she returns to packing her belongings. Her hands tremble as she folds her clothes. "After the fight between Jack and Blake, I need to leave."

"What fight?"

Sharon gapes at me like I'm high. "You don't remember? It happened just last weekend."

I laugh, relieved I've found the source of her distress. "You're upset over *that*? Sharon, it was a disagreement between siblings."

"It was bad. I've never seen anything like that before."

I almost roll my eyes. "No, it wasn't. I mean, sure, Jack got a bit carried away. Believe me, I gave him hell for it. He's learned his lesson."

"It was brutal," she says, zipping the suitcase. "The screaming...the blood. It terrified me."

"Brothers argue. It means nothing."

"Jack put Blake in the *hospital*."

"He went to urgent care. Trust me, I'm a doctor. Most of what you saw was swelling. It looked a lot worse than it was."

Sharon lifts the bag from the bed, stony-faced. She

throws her coat over her shoulder. "I've already told Jack I'm quitting."

I follow her to the front door. "Listen, I understand it was scary, but I promise you it's okay. We've discussed it, and it won't happen again."

Sharon grabs the doorknob. "Sorry."

Frustration smolders inside me as she rushes out of the house, her tall, slender frame disappearing down the staircase. Heat boils in my belly. Why does Jack ruin everything?

I storm down the hall and barge into his office.

Jack closes his laptop's lid and gets out from behind his desk. "Hey. What's up?"

"Why did you fight with Blake?"

He runs a hand through his disheveled hair. "Because he's the plague of my life."

I gesture outside. "Sharon left because of you!"

"I know, baby. I'm sorry. I didn't mean for our argument to escalate like that." Jack strolls around the desk, frowning. "Blake said something, and I couldn't hold back."

"Couldn't hold back? Are you a child?"

He shrugs. "We've never gotten along."

"That's your excuse for scaring away our maid? For acting like a complete idiot?"

He grinds his jaw. "You didn't hear what he said."

"And it warranted beating the stuffing out of your brother?"

His expression clouds over. "It was a disagreement."

I place my hands on my hips. "What was it about?"

"We had this conversation a week ago."

"Yes, and you gave me vague answers then, too. I want the truth."

He hesitates. "It's nothing...family stuff."

"Well, I hope making a spectacle in front of your father and our friends was worth it. You are so selfish sometimes. I just can't with you." My voice breaks as a wave of devastation crashes into me. "You know how depressed I've been. It's been so hard for me to get out of bed. Sharon helped me. She was my friend."

And now she's gone forever, just like my baby boy. Pain squeezes my heart. Tears flood my gaze as Jack takes my shoulders.

"She wasn't your friend. She was your project."

I wrench out of his grip. "What does it matter? Having her here was a distraction, and *because of you*, I don't have that anymore."

"You're right. I apologize. I'll make it up to you," he murmurs, pulling me close. He kisses me gently, soothing the ache in my chest.

I need to fill the void where my baby should be. My fingers dive into Jack's hair, curling around his neck. I crush my lips against his. I barely come up to breathe, my palms gliding over his broad pecs. I miss my husband. As our kiss deepens, I play with the waistband of his jeans, but Jack closes his hand over my wrist, stopping me.

He pulls back. "I can't. I have to work."

Heat stings my cheeks. "There's always an excuse."

"You barged into my office in the middle of the day."

"That never used to stop you before," I hiss, turning my back on him. "But I guess you have your needs fulfilled elsewhere."

He grabs my shoulder, whirling me around. "I never cheated on you. How many times do I have to say it?"

The pain splintering in his earnest gaze stabs my gut with shame. I love him so much. I don't want to believe he's unfaithful, but as weeks fly by without him touching me and with Blake's warning still echoing in my ear, I can't help but wonder.

"I need this. *Please*." I grasp his shirt collar, leaning forward. "I want to try for another baby."

Instantly, he's on guard. He stiffens, his tone robotic. "We need to give ourselves more time to heal."

"I can't wait. I feel so empty inside."

Jack cups my face in his hands. "Trying for another baby right now is not the best decision for us. We'll work through this together, and when we're *both* ready, we'll try again."

"You keep saying that, but *when*?"

"Maybe next year."

I step out of his embrace, my stomach boiling. "It feels like you're pushing it off indefinitely."

"Jesus. I'm not."

"Are you even sure you want to be a father?"

He flinches. "Of course. I'm just... I'm scared. What if it happens again?"

"I see. It's easier for you if I suffer."

"What makes you think any of this is easy for me?" he says in a low, tormented voice. "I love you, and I want to be there for you, but I need time, too."

Blake has been there for me more than my husband these past few months. He's been a constant source of support, helping me grieve in ways that Jack hasn't—

sending me food, forcing me to go out when all I wanted to do was lie down and cry. He's listened to me vent in long phone calls, never asking for anything in return.

I try to hold back the pain, but it seeps into my words. "You're not there for me."

"Because I'm drowning in work."

"You don't understand what Blake has done for me. He's helped me through some of the darkest moments of my life."

"What the hell are you saying?"

"You haven't been a good husband. You have to put work aside to support me, or this will never last."

Jack looks away, his lips thinning. "If I agree to that, you'll have to stop bringing up my brother. And you won't hang out with him anymore."

"Why?"

"He's poisoning you against me," he says in an unyielding voice. "I don't trust him around you. He's jealous of me. Growing up, he's always felt that I get everything while he gets nothing, and now that our roles are reversed, it's only made it worse."

"I've never noticed that about him."

His pleading gaze crashes into mine. "He knows how much I love you. So when he sees us together, it brings out this toxic, competitive crap that my father groomed in us."

I frown, finding that hard to believe.

"I know it doesn't seem like it, but I have your best interests at heart."

My mind reels. Is Blake as untrustworthy as Jack claims? What about all Blake's done for me? He was a shoulder to cry on when I needed it most. Maybe we've been crossing a boundary, but that's not a reason to cut him out of my life.

But I can't ignore Jack's sincerity. He may be wrong about Blake, but our relationship needs to stay in a healthy place. Taking a deep breath, I finally respond. "Okay. I'll stop hanging out with Blake."

He grabs me, enveloping me in his embrace. He presses his lips against my ear, whispering. "I love you. I promise I'll be there for you more."

"I love you, too."

He kisses me, and all my worries drift away. No matter what lurks ahead, Jack will always have my back, just like I'll have his. Our bond is unbreakable.

TWENTY-NINE
NAOMI

My nursery is coming together nicely.

This is one of my favorite experiences of motherhood. The nesting. The *excitement*. Picking out names. Fighting over wallpaper. It's a joyful time. At least, it is for me.

Grace is indisposed at the moment, so I'm preparing the nursery for her. She'll be over the moon with the finished results. I gutted the room. Threw out everything—the cribs, the board books, all of it. Too much bad juju. Then I had the painter come in and redo the walls. I tried asking for Grace's input, but she's been uncooperative with my questions, so I decided on a neutral color that fits with the rest of my house. I've already picked out the accent colors—yellow and purple—to symbolize Grace. She's a college girl, so using her school's football colors made sense.

I am so grateful for her. With her around, I feel better. More grounded. I don't spend nearly as many days crying. Life is not only bearable but good, because I have her and the baby to look out for. She keeps me busy. I've been very vigilant since she moved in. I've been monitoring her Internet usage, checking out the mom blogs she's been reading, and *yikes*. I limited her access to Google from the guest network before turning it off completely. Earlier this week, I intercepted a few books for new moms that Grace ordered. They went straight into the trash.

I've also been preparing for the delivery. I remember my OB/GYN rotation like it was yesterday, but anything could go wrong. Giving birth at home comes with risks. I can't just get a kiddie pool and hope for the best. I'll need fetal dopplers. Forceps. Scalpels. Suturing needles. The list goes on and on. Most can be bought online. I stock up on wound care items at the local medical supply store. I made a cart of supplies and keep it next to the butler's pantry.

I glance into the camera feed in the app on my phone. She spends a lot of time lying in wait at the top of the stairs.

Hand on the doorknob, I watch the screen. Grace paces in front of the television, a lioness in distress. Perfect. She's downstairs. Quickly, I put my cell away. Then I open the door.

Grace's dark head whirls in my direction. I grab the tray. She hobbles upstairs, her expression murderous. I throw the tray aside and yank the door closed, locking it. Her body smashes into the frame a few seconds too late.

Jesus, she's relentless.

Shaking, I pick up the tray. It's strangely heavy. I look

down, gasping at the untouched food. "You didn't eat. Are you okay?"

The door vibrates with a violent slam. "I'm sick of this. Give me a fried chicken sandwich with mayo."

"We have to change how you eat. It's unhealthy."

"So is locking up people against their will."

I swallow hard. "I'm doing right by your baby. That means no more fried garbage and absolutely zero refined sugars."

"You're starving me with this disgusting crap."

I click my tongue. "That's a ridiculous lie. You have plenty to eat."

"Yeah, but I can't stand half this stuff. It's too bland. Raw avocado makes me nauseous. *I don't like it.*"

I roll my eyes. "You're not used to it, that's all."

A loud groan escapes through the door. "God, you are so out of touch with reality."

My hackles raise. "You're the one who needs to search inward. You're acting like a spoiled brat. This is good food. It might not be as tasty as Taco Bell, but it is way better than what you were eating."

"I'll go on a hunger strike if this continues."

My teeth hurt from clenching my jaw. "Fine. Then I'll put you on an involuntary psychiatric hold and feed you calories through an IV. Is that what you want?"

"Yes," she snarls. "I'll get out of here. Then I'll tell the doctors you kidnapped me, and you'll go to jail."

"Is your pride worth putting the baby's life at risk?" I blow out a tense stream of air when she doesn't respond. "You will be healthy for this baby. Whether or not you like it. I'll come back with something else."

"Don't bother."

I roll my eyes, heading toward the kitchen. I dump the tray's contents in the trash. Then I slip into my waistcoat and open the bottle of Ativan. I swallow two pills, hoping it'll numb the throbbing pain between my temples.

She's such a child. I'm doing her a favor. A woman with her maturity can't take care of an infant. Once she gives birth, she'll realize how difficult it is to raise a baby alone. My only reservation is lying to my brother-in-law. He's capable of hiring a full-time nanny, but they won't love her more than me. I doubt he'll be too upset about my lie. Once he sees Jack and me with his daughter, he'll agree it's for the best. If he finds out.

I fix Grace's snack on a paper plate: whole grain crackers topped with cream cheese and smoked salmon. It's a compromise. Watching the camera feed, I wait until she's back downstairs before dropping the tray behind the door. Her haughty glare scours the staircase, but she doesn't move. Maybe she'll make good on her threat. I fiddle with my shirt. She *has* to eat.

My phone lights up with Jack's face.

I answer the call. "Hey."

"Hi. How are you?"

His warm baritone is like slipping into a hot bath. I smile, heading into the family room. "Not bad. I miss you, though."

"Yeah? I miss you, too."

I sit on the couch. "Then come back."

"Is Grace still there?"

I bite my lip.

Jack lets out a heavy sigh. "You can't keep her forever. Let her go. You helped a person in need, but now it's time for her to leave."

"I can't. She needs me."

"No, she doesn't," he says, his sharp tone making me flinch. "There are plenty of social services, even if she didn't have a filthy rich baby daddy."

I cross my legs. "Why can't she stay?"

"Because I don't like what it's doing to you. You're too attached to the maid. It's like...you're projecting yourself onto this pregnant girl."

"I'm not. I swear."

"I watch you with her. You are *way* too involved."

If I were hooked up to my monitor, my blood pressure would spike. I hate when he comments on my behavior. He has no idea what he's talking about.

"I only want the best for the baby, and I have the means to provide it. What's wrong with that?"

"Nothing, but this is my *brother's* kid. You...you realize that, right?"

Heat steals into my face. I know what he's getting at. "Yes. I'm quite aware."

"Don't get mad at me."

"Well, it's hard not to. You think I can't hear the accusation in your voice? I'm not crazy for helping Grace. I had to. Blake wasn't stepping up to the plate. He couldn't care less about his baby."

"Not our problem," he says coldly. "Let him deal with it."

"I don't mind helping. Besides, it'll show him that... that I'm good with his daughter."

"Why does that matter?"

"We could adopt her." My breathing hitches as Jack falls into silence, always a danger sign. "We'll be much better parents than him and *her*. We have the perfect house, incredible schools, and a fantastic neighborhood. More importantly, we want this."

"That's a gigantic leap."

My grip tightens on the phone. "It's what needs to happen. Can't you see that?"

His sigh crackles through the line. "You can't coerce that girl into doing this. That's not fair to her or the child."

"Fair? Blake and Grace hardly know each other! How is it fair to bring a baby into a situation where the parents are strangers?"

Jack hesitates before responding. "Look, I understand your concerns, but it's their choice to make. We can't take someone else's child and raise it as our own just because we think we'd do a better job."

My free hand clenches into a fist. "But we would be amazing parents. We'd give that baby everything she needs and more."

He exhales slowly. "I'm not denying that, but we need to respect their decision. We can't impose our will on them."

I bite back the frustration threatening to spill over. "Then we'll show them it's the sensible decision, that providing their baby with a loving home with us is what's best for everyone involved."

Jack's voice is weary. "This isn't a simple solution. You can't force them to do what you want."

My eyes fill with tears, and I struggle not to cry. "I... I just want to help."

"I know," he murmurs, softening. "But sometimes the best way to help is to let people figure things out on their own. Let's be there for them as family."

"But he's your brother. Adopting that baby will be almost like having one of our own. It solves all our problems. Blake is the face of the company. He needs to bury this before it becomes public knowledge, right? We can help him. Nobody has to know she was adopted. We'll say we did IVF with a surrogate."

"For Christ's sake. Stop it. You will never convince that girl to give up her child."

"We'll compensate her generously."

"Jesus. *No*. This won't work out the way you're imagining. I'm sorry, babe. I know it hurts, but this is something you need to accept. Blake won't give up his parental rights, and neither will Grace. So drop it."

My insides churn. "Are you coming home?"

"Are you kicking out Grace?"

I chew on my lip.

Jack makes a contemptuous sound. For too long, I press the phone into my ear, hoping I'll hear more than dead air. Then I glance at the blank screen.

He's hung up.

It's as though he sliced open an unhealed wound. Jack never used to disrespect me like this. Before the stillbirth, he was the model husband. He doted on me. He made me feel cherished and loved, but I barely recognize him anymore. Jack doesn't encourage me. He avoids me.

Maybe the only thing holding our marriage together is trauma.

Tears well up in my eyes. I need to be a mother. Jack will never be ready to have another child. If he won't listen to reason, I'll take matters into my own hands. I'll provide that baby the life she deserves. Nothing will get in my way.

THIRTY
GRACE

I'll strangle Naomi.

She deserves it for forcing me to eat this crap. How healthy can this food be if it makes me feel terrible? As I choke down today's smoothie—spinach, kale, yogurt, beets, and unsweetened almond milk—my stomach churns. Last night's meal is not sitting well with me, but it was either that or starve.

I slam the plastic cup down and climb the stairs, returning to my work. I grab the bent bobby pin I've been using as a lockpick. So far, no luck.

I shove the pin into the keyhole, trying to bend it all through. My hands shake, making it even more difficult. I bite my lip, focusing on the stupid lock. Each failed attempt enrages me. I can't stand being trapped, forced to eat disgusting meals.

Should I have seen this coming?

Naomi seemed like a good person. She treated me like a sister, and I was so desperate for support that I ignored the red flags. God, I have to get out of here.

Naomi's not well. I can't risk another day of being at her mercy.

Think, damn it. What can you use?

I glance at the door. Lock picking isn't effective. But if I remove the doorknob, I can disable the lock. With enough force, it'll come off. I need a lever. I could get a broom, position the fulcrum next to the door, and *pop*.

No. Too complicated. I know what *needs* to be done. I just don't want to do it.

As I trudge downstairs, I pick up a shard of the shattered mirror. I wrap a towel around the jagged edges for a makeshift handle. I hate violence. I've never so much as thrown a punch at someone, and now I'm fashioning shivs like a convict. How did it come to this? I'll have to hurt Naomi to escape this basement. I haven't made my peace with that.

It's not like you're killing her. Clearing my throat, I knock on the door. "Naomi?"

No response. She must be in another room.

I give the door a sharp rap. "Help!"

My thighs tense as rapid footsteps echo through the ceiling. It's early. She isn't done with her skincare routine. I imagine her in that loud Versace robe, hand on her hip as her voice floats through the crack under the door, as pleasant as always.

"Yes? What is it?"

I lick my dry lips. "I'm spotting."

"When did it start?"

"Last night, I think. I woke up and there was some blood. It's not flowing, but we shouldn't take any chances. Anything could happen."

Any second, she'll open the door. It'll swing outward. She'll step through. She'll reach for the railing, exposing vulnerable blue veins under her wrist. Then I'll slash.

A bead of sweat rolls down my neck.

"It's probably nothing, but I should check you anyway. Head downstairs. I'll join you in a minute. I need to gather supplies. Gloves, a gown, and a speculum."

I grip my shiv tighter. "A what?"

"A speculum. It's what they use in gynecology exams."

Be cool, Grace. "My bad. I didn't realize you had that equipment."

"Oh yes. With your condition, you'll need to be monitored closely."

I almost drop the piece of mirror. An absurd image of me in a paper gown, lying over the coffee table, burns into my retinas. Is she assuming I'll consent to that?

"I'm not sure I'm comfortable with that."

"What do you mean?" she asks, sounding genuinely confused. "If you're bleeding, I have to examine you."

"All due respect, but I'd rather visit my board-certified gynecologist. And didn't you have your medical license revoked? I'm sorry, but I can't leave my baby's health to chance."

A long moment passes in which the only sound is my frantic heartbeat. Naomi's cold chuckle breezes through the door.

"I see you've been reading tabloids. I'm a doctor, and a damned good one. Just because my license isn't active doesn't mean I can't deliver your baby."

"That's exactly what it means," I snarl, gripping the shard so hard it cuts into my fingers.

"It'll be fine. I'm trained. I've done rotations through many different specialties in med school, including OB/GYN. In small towns, it's common for primary care physicians to deliver babies."

"I doubt that."

"I can do this," she bursts, overriding my objections. "Giving birth is scary. I get it. But I'm more than qualified. Since you moved in, I've been taking CEs. Continuing Education classes. I've completed delivery courses, hands-on workshops, and I've also been poring over the latest medical journals, just in case."

So the entire time, she planned to steal my child. I picture her in a white lab coat, brushing up on skills she would need for my pregnancy. *Wow.* The nerve of this crazy bitch. I glare at the door, willing it to open so I can slash her throat.

Naomi lists other programs, ticking them off. "I've invested hundreds of hours in this. I'm giving this my full attention."

"And yet, you'd rather lock me up than allow professionals to evaluate me."

"I am a Stanford-educated doctor."

"What will you do when I go into labor?" I ask, hysteria weaving through my words. "Do you even *have* a plan? What if I start hemorrhaging?"

"I have all the equipment to handle any major complications. Unlike you, I'm extremely vigilant. I won't let your baby down."

My baby. My baby. She can't stop harping about a baby that isn't hers.

"You can't do this. I'm not talking about your qualifications. You're not in your right mind. You're forcing a woman to give birth in captivity, for God's sake! That's sick."

"It's only temporary, and you'll be given the best medical care. If that makes me a monster in your eyes, so be it. But I'm doing what's necessary."

A vein in my temple pulses. If she cared about the baby, she'd never jeopardize her life. There's something else she's not telling me. As it dawns on me, I grind my teeth. My cheeks blister. I seize the doorknob and wrench. I bash my shoulder into the frame, screaming.

"Stop doing that," she shouts, slapping the door. "Stress is bad for the baby. Your risk of preterm birth is much higher. Take a few deep breaths and calm down."

"I can't. Because I'm stuck in your basement. *I want out of your house.*" I body-slam the door, hurting my arm. "You can't keep me here, damn it. It's cruel."

"Cruelty would be leaving you to fend for yourself in a homeless shelter."

"Blake will help me."

"*Blake?*" Naomi laughs. It's short-lived, but it rakes my neck. "He cares more about his stock portfolio than your baby."

I ball my fists. "You're lying."

"I just saw him. I told him you moved out, and he didn't bat an eye."

"Bullshit," I snarl.

"Sweetie, let me give you insight into the world of

Hamilton men. Jack said his father deposited two hundred thousand dollars in his mother's bank account when she got pregnant. Money was the only reason Jack was born. Do you think Blake will be any different?"

"You don't know him like I do."

"Oh, please. If anything, I know him better. Men like Blake will say anything to control girls like you. They're manipulative, and they don't change."

"You're one to talk. You kidnapped me, you're feeding me crap, and you're playing doctor with my baby."

Naomi's voice hardens. "You can't fathom the pain of losing a child. I'll do whatever it takes to protect her. Eventually, you'll thank me for it."

I shake my head. She's a sick, twisted woman, and there's no reasoning with her. My only hope is breaking free, escaping this nightmare, and getting as far away from Naomi as possible.

"I'll never thank you for this," I hiss through gritted teeth. "You're insane, and you'll never lay a finger on my baby."

"We'll see about that," Naomi says coldly.

Her footsteps retreat.

I slump against the door, my fist tightening over the mirror. I never had an opportunity to strike. *Good.* I need more time to think about what I'll do and how I'll do it. Being stuck down here is more dangerous than I imagined. I'm running out of options. If I want to save myself, I have to do this.

Naomi must die.

THIRTY-ONE
NAOMI
MONTHS AGO

I don't recognize myself anymore. I feel as though I'm looking inside an aquarium of strange fish. As I stand in a room filled with people whose company I dislike, the grandiosity of our house seems surreal. A crystal chandelier casts a warm glow on polished hardwood floors and floral decorations. A lively jazz tune fills the foyer, courtesy of a local band. The Madisons and the Yorks, wealthy private equity group owners, complain to my father-in-law about Seattle's homeless problem. They vape and sip vodka sodas while discussing the imminent end of the world. Artificial intelligence will wipe out humanity. Society is collapsing. China and Russia are coming for us. The conversations center on one common theme—themselves.

These people used to intimidate me until I recognized the deep flaws in these so-called elites. When I got married, I promised myself that wealth wouldn't change me. No matter what, I'd be the same principled girl I was before I met him. And yet, everything changed the moment I whispered, "I do." A leave of absence from my job that was supposed to be temporary has become permanent. Jack said my work was taking a toll on my emotional health and that being a primary care physician wasn't fit for a woman of my status. Because I haven't renewed my license in years, everybody assumes I lost it due to malpractice.

At social functions, I'm treated like a trinket on Jack's arm. Nobody asks about what I'm doing with my life. They don't care. I have no identity. I am an extension of Jack. A childless trophy wife who spends most of her time maintaining an illusion of perfection.

I glance around the room, my heart aching. Jack swore he'd be here, but as usual, he's let me down.

A raven-haired girl in a stunning floor-length pink gown slides past a coterie of rosé drinkers. Her catlike gaze finds me, her ruby mouth curling.

"Naomi. Hi."

I force on a smile. "Thank you for coming, Brandi."

"Of course. I wouldn't miss it for the world." She kisses the air beside my cheek. "The cause is so important."

The charity is for helping bereaved parents cope with the loss of a child. Hosting the event seemed like a good idea, but it's taking everything in me not to cry. Reminders of my grief attack me from every corner.

"This is great," she gushes, grabbing a flute of champagne from a passing waiter. "The band is fantastic. You've done an incredible job."

"Thanks. I'm glad you're enjoying it."

THE MAID

"Oh yes. I'm looking forward to the auction. I hear there is some amazing artwork up for grabs."

"Yes. We're fortunate to have very generous donors. My father-in-law donated several pieces from Hollowell. Jack threw in a luxury vacation package and rare sports memorabilia."

"Wow, that's incredible."

She shifts a hand over her clutch, beaming, but her enthusiasm feels insincere. Like everybody else, she's here because it's an opportunity to mingle with Jack Hamilton, Sr. Her dad, Dave Madison, never misses a chance to suck up to him.

Brandi frowns, gazing around the room. "Where's Jack? I haven't seen him."

Probably out with his girlfriend. I tip my tumbler back, swallowing more gin. "He's been held up at work, but he should be here soon."

"On a Friday?"

"Yes, unfortunately. He had to attend a conference."

She raises a brow. "What for?"

I clench my mouth tighter. "Discussing the latest trends, technological advancements, that sort of thing. He needs to stay informed in the business."

Brandi nods. "Oh. I hope he can make it."

"Me too," I say, struggling not to sound bitter. "He really wanted to be here."

"How are you two doing?"

"Great. It's our fifth anniversary in May."

She grins. "I'm so happy to hear that. You and Jack have such a solid foundation."

"Thank you."

I tap my nail on the glass, fighting the urge to fidget. Brandi's smile gives me hives. It's like I'm the punchline of a joke that only she knows. What if she's aware of my husband's extracurricular activities?

Panic riots in my chest. All I have left is the image I've cultivated. If she finds out my relationship with Jack is anything but perfect, this *harpy* will spill every detail in a group text to our mutual friends. She'll use it as ammunition.

As the evening progresses, guests move into the dining room. My mind keeps wandering to Jack. He told me he was at a conference, but can I believe him? I can't shake that his absence is more than just a work commitment.

The chatter swells to an overwhelming cacophony, amplifying my nerves.

I open my phone.

> Where the hell are you?
>
> Are you with her?

I glare at the screen, but his reply never comes.

This is my fault. After Jack refused to try for another baby, I stopped being intimate with him. Opening our relationship was the only way to save my marriage. He does what he wants, and I do my best to ignore the stabbing in my heart. I've dulled the pain, but sometimes a gut punch will sock me in the belly when I'm not expecting it—like now.

I clutch my glass so hard, I picture the stem breaking. Excusing myself, I rush to the toilet and lock the door. As

I lean against the cool marble countertop, tears burst out of me. This is torture. This has been nothing but horrible reminders—my loss, my failing marriage.

My phone vibrates, casting a blue glow in the dimly lit bathroom. But it isn't Jack. A name I haven't seen in months flashes on the screen.

I answer the call. "Blake?"

"*Hey.* I need your help."

THIRTY-TWO
NAOMI

I'm having a baby. I'm so excited. It's happening, and I won't have to relive the trauma of childbirth. I float through clouds of euphoria all day. This is the best I've felt in years, and it'll be even better when my baby is in my arms. In a few months, our lives will completely change.

After Grace surrenders her rights and gives me full custody, we'll devote ourselves to the baby, which means it'll be over between Jack and his side piece. I've put up with Jack's bullshit for far too long. I can't raise a child in a dysfunctional marriage. He'll start behaving like my husband or I'm done. I have more than enough evidence to claim infidelity if I file for divorce, which will give me a huge lump of cash. I'll use some of it to compensate Grace.

> Come back.

> Jack, I'm serious. I need you now.

I inhale my third glass of wine as I wait for his reply. My sluggish thoughts swim together as I reach for the bottle. I lift my drink, hesitating. Do I want to be one of *those* moms? Drinking the pain away? If Jack has to mend his ways, so do I.

I set down my wine as the doorbell rings.

Groaning, I slide off my recliner and head to the foyer. I hope it's not the neighbor. I open the door, frowning at my visitor.

A frazzled Brandi stands on my porch in a pink coat, clutching her Prada bag's straps tightly. Her hostile glare rakes me, head to toe.

What is *she* doing here?

I don't see Brandi except at social functions with Jack's father and his cronies, and when we're in the same room I make a point of avoiding her. Since we met, I've felt uneasy around her, a feeling not helped by her stiff smiles and unflinching stares.

"Hi. We should talk."

My stomach tenses. "About what?"

Her lipstick-smudged teeth pull into a smile. "You know why I'm here."

"Actually, I don't." I grasp the door, closing it. "I'm busy, so you'll have to drop by later."

"I'm fucking your husband."

I swallow hard, rocked by a hot swoop of anguish. I asked Jack if Brandi was the other woman. He denied it. This can't be. Jack wouldn't lie. He has no reason to mislead me. A breathless malaise wraps my body.

She grabs the door, wrenching it out of my grip. She steps inside and closes it. "Nice place."

"Th-thanks."

Thanks? What the hell is wrong with me?

Why am I not grabbing this vulture by her throat and screaming at her for touching my husband? I want to force her out, but the words don't come.

"I've always admired this house," she says, a malicious glint playing in her eyes. "The first time Jack brought me here, I made him give me a tour."

My cheeks flush. "Is that all you have to say to me?"

"I want your husband."

I gape at her, taken aback by her sangfroid. There's no blustered apology, no downward gaze, no shame. Meanwhile, my palms are slipping off my jeans and my face probably looks like a five-alarm fire.

"Don't be offended," she scoffs, strolling into my kitchen. "Jack told me the entire story. You gave him a green light to sleep with other women."

I need to get her out of here. I open my mouth to say something, but she leans over the island, plucking almonds from a bowl. Then she pops them into her mouth. Paralyzed, I watch her make herself at home like she's undoubtedly done many times.

"It's obvious you two aren't working out. You don't take care of his needs." She holds up her hands, smirking. "I can't imagine why you'd ignore a hunk like Jack, but *whatever*."

Did he tell her everything? The thought of Jack confiding in this woman makes my skin itch. She reaches for another almond. I grab the bowl, yanking it out of her grip.

"Get the hell out of my house."

Brandi reacts like I've commented on the weather. She picks an invisible speck from her sleeve. "It's nice to see that you have a backbone, but I'm not the bad guy."

"Really? You're sleeping with my husband."

She raises a brow. "Only because you gave me the opportunity."

"That doesn't mean I want to talk to you. Ever."

Sighing, she drums her fingers on the marble. "I know Jack and I have caused you pain, and we're sorry for that, but you only have yourself to blame."

"*We?* Don't you dare say *we*. You and my husband aren't *we*. You're nothing. You're his blow-up doll."

"Unfortunately, it's not that simple. We have a history. We met each other years ago. You see, our families have so much in common. We used to be good friends. And when we started sleeping together, our friendship deepened into something more."

"Well, it's over. I won't allow him to be with you anymore."

She smirks, stabbing ice through my heart. "This may not suit the narrative in your brain, but your husband won't stop seeing me. He knows what he wants and takes it, over and over."

My vision clouds over with violent fantasies as Brandi reaches across the counter and pats my arm. I loathe this woman, but I hate Jack even more. She thinks she has a chance, which means he must've given her hope. Is he planning to leave me?

I look down to stop the tears from rolling down my cheek.

Brandi shakes her head, smiling. "You're more pathetic than I thought."

I clench my fists. I'm aching to grab her throat and squeeze the life out of her smug face. If I kill her, it'll be his problem. Perhaps I should. He deserves to reap the consequences for screwing other women. But as satisfying as it'd be to present Jack with the corpse of his mistress, I'm not a murderer.

Once Jack gets home, I'll tell him it's over between them. I should feel sorry for this girl. She isn't fit to shop for my groceries, much less replace me as Mrs. Hamilton. I fight hard against tears, straightening my back.

"Get out, or I'm calling the—"

A shout booms into the kitchen.

Brandi's attention snaps to the butler's pantry. "What was that?"

Shit. I hold my breath, hoping she'll drop it, but Grace's muffled cry echoes into the kitchen, followed by a thud.

"Oh, that's just...the dog. We've been having trouble with her getting into things lately." Panic wells in my throat, but I force my voice to steady. "So I locked her up."

Her eyes narrow. "Huh. Doesn't sound like a dog."

"She's a husky. They're very dramatic."

She folds her arms. "I didn't know you had one."

I have to get her out of here. "Yeah, well, it's none of your business and frankly, I'm done with this conversation. I'd like you to leave."

She purses her lips and frowns. Then hammering

fists bash into the door of the butler's pantry. Brandi whirls on me. "Okay. What is going on?"

"I—I want you to go." I grab her arm, steering her to the exit. "We can talk about it later."

"There's somebody down there," she says, ripping out of my grasp. "What are you hiding?"

"I'm not—Brandi!"

She stomps toward the butler's pantry. I follow her, my pulse thundering. She can't reach the basement. If she finds Grace, everything I've worked for will be for nothing. My dream will collapse. A sheer black fright swoops through me as she reaches the door.

I lunge at Brandi, grabbing her shoulders and shoving her back. She pushes me away with an indignant glare. I launch at her, digging my fingers into her eyes. She slaps me, the blow stunning me. We fight, clawing at each other's hair and clothes. She's strong. She's probably just as desperate as I am, but Jack is mine. If I can't have him, neither can she. And I won't let her destroy my chance for a child.

She hurls a vase at me. Misses. It shatters just as the door to the basement creaks open. She's turning the knob.

My hand wraps around a candlestick, its weight reassuring in my grasp. I spin around as she opens the door, a triumphant smile blooming across her face. Then I bring down the candlestick with all the force I can muster. The heavy pewter connects with a sickening thud against her head. She staggers backward, a dazed look crossing her face.

Then her knees buckle and she crumples to the ground.

THIRTY-THREE
GRACE

The doorknob turns.

I haul myself upstairs, but it slams shut. Then a deafening bang hits the ceiling.

What is going on up there? It's like Jack and Naomi are in a cage match. Is he hitting her? My blood chills at the thought of Jack laying a hand on Naomi. It's impossible to imagine him doing that. As awful as he is to me, he's a simp to his wife.

But these are volatile people. One minute, we're getting along fine. The next, I'm locked in their basement. A bone-chilling silence chokes the air, and a woman I don't recognize shouts.

"You'll pay for that, bitch!"

Who the hell is that? Shouting seeps through the ceiling, a turbulent back-and-forth that puts me on edge. Something is very wrong. I don't want to be around for the fallout. I have to break free. I rush downstairs.

What can you use? Think.

My gaze lands on a butter knife. Maybe it can be

used like a screwdriver. Grabbing it, I hurry to the door. I have to remove the hinges. I try sliding the knife under a nail, but the blade is too thick. I set it down and rush back downstairs. My pulse races as I sprint into the bathroom, rummaging through the drawers. Nail clipper. *Yes*. I grab it and sprint upstairs to the door.

Raised voices echo above me as I close the clippers on the head of the nail. I yank and twist. It's difficult. They keep slipping. Gritting my teeth, I wrench hard. The nail retreats a fraction. Then I get the knife and wedge it under the small gap. I take off my shoe, hammer the clippers, knocking the nail loose, then I pull. It slowly slips out of the hole.

I gape at it, panting.

On the other side of the door, Naomi screams. *Damn*. Running out of time. I attack the door hinge with renewed vigor. The second nail flies out as the yelling reaches a crescendo, and then the ceiling trembles with a thump...like a body hitting the floor.

I shake off the fear. *Keep going*. I slide the bent butter knife under the hinge. If I can remove two of them, I can squeeze through.

Then the lock clicks.

Is it unlocked? I face the wall, my heart thundering. I palm the doorknob. I push, and it swings outward. Someone unlocked the door. Swallowing my relief, I step into the house. I'm free. Just like that.

The hair stands on my neck as I leave the butler's pantry. It's silent. I strain to hear something, but there's nothing but my frantic heartbeat. Did Naomi throw Jack out?

I enter the kitchen, my feet slipping over water.

A toppled chair blocks the doorway. A vase lies shattered, its water and flowers creating a small puddle. Naomi sprawls on the floor like a rag doll, eyes closed. My throat tightens. I rush forward and kneel beside her.

"Oh my God. Is she dead?"

"Not yet."

I whirl around, facing the owner of that voice. It's that girl Jack's seeing behind Naomi's back. Brandi. She's battered and bruised, but there's no mistaking that haughty glare under the nest of ebony hair. A red shadow forms under one eye. Blood trickles down her lip, her expression unreadable.

Alarmed, I turn my attention to Naomi. I tap her cheek. I grab her jaw and shake her, but she doesn't stir.

"What'd you do to her?"

"She deserved what she got. She attacked me." Her gaze flicks from Naomi to my belly. "She didn't want me to find out you were here."

"That's because she locked me in the basement."

"*Naomi* did this to you?" she asks, eyes widening. "Hang on, you're the maid. You saw Jack and I weeks ago."

I swallow hard, hesitating. The silence stretches between us like a taut wire.

"That's right."

Her head tilts. "They've been keeping you captive?"

"Naomi has."

"*Why?*"

I bite my lip, unsure of how much to reveal. "It's a long story. But she's...been using my pregnancy against me. Threatening to take my baby away from me if I don't do what she says."

Brandi strokes her chin. "Huh."

"Shouldn't we call an ambulance? She needs help."

Brandi takes a deep breath, her attention flicking to the unconscious Naomi. "She's fine. Just knocked out."

I grab Naomi's cell phone from her pocket to dial 911, but Brandi plucks it out of my hand.

"What the—give it back!"

Brandi frowns. "Let's hold off on calling anyone."

"What the hell are you doing?" I shout as she pockets the phone. "She needs a doctor *now*."

"No, we need to slow down and figure this out." Brandi crosses her arms, staring at the ceiling. "If Jack finds out I attacked his wife, it'll be a disaster. He'll never speak to me again, and I'll be charged with assault. And you...well, the Hamiltons will make sure your life is a living hell."

"How?"

"If you bring the police into this and tell them you were held captive by Jack's crazy wife, his father will use his connections to discredit you. They won't hesitate to ruin you."

"So what do you propose?"

Her eyes narrow, and she steps closer. "We'll call Jack Sr. He'll sort this whole thing out. You'll admit to hitting Naomi. Say it was self-defense. She locked you up and threatened you. You had no choice but to fight back."

I stare at her. "You're asking *me* to take the blame?"

"It's the best option for everybody. Jack and Naomi

won't face any charges, and you'll get a nice payday from Jack Sr."

The nerve of this girl. "So...you want me to be your scapegoat."

She waves her hands. "No. That's not what I'm saying."

"It is, but I'm not falling on my sword for Jack's lover."

She bristles. "Look, maybe you don't get it. There will be your version of the story, and there will be mine. Which do you think people will believe?"

I sneer. "You're covered in bruises."

"I'll be gone before they get here."

"Then Naomi will back me up."

"You sure about that?" she asks, sliding her hand on her hip. "Doesn't she have every reason in the world to put you in a jail cell?"

My heart pounds. "Damn it."

"Go. I'll take care of it." Brandi wipes blood off her chin, smearing it on the counter. "I'll...tell Jack something."

Leave her alone with Naomi?

My stomach churns. "I can't do that."

"Why not?" she growls.

"Because I don't trust you."

Brandi's mouth pulls into a grin that fails to reach her eyes. "What's your name?"

"Grace."

"*Grace*, everything is fine. Just go."

I shake my head.

"Don't be an idiot. These people don't care about

you. The fact she locked you up says it all. You're just the help."

I open my palm. "Give me the phone. I'm calling the police."

"Oh yeah? What'll you say to them? That she forced you to live downstairs?" Her nasty chuckle fills the room. "Nobody will believe you. I'm skeptical, and I'm the one that unlocked the door."

"I've been there for a few days."

"Right." Brandi bends over, picking up a candlestick. "But why would she do that? She's not the type to keep someone captive."

"Because she's lost her damn mind. She's desperate to control me and my baby." I wave off Brandi's smoldering expression, turning toward Naomi. "I'm calling the police."

"That won't work for me."

"Well, too bad. You're not blaming me so you can keep screwing Naomi's husband."

Brandi's eyes flash. She lunges forward with the candlestick, and searing pain explodes in my skull. My vision blurs. I slam into the floor as white-hot sensations burn through me, piercing my skull like tiny ice picks. I clutch my head, moaning.

An icy grip seizes my ankles and smashes them together. I try to cling to consciousness, but darkness crawls over my sight. Then I'm yanked away from Naomi's lifeless form, dragged through the doors of the house and into a new nightmare.

THIRTY-FOUR
GRACE

The psycho shoved me into a *trunk*.

I have no memory of being lifted into a car, but she must have done it. My eyes open to darkness as the floor rumbles. A gag muffles my gasp, which I can't pull out because my hands are bound behind my back. I can't break free. The string binding my wrists won't give. It's so tight, my palms sting as though with needles. I am powerless. I can't stop myself from rolling with every tap of the brakes.

I oscillate between denial and shock. I thought nobody could top Naomi's crazy until Brandi threw me in the trunk like a sack of gym clothes. A sour taste forms in my mouth. Brandi will reach her destination soon. She'll exit the car, whip out a knife, and stab me. Vomit burns my throat. Something must've misled her. She has no reason to want me dead, but I'm not dealing with a normal person. I have to get out of here.

All modern cars have a glow-in-the-dark handle in case of kidnappings. I search the corners, but I don't see one. Damn. This can't be Brandi's Lamborghini. I'm in an older car, probably Jack's vintage BMW.

Working for the Hamiltons was such a mistake. I swear to God, I'm done with these lunatics. I'll never darken their doorstep again. I'll raise my kid in poverty, so long as I'm far away from these people.

My feet slam into the trunk's lid. I aim for the taillights, but the car veers onto rougher terrain. The rocky ground sends painful jolts through my body. Our speed increases, and the bumpy ride becomes unbearable. Little flutters pummel my stomach. Is the baby okay? Where the hell is she headed?

Finally, the car jerks to a stop. Footsteps crunch gravel, growing closer. *Shoot*. I roll onto my back as the trunk opens. Bright light floods my vision, and I squint.

Brandi's features swim into focus—ruby-red pout, pale skin, dark eyebrows arching high. She grabs a handful of my hair and yanks me out of the trunk. She rips the gag from my mouth, saliva dribbling out. It slides down my chin as Brandi chuckles.

"Hope the ride wasn't too rocky. I'm not good at driving a manual."

Her taunt flies over my head as I take in our surroundings. We're in the middle of nowhere. Trees everywhere. I can barely make out the sky above us. It's blocked by a canopy of green, and the forest is as silent as a cemetery. No honking horns or zooming cars. Nobody's around.

A chill crawls down my spine.

Brandi strolls to the front of Jack's car—the BMW, just as I thought—grabbing something from the passenger seat. She kicks the door shut, lifting a shovel over her shoulder. My hands wrench against the string encircling my wrists.

"Where's the Lambo?"

"At home," she mutters. "I couldn't take it to the house. Jack would've spotted it from his security cameras and stopped me."

"Stopped you from *what*? Why am I here?"

She scoffs. "Playing dumb?"

"No. Honest to God, I have no idea—*Brandi, put it down.*"

She approaches me with the shovel. I back away in an absurd hopping motion, stumbling over a branch. The world tilts as I crash into a pile of leaves. My shoulder breaks the fall, smashing into the earth. Groaning, I roll to my side.

Brandi laughs, swinging. She misses, striking the tree above my head. The vibration from the impact rattles my teeth. Hissing, I strain against my bindings.

"Brandi, don't do this. Let's talk." I blow out my cheeks, heart hammering. "We could both benefit from a discussion. Tell me what's bothering you."

Her upper lip curls into a snarl. "Jack Hamilton is a selfish jerk, and he's been making a fool of me for too long. Today, he gets what's coming to him."

"What do you mean? How did you even get all this stuff?"

"I grabbed a few things from his garage. Then I put you inside his car. I figured I'd get rid of two things he loves."

She thinks Jack loves me? "What makes you think he cares about me?"

"I want to know how," she seethes, lifting the shovel so the blade hovers above my nose. "When. Why. *Everything.*"

"H-how what?"

"How what?" she mocks in a shrill voice. "You think I'm stupid? You've been sleeping with him."

"What?"

She tosses the shovel aside and wrenches me to a seated position, her breath hot on my face. She shakes me, her nails digging into my flesh. "Tell me the truth."

"I didn't touch him!"

She sneers. "Right. That bump in your belly is just a cyst."

"It's not his baby."

"Stop lying!" she screams, flecks of spit landing on my forehead. "He's hiding you in the basement like a dirty little secret. It's his. He's protecting himself from the scandal."

"No, that's not it."

"Then *what?*"

"I-I needed a home," I burst, my bound hands groping for a rock. "I applied to the job, and they hired me."

"Jack would never do that."

"H-his *wife* insisted. She has a soft spot for pregnancies," I hiss through my teeth. "Naomi wants a baby more than anything. She convinced Jack to hire me. They're helping me out. That's all."

"Because you're having his kid."

THE MAID

"It's not his. I'd never sleep with Jack. He's been a jerk to me since the day we met." Heat climbs my neck as I channel all my rage for Jack. "He tells me all the time how stupid I am. That I'm lucky to work for him. How if it wasn't for his wife, he never would have hired me. I have no interest in him. I swear."

A brittle silence stretches between us. Her expression lightens. For a moment, it's almost like she's convinced. I can practically see the gears turning in her head. Then she snorts, shaking her head.

"Your story is such a crock of bull."

"Give me a Bible, and I'll swear on it."

"It's Jack's baby," she says firmly. "And he's adopting it. Isn't he? I can't believe he'd do this. He's supposed to love *me*."

Brandi releases me, and I fall against the trunk. Her posture crumbles and her eyes glisten. For God's sake. I can handle getting kidnapped by Jack's lover but apparently, listening to her cry over him is too much.

"Why are you pining for that drunken loser?"

Brandi swipes the tears off her cheeks, her bloodshot gaze darkening. "Insulting my man isn't doing you any favors."

"But it's the truth. He's not a good person."

"Please. You want him for yourself. You *seduced* Jack." She points at me. "You're trying to trap him, so he trapped *you*."

"Oh my God. That is *not* what happened."

Brandi seizes the shovel from the ground. "If that baby comes out, Jack and I are done."

My throat tightens. "Let's not get crazy. I'm pregnant."

"I don't care."

"Brandi, wait. This is a misunderstanding." My fingers close over something hard and round. I twist it, rubbing the jagged edge over the string. "We'll talk to Jack together. He'll back up my story."

She shakes her head. "I won't let you manipulate him."

I saw through my restraints. This can't happen to me. I have to keep talking. She has to believe I'm not the enemy, but how can I make her see the truth when she's blinded by jealousy?

I swallow tightly. "Think about it. If Jack were the father, why would Naomi give me a guest room in her house? What woman would tolerate that?"

"One that lets her husband sleep around."

"This is much worse," I blurt, stalling for time. "She wouldn't risk her reputation like that."

Brandi hesitates. Doubt flickers in her eyes, and then she snaps to rage. "You're a scheming little skank. You must've lied to her."

"I haven't." I grit my teeth, flexing my hands against the rope. "Give me a chance to prove it."

"So you're saying that the baby isn't his, but Jack let you stay in his home anyway?"

I bite my lip. "Yes."

She laughs hollowly. "I don't know why I'm listening to you."

"I'm not lying."

"Just freaking admit it. You thought you could trap

him. You want to steal my man." She closes the distance between us, screaming, veins standing out on her neck. "But you don't deserve him. He's mine."

"Please let me go. We'll sort this out with Jack."

"I can't trust him," she hisses. "He's weak. He can't commit to a decision. That's why he's juggling me in between placating his wife. He'd rather lead me on for months than rip off the Band-Aid. It's also why he stuck you in a basement instead of doing what's necessary."

"Which is what—*killing me?* Do you hear yourself?"

I try to wriggle myself free, but the fibers binding me are still too strong. A thrill touches my spine. Is this how I'll die, at the hands of a jealous mistress?

"*I'm not your enemy*. I only care about raising my baby in peace." The string holding my wrists loosens, and I nearly cry out with relief. "You don't have to murder me to get Jack. I'll leave town."

Brandi seems to weigh it over, her grip on the shovel wavering. "You will?"

"I'll do whatever it takes."

She glares at me. "How do I know you won't sue him for child support?"

"You don't, but even if I did, that doesn't make him any less yours." My stomach tenses as I lean forward. "I'm not a threat to you. I'm not Jack's type."

"What if I agree?"

"You'll untie my ankles and drop me off at the closest train station. I know it involves trust, but if our roles were reversed, that's what I'd pick."

"You're just trying to save your neck."

"Sure, but I'm not wrong. Letting me go is better than looking over your shoulder for the rest of your life."

She glowers at me. Then she sighs, throwing the shovel aside. Kneeling, she brandishes a knife. A quick slice through the strings frees my legs. Brandi gets up.

Keeping my hands concealed, I stand. The shovel lies beside a tree. As long as Brandi is in the picture, my baby will never be safe. She's unpredictable and dangerous. She might come after us again.

My heart pounding, I wait. Brandi turns around, heading to the car. I lunge for the shovel and grasp it tightly. I can't let her react.

I aim at her head. The blade strikes the base of her skull. Brandi reels, and I swing in another wide arc. It crashes into her temple with an awful crunch. Brandi hits the ground hard, and I toss aside the shovel. Dirt splatters her expensive pink coat. Leaves and twigs nestle in her hair. Her manicured ombre fingernails stab the earth. A gash pulses blood onto her neck. Pain hits me below the navel, and my throat tightens. Did I hurt the baby? I hold my belly, trying to calm her. When the kicks subside, I return my attention to Brandi.

Biting my lip, I inspect her wound. It's pretty serious. If she's not dead, she will be in a minute. That's what I wanted. The nutcase is out of commission. With Jack's car in my reach, I'm home free. All I need is the courage to see my plan through. By the time I get to a phone, she'll be toast. I'll make an anonymous call to the police. They'll discover her body, but I'll be long gone.

Hopefully, out of the country.

I root through her pockets, grabbing her keys. A mini

leather purse dangles from her keychain. My fist trembles, and I break. *Jesus*. Listen to me. I sound like a psychopath. I'm not a murderer. This isn't who I am. She's insane, but that doesn't mean she deserves death. I have to do the right thing.

I pat her coat for a phone, but don't find one. Never mind, I'll go to the closest convenience store. I stomp through the trail, reaching the BMW in seconds. Elation runs through my veins as I rip open the door and slide into the seat. I jam the keys in the ignition and twist them, but as I grab the gear shift, my stomach drops.

Oh, no. It's a manual transmission. I've never learned how to drive a stick, but it can't be that hard. Crap. I step on the clutch, trying to remember how it works. I press it down and hit the gas. The dashboard lights flicker, and the engine turns off. Damn. It stalled.

I try again and again, but I can't make it cooperate. I pound my fists into the steering wheel. I lay on the horn. Brandi's going to die because of Jack's stupid hobby. I unbuckle myself and get out, slamming my foot into the door. *Go to hell, Jack*. I seize a giant rock from the road, hurling it at the windshield. It shatters the seats with glass.

My chest pulses as I glance down the street. Someone will pass by. I'll flag them down. I stand in front of the trailhead sign and wait. Headlights beam through the mist as a car roars through. I wave my arms, yelling.

The car slows, and I sag with relief. The door opens, and out steps the last person I want to see. Out of all the people I could have flagged down, fate threw me a cruel twist.

THIRTY-FIVE
NAOMI

"Wake up, sweetheart."

My vision swims in a blurry haze, sharpening into my kitchen. The white roses I just got from the florist lay scattered, drowning in a puddle of water. How did they get there? A volatile image of a raven-haired girl in my pounding head.

"Are you okay?"

Jack's apprehensive face floats above mine. Only my husband would walk into our home, see me passed out on the floor, and ask such a stupid question. Groaning, I massage my temples.

"Yeah."

"Thank God. I was so worried." He strokes my hair, and his puzzled frown deepens. "You're bleeding. Did you girls fight?"

"Look at the place. What do you think?"

Jack helps me upright, his hand at my back steadying me. He cradles my jaw, his lips brushing my forehead, and my stomach churns with a confusing swirl of emotions.

"Talk to me."

I pull myself free of his arms. "Where is she?"

"No idea. The maid's car is gone."

"Not Grace. *Brandi*."

Jack gapes at me, rubbing his brow. I've yet to scream at him, but his feigned confusion sends me over the edge. A stinging pain wraps my chest like barbed wire. It tightens over my ribs, squeezing the growing pressure inside me. Heat lashes up my arm. My hand whirls, slamming into his jaw.

He staggers. He touches his flushing cheek, his mouth gaping. I've never hit him before, not even when he demanded that we open our relationship.

"Your girlfriend showed up," I begin in a low voice, breathing hard. "I support you. I let you do whatever the hell you please. I *share you* with other women, but no. That's not enough for Jack Hamilton. You screw your side piece *here*. In my bed. *How dare you?*"

"Babe, I know. I didn't want to, but—"

I laugh bitterly, and he flinches. "You threatened our marriage. You were going to leave unless I agreed to what you wanted. She knew where everything was *in my house*. Do you have any clue how humiliating that was for me?"

"I'm so sorry," he chokes out, his eyes glistening. "I never invited her over, but...she didn't respect our rules. It got worse after she fell in love with me. I broke it off so many times. She wouldn't listen. She wanted to confront you. I couldn't let that happen."

THE MAID

"So you kept screwing her," I drawl, disgust pitting my stomach. "While lying to my face."

"Telling you the truth would've been like rubbing salt in the wound."

"No. You just didn't have the guts to come clean."

A tear trickles down his hollow cheek. "I told her the house was off limits. I would never disrespect you."

"You are so like your father. Full of it."

"I swear to God, I'm not. I never meant for this."

"You brought this drama into our lives. An open relationship means you satisfy your needs elsewhere, not bring them home with you. This was supposed to be our sanctuary. You violated it."

"I'm sorry."

"I don't care," I shout, and he winces. "I loved you with all my heart. Even though it wasn't what I wanted, I tried to be okay with other women sharing my husband. I turned into one of those miserable Stepford wives, numbing myself with drugs and alcohol just to escape my existence."

"Then why did you agree?"

As I gaze into Jack's tortured eyes, the reasons run through my head: I thought it would save us, I was sick of him bothering me for sex, and naively, I hoped he'd fulfill my dream. But all I did was enable him to chase after his needs and completely ignore mine.

Elbowing him out of the way, I stomp toward our bedroom. I grab my suitcase and yank it over the bed as Jack hovers nearby, whimpering.

"Where are you going?"

"Out," I deadpan. "I'm done."

"What do you mean?"

"As in, I'm filing for divorce." I open a drawer, and I start packing. "I can't be in this marriage anymore."

He whitens. "No. We'll go to counseling. We'll do anything but that."

"I'd rather die than stay married to you."

"Please don't say that. We can fix this. I'll stop seeing her."

My mouth pressed into a tight line, I twist off my wedding ring and leave it on the nightstand. Jack raises and lowers his arms, slapping his sides.

"You can't punish me for what *she* did. That's not fair. None of this is what I wanted."

"Oh. I guess she forced you into it?"

An ugly flush claims Jack's neck. "You know what I mean. I love you. I only want you."

Such pretty, empty words. I zip up the suitcase. I pull it off the bed, but Jack moves in front of the doorway, blocking me.

"Take responsibility for your part in this. You won't touch me," he says, the devastation in his voice almost buckling my resolve. "Not unless it's to make a baby, and I'm not ready. Neither are you."

"Don't tell me what I'm ready for."

"You're not well. You never dealt with the stillbirth. Ever since it happened, I've begged you to see a therapist. You ignored me. Your stay in the hospital helped a little, but it wasn't enough."

"I'm too crazy to have children—that's your excuse? Are you kidding me?" Judging by his steely expression, he's not. Disgust pits my stomach. "Get out of my way."

"I love you," he growls, seizing my arm. "I have never stopped loving you."

"You don't love me. You let that vulture come to our house so she can scream at me, belittle me, make me feel like the dumbest wife that ever lived, attack me, interfere with my private business."

Oh no. I forgot about—

"Grace." I abandon the suitcase, blood pooling in my feet. "Where is she?"

He blinks. "What?"

I shove aside a bewildered Jack and reenter the foyer. "Where did she go?"

"I don't know."

I sprint to the basement door, but the door is hanging off its hinges. She must've escaped. Then what? What happened after she found me? I race into the garage and flip the switch. Lights illuminate the faded paint of Grace's Toyota. Her car is still here.

Jack peers outside. "Where the hell's my BMW?"

I face him, gritting my teeth. "Brandi must've taken it. She attacked Grace and drove off."

"She wouldn't do that. She's not violent."

"Who do you think knocked me out?" I gingerly touch my neck, feeling the tender patch of skin. A blurry memory assaults me. "She strangled me. Your...*girlfriend* almost killed me."

He pulls me into a tight embrace. The tension in his muscles coils like a spring. "I'm so sorry. I had no idea she was capable of this."

"Jack," I whisper, my voice shaking. "We have to find her."

"I have a GPS tag on every car. We'll follow the signal." Jack takes out his phone and taps a few buttons, bringing up a map with a blinking dot. "Come on, let's go."

We rush outside and climb into Jack's Bentley. He starts the engine, its roar heightening the tension as we head east. I glance at Jack. He grips the steering wheel with white-knuckled intensity.

The signal leads us out of the city and into the dark countryside. The further we get, the more sick I feel. Agony gnaws at my insides. What if we're too late? I push that terrifying thought from my mind, but it clings to me like a cold blanket.

"Why would she drive all the way here?"

Jack doesn't answer, but the fear lies stark in his eyes. He knows what's at stake. As we follow a winding road, we spot a woman waving beside the missing BMW. It's Grace. Jack parks and turns off the engine. Then he rolls down the window, staring at the ground littered with glass.

"What the hell did you do to my car?" he roars.

Grace stiffens.

Jack gets out, his jaw agape. "That's a nineteen-fifty-seven Cabriolet. Do you know how much that costs?"

Grace shrugs.

"What did I do to deserve this?" he demands. "I let you into my home. I feed you, and this is the thanks I get? You're paying for this. *Hey!*"

Jack's shout cuts off as Grace runs into the woods. He sprints after her. They disappear into the forest, but a moment later, Jack comes out with her pinned to his chest. He drags her along, red-faced. She sinks her teeth into his arm like a rabid animal. Jack yelps, hurling her down.

I exit the car, yelling. "Don't hurt her!"

"That little *viper*. Did you see what she did to my car?" Jack gestures at it wildly. "Did you?"

"Yes, Jack. I have two eyes."

He goes on and on, complaining about the damage, but I couldn't care less. Frankly, he deserves a dose of karma after his many indiscretions. Grimacing, he wipes his arm. "And on top of that, I'm bleeding. I'll need a tetanus shot—"

"Where's Brandi?" I ask Grace.

"She's in there." Grace stands, pointing at the trailhead. "She's not...doing too good. She needs help."

Jack gives me a significant look and shoves her in front of him. "Lead the way."

We follow her. Grace leads us down the path. My gaze darts from shadow to shadow, every step filling me with growing unease. A twig snaps, and my body seizes. The darkness around us seems to pulse.

As Jack rounds the corner, he gasps, and his panic strangles my throat. Then I take in the horrifying scene. This changes everything. There's no turning back now.

THIRTY-SIX
GRACE

Naomi rushes to Brandi's aid. She peels strands of black hair from Brandi's neck and prods her skin. "She's alive, but her pulse is weak."

"What does that mean?"

Naomi ignores me, ripping off her jacket to make a pillow for Brandi's head. Then she tears a sleeve off her blouse, winding it around her skull. "This should help with the bleeding, but the swelling looks bad. We need to get her to a hospital as soon as possible. She could have a concussion or worse."

Jack makes a noncommittal sound, apparently far more interested in the local flora. As his wife tries to save his girlfriend's life, Jack stares at a tree. He seems riveted by the crawling ivy. Perhaps the visual of Naomi tending to Brandi is too humiliating.

I crouch beside Naomi. "Is she all right?"

Naomi shines her phone's light into her eyes. "Her pupils are responding, but she could still have a traumatic brain injury."

Relief unclenches my stomach. "So we'll call an ambulance."

Naomi takes out her phone. "I'll do it."

"Hold on." Jack rushes to his wife's side, smothering her hand with his before she dials. "Let's think about this, babe. We don't *have* to call for help. She'll wake up and do that herself."

Naomi grits her teeth. "How? She has no phone."

Jack frowns. "It's here somewhere. She doesn't leave the house without it."

"She needs medical attention right away."

"I'm not saying she *won't* have it," he forces out, his cheeks flushed. "Only that us calling is unnecessary."

"If she has a skull fracture and she doesn't get to a hospital, she's dead."

"I know, but look. Our circumstances are pretty dire, too." Jack slides the phone out of Naomi's grip. "We're looking at several decades in prison."

"For what?"

He gestures at me. "Kidnapping *her*."

Naomi scoffs. "Your girlfriend shoved her in a trunk."

"You...did the same thing. You locked her in the basement." Jack holds up his hands when Naomi protests loudly. "It doesn't matter why you did it. Laws are laws."

Her brow furrows. Jack lets out a frustrated sigh.

"Do I have to spell this out? We can't be here when EMS arrives. Grace will tell them what you did. They'll tell the police. If that happens, you're going to jail."

Naomi shakes her head as though warding off a tiresome fly. "It means a lot to me that you want to protect me, but we can't let Brandi bleed to death."

"No, baby. We'll call for help." Jack tucks her phone in his back pocket. "We just won't be here when they arrive."

Naomi bites her lip.

"It'll be fine. She'll pull out of this." He pats her arm like she's a child in need of comfort. "I wish we could wait for them, I do, but we have to think of the greater good."

"Good...how can it be good to leave her stranded?"

"We don't have a choice," he murmurs. "We have to go."

Naomi looks uncomfortable, but not enough to put her foot down. As she gets up, Jack uses his phone to dial 911. We listen as he rattles off our location, Brandi's condition, and that she needs an ambulance. Then he hangs up.

"They're coming?" asks Naomi.

"Yup," he says, and a stone sinks in my gut. "Be here in a few minutes. Which means we gotta get out of here."

That's my cue to run. I don't stand a chance in outrunning Jack in my condition, but I have to try.

Naomi heads toward the cars. Jack picks up the shovel. I sprint in the opposite direction, but he catches me by the elbow. He swings me around like a toy and tosses me in front of him.

Swift heat coils my throat. If only the shovel wasn't in his hand. Jack shoves me forward.

"Don't be mad at me. I didn't do this to you."

"But you sure as hell enabled it."

He gazes at me, exhaustion lining his face. "I did everything I could to make you quit."

"Making me paint the guest room, forcing me to rewash windows, and making me sleep in a cold basement. That was...charity?"

"I was sparing you," he hisses.

"By causing me pain."

Jack shrugs. "If it made you leave, it would've been worth it."

"And the last maid? Did you ruin her life?"

"Nope," he says. "It was an empty threat."

I replay the last few weeks, stunned that his loathsome behavior might've been an act. Couldn't he have told me Naomi was crazy? Of course not. Exposing his wife as a maniac was out of the question. The Hamiltons can't afford the world to know the depth of Naomi's madness.

But I'm not staying quiet. Once I tell my story, they're done. There's no coming back from imprisoning a poor, pregnant woman in your house. Jack has every reason to silence me.

I dig in my heels as we approach the cars. My elbow sinks into his gut, but he sighs like he's had a long morning. He pins me on the hood of the BMW, hands on his hips.

"Get rid of the glass."

I grimace. "How am I supposed to do that?"

"I don't give a damn, but I want it off my seats."

Naomi socks her husband on the shoulder. "Enough. This isn't her fault."

Jack seems to realize that, but the broken windshield grates on him. Perhaps it's one blow to his pride too many. A vein pulses on his neck. His eyes rake me like rusted nails. He's at his breaking point.

One wrong move, and I'm dead.

THIRTY-SEVEN
NAOMI

Jack put Grace in the trunk. I didn't want to do that, but we didn't have a choice. Grace was completely uncooperative. I drove the Bentley. He took the BMW. Once we get home, Jack forces Grace downstairs. She does not go quietly. She protests, kicks, and screams her way down, adding a few more bite marks to my husband's arm. Lovely. I can't wait to come up with excuses for that.

As Jack replaces the screws on the basement door hinges, Grace sits on the bottom step of the staircase. Tears streak her round cheeks as she drags a quilt around her shoulders. She's the picture of innocence, and my heart breaks.

What am I doing wrong? I help and *help*, but everything makes her miserable. Haven't I given this girl what she needs? I swear, she is searching for a reason to be sad. She seems so entitled, but maybe it's her generation.

I fixed her a salmon dinner with wild rice and greens from our garden. She barely touched it, so I caved and bought fried chicken from that place she loves. I thought she'd be *grateful*, but *no*. She hurls the food at us like a savage. Now the house stinks of mashed potatoes and gravy.

I finish two glasses of rosé. My world swims in a gray haze as Jack returns with the power drill.

"Door is repaired. Your pet is locked downstairs."

"Damn it, Jack. Stop calling her that."

He rakes his hair, huffing. "That's what she is."

I bite back a retort as he wrenches open the fridge. He grabs a beer, twisting off the cap. It rattles on the counter as he guzzles it, grabbing another. Glowering at me, he throws himself on the couch beside me and turns on ESPN.

"What are you doing?" I ask.

"I need a few hours of zoning out after the hell you put me through today." He increases the volume, presumably to drown out Grace's sobbing filtering through the floor vent. "A fine mess you've thrown us in."

"Oh, it's all my fault?"

"Yes," he snarls, whirling around. "You kidnapped that girl. What in the ever-loving hell were you thinking?"

"I had it all under control until *she* showed up. I was going to help her. It would've been good..." I lose my train of thought as Jack gapes at me, wide-eyed. "She... she was taking risks with her pregnancy. This way, she's safe."

Jack puts down the remote like it's the detonator to a bomb. He rubs his face. Breathes into his hands. Then he lifts his head, his glassy eyes seeking mine.

"I've stuck by you for years. I've sacrificed my happiness for you. But you need help. I'll hire the best doctors. I'll make some calls to a great hospital."

"No."

"Baby, I need you to get better."

"*No*. You talked me into doing that once, and it was the worst decision of my life. You forced me in there so you could cheat."

"That's not true."

Yes, it is. When I confronted him about Blake's accusation, he denied everything. I used to believe him...but I don't anymore. I barely recognize the man sitting next to me.

Shaking my head, I wipe my eyes. "We used to be good together. Now look at us."

Jack's arms pull me into a hug. His gentle hand takes my shoulder. He cradles my face, his lips brushing my forehead.

This is nice. I'm in no hurry to shatter this moment. I feel loved. It reminds me of the old days, when Jack and I were inseparable.

"I love you, Naomi."

"You don't mean it. You never have." My face screws up. "It's all ruined."

"Don't be upset, sweetheart. Please. I'll fix it. I love you so much."

He presses his soft lips onto mine.

I lean into the kiss, clutching his hair. Our mouths meet again and again, every stroke hungrier than the last. Blinded by the electricity humming through my body, I fall backward. Jack's body covers me. His scorching kisses travel down my neck as he undresses me. He rips off my clothes with wild abandonment. All I can think is —*finally*.

We stumble to bed and make love, and it's beautiful. The best we've had in years. Pure bliss. Afterward, we lay in each other's arms. Trauma forced us apart, but it's also what bound us back together. We're connected. I'm in love again. It feels like a mountain of stress is off my shoulders.

How could I think of leaving him?

Jack is my partner. I swore to soldier through the tough times with him. I promised him a lifetime. He's right—I can't give up.

The doorbell's ringing interrupts our peace.

THIRTY-EIGHT
NAOMI

Blake's at the door.

We spot him on our security system. Jack checks his phone. The screen blazes with a live video of his agitated brother. Blake punches in the code that I changed a few days ago, jiggling the doorknob. He paces the porch. He peers through the windows, shouting.

"I know you're home."

Growling, Jack rips off the bed linens and swings out of bed. He dresses in jogger pants. As I slip into my clothes, the sparks from our postcoital bliss dissipate like smoke.

My stomach churns. "Maybe we should ignore him."

Jack sighs. "I'd love to, but he's not leaving."

"What'll we do?"

"We'll blow him off."

Gritting my teeth, I nod. The last thing I need is a conversation with Blake. I follow Jack into the foyer, bracing myself.

He wrenches open the door.

The tension radiating from Blake's rigid stance is palpable. He looks mad, but not enough to kick down the door. His clenched jaw tics. His eyes, usually a warm brown, seem darker as they bore into mine.

"I want to know what happened to Grace."

Jack frowns. "The maid? She's not here."

"You know damn well what her name is," he retorts, his voice dripping with fury. "Where is she?"

"*Grace* is gone."

"*Where?*" he bellows, making me flinch. "I've called every shelter and hospital in Seattle. I've driven past encampments. Nobody has seen her. I don't know if she's okay or if she's living under an interstate somewhere."

"Buddy, relax. She's probably fine."

"I've been to her parents' house. They have no idea where she is. They passed along her friends' information to me, but they haven't heard from her, either."

Jack scratches his neck. "I bet she moved to a cheaper city. Tacoma, maybe."

"No. She wouldn't do that."

Tutting, Jack crosses his arms. "Don't tell me you've caught feelings for her."

"She's carrying my baby!"

"So? You should be celebrating." Jack smirks, and I wince. "Now you don't have to face Dad with your mistake."

"For once, put your petty feelings for me aside," Blake snarls, grabbing the door frame. "What *happened?*"

Jack gestures to the road. "She left."

"Tell me the full story while I look through her room."

Jack shakes his head. "Why can't you accept that she wants nothing to do with you? She dodged a bullet, and deep down, you know that. Dad will never allow a *maid* to join our family."

"I don't care."

"You're not thinking straight," says Jack in his rolling baritone. "You're only upset because she slipped through your fingers, but her disappearing is a good thing. Dad never has to find out."

"Naomi, where's Grace?"

Downstairs, taking a nap. At least, that's what she was doing when I checked on her fifteen minutes ago. I pin my arms against my queasy stomach. "No clue."

Blake takes a reckless step forward, forcing Jack to push him back. "The day after you called me in a towering rage, Grace went radio silent. I haven't heard a word from her since."

"We have nothing to do with her disappearance," I say, trying to keep my voice steady. "She's not here. You need to accept that."

"I'm not leaving until I search the house."

Jack snorts. "You can't just barge in whenever you want."

"Honey, let him through."

"But—"

"Let him through." I back away, my heart thundering. "He'll realize how silly he's behaving and go home."

Blake's shoulder slams into Jack as he barges inside, screaming her name. He races upstairs. He flings open closet doors, gaping at the empty hangers and dresser.

Undeterred, he checks the bathroom and the master bedroom before heading downstairs to the living room.

As Blake searches, Jack and I follow him. The silence between us is deafening. I hunt for something to fill the void, but I'm glued to Blake's every move. He opens closets, peeks under beds, and peers behind furniture. The intensity of his search both unnerves and saddens me. I'm responsible for his pain.

Then Blake heads for the garage.

Jack charges after him. "Come on. You've seen enough."

I exchange a nervous glance with Jack, but there's no stopping his brother now. As Blake stomps through, his gaze falls on Grace's Toyota.

"You lying pieces of shit!" He whirls on us, shouting. "Her car is right here. Where is she?"

Jack steps in, hands raised. "Listen—"

"*Where is she?*"

"She's safe, okay? But she asked us not to tell you anything."

Blake shoves him aside. "I'm calling the police."

Just as he takes out his phone, a muffled scream echoes through the ductwork. I ball my hands into fists, inwardly groaning. She has the worst possible timing.

Blake sprints into the house. "Where are you?"

Her pounding rattles the door in the butler's pantry.

Jack tries to block his path, but Blake hurls him aside. He reaches the door and wrenches the handle. Jack grabs his arm. Blake yanks free, shedding his jacket, and socks him in the jaw. Jack staggers back, crashing into built-in shelves. Photo frames topple. Jack regains his footing and retaliates with a vicious left hook. Jack tackles his brother, but Blake rolls, reversing their positions. He pins Jack to the floor and pummels his head.

Oh my God.

Blake, still grappling with him, screams at me. "Open the damned door!"

I hesitate, my insides ripped apart.

My brother-in-law has always been good to me, but he failed Grace. Is it right to let him in her life? But if I don't, Jack could be seriously injured. I have to do something.

I rush to the door and fumble with the lock, my hands shaking. It clicks and I swing it wide.

Jack gets up and shoves Blake toward the doorway, who loses his balance. His arms act like windmills before he clutches at the wall, slick from the mess Grace made, and misses the railing. His body crashes on the steps and slams into the cement floor.

Jack closes the door and locks it. His chest heaving, he turns to me. "We'll figure it out later."

I nod, my throat tightening. I've only seen them fight like that once, and it scared me to death. He could've killed Jack. Maybe keeping him downstairs is wise. For our safety, he needs to be confined. It won't be forever. He'll cool off, see how well she's being taken care of, and back off.

Blake will understand. He just needs time.

THIRTY-NINE
GRACE

The door swings open.

A man flies down. I dive out of the way as he hurtles toward me. He smashes down the steps, landing with a loud groan on the concrete. He picks himself up, swearing profusely, brushing back his chestnut locks. A handsome face glows through the darkness.

I gape at Blake. "What are you doing here?"

His attention snaps to the door as it's slammed shut. Breathing hard, he gets up. Grabbing the railing, he launches upstairs, bellowing a tirade that makes me blush. He slams his feet into the wood, ripping at the door like a caged panther. He hurls his body into the frame. When that doesn't work, he descends the staircase and tries to rip out the ductwork with his bare hands.

"You're both going to jail for this," he taunts, slamming his fist into the wall. "I'll hire the best attorney. I'll sue you both. You'll lose this house."

"*Blake.*"

"I'll burn it down and piss on the ashes!"

He goes on and on, barking detailed threats at the ceiling. And at first, it's satisfying to witness. I'm not crazy. What they're doing *is* wrong. Throwing gravy on the walls isn't as bad as the havoc Blake looks prepared to unleash. As Blake draws breath for a fresh round of insults, I take his hand.

He whirls at me, but his expression loses its ferociousness. He grabs me, pulling me into his chest. I'm so stunned that he's here, that I don't register the hug until he whispers my name.

"Grace. I finally found you."

"I-I didn't know you were looking."

"You stopped responding to my calls. I thought I'd made you upset again. So I waited as long as I could stand and came here." Blake pulls away, his tender gaze sweeping over me. "When Naomi told me you moved out, I had no idea what to think."

I swallow hard. "I-I never moved out."

His brow furrows. Slowly, his arms glide down my back. One stays wrapped around me as he seems to take stock of our surroundings. His hold on me tightens as he passes the couch, the bed behind the stairs.

"What *is* this place?"

"This is where I've been living."

He frowns. "You're kidding."

"Afraid not."

The comforting grip around my waist disappears as he explores the room. He kicks the space heater on its side. Seething with displeasure, he glowers at the ceiling. "What the hell is going on?"

"I honestly don't know anymore."

He approaches the bed under the staircase, his jaw hanging. "How long have you been here?"

"Um...Well, Jack didn't want me upstairs, so I've been here since I got my job." I rub my arm, alarmed by the tension gripping his face. "I-It was my only option."

"I gave you options," he bursts, exasperated. "Plenty of them. Why didn't you take one?"

"How could I trust you?" I shoot back, nettled by his accusing tone. "You didn't back up your words with actions until it was too late."

"So you stayed with a man who put you *here*?"

"Better the devil you know than the devil you don't."

His anger seems to deflate when he sits on the couch, and then he explodes. "I can't believe they put you in the basement, and not in one of the three empty guest rooms."

"It doesn't matter."

"Yes, it does," he snarls, firing up again. "They won't get away with this. I promise you. I will do everything in my power to make them suffer."

"Whatever."

Blake sighs. "So...what happened?"

I tell him the full story, starting with Jack's freakout when he discovered the baby's paternity. When I describe how Naomi locked me in the basement, he cracks his knuckles.

"Damn her. I knew something was off." Blake launches off the couch, pacing. "I should've found you sooner."

"Don't beat yourself up. It wasn't that bad. Aside

from being force fed green smoothies and being told I'm a bad mother."

Blake groans, completing another lap around the basement. "She's lost it."

"Would you sit down? You're making me dizzy."

"My phone was in my jacket. We need to find a way out."

"Believe me. I've tried." I take his hand, guiding him to the couch. I sit. He slumps into the cushions beside me with a sigh.

"I should've found you sooner."

"You had no reason to suspect her."

He looks at me intently. "Did they hurt you?"

"Not physically, no."

Blake grasps my hand and squeezes. My heart skips as his fingers trace my knuckles. "Why did you look for me?"

"I've been worried," he says finally. "I had to find you. I looked everywhere—hospitals, shelters. I visited your parents."

A lump lodges in my throat. "How did you find them?"

He waves a hand. "I ran a background check on you. It gave me all your previous addresses."

"I see...and how did it go?"

He makes an indistinct sound. "They didn't believe that I was the father. Then I showed them the ultrasound picture with your name, and they agreed to talk to me. But they didn't give me any useful information."

"I see."

"After I'd searched every place I could think of, my

instincts kept pulling me here. Naomi and Jack." He spits out their names like poison. "The lying bastards."

"Naomi said you'd abandoned me."

"She'll pay for that, too."

"Have I ever told you that your family's insane?"

His mouth quirks. "I'm sorry about this. I can't even imagine what you must've gone through."

A dart of pain launches into my chest, and a tear slides down my cheek.

"I-It's been hard. I was losing hope."

"Oh, sweetheart. I'm so sorry."

Blake pulls me into a tight hug, and I cling to him. I bury myself in his embrace, breathing in his scent. He's like a furnace, and I soak in the warmth.

"I'm glad you're safe."

"Thanks for not giving up on me."

He squeezes me. "We'll make it through this mess. Everything will work out."

No, it won't.

His lips find my temple, and I melt. I want to surrender to the warmth growing inside me, but I can't. I dig into his back, trembling.

"You don't need to be so scared," he says, pulling back to cup my cheeks. "Jack knows he's in over his head. He can't keep us both here."

"Even if I get out, I'm in trouble."

His lip curls. "For what? Shoplifting?"

"Something a lot worse."

My vision fills with horrifying stills of Brandi's body. Blake's mouth flattens to a grim line. Then he strokes my hair, and while the images don't vanish, they fade in severity.

"We'll talk about it later," he murmurs, rubbing my back. "Right now, we only have to worry about one thing—getting out of here."

FORTY
NAOMI

Brandi is missing. Three days after my husband "called 911," I stumble on an article about her. *Bellevue police are asking for the public's help in locating Brandi Madison, who was last seen Friday evening at a Sounders game.* It describes the twenty-five-year-old darling of the Madison family. Her sad story is shared all over social media. Bold headlines sit underneath a portrait of a grinning Brandi.

I'm angry. Not because she's dead—although that's another black mark on Jack's record—but because he lied to me. How many times have I said that lying was a dealbreaker? He thinks he can get away with it, doesn't he? I keep giving him a pass because I'm such a doormat. That ends today.

The front door opens, announcing his return after his five-kilometer run. Jack strolls into the kitchen, whistling. He bangs a giant tub of protein on the counter. He's a fanatic about whey powder, even though it's loaded with terrible ingredients.

I set my tablet on the coffee table, my stomach tightening. "We have a situation."

"Yeah. My brother is in our basement."

Jack drinks his shake and opens the fridge. He takes out a Styrofoam box with leftover fried chicken and eats it cold.

"No, I mean...it looks like the ambulance never reached Brandi. Her parents filed a missing persons report. That means she's dead in those woods."

"Babe, I get it. But I don't know what you want from me."

"An explanation."

"To what?"

I grit my teeth. "Why didn't they find her?"

"Beats me. I gave them clear directions."

I wait for him to express the slightest drop of remorse, but all he cares about is stuffing his face. He inhales a chicken leg. When he reaches for a dinner roll, anger twists low in my gut.

"That's all you have to say?"

He shrugs. "It's a shame they never found her."

"I'm glad she's dead, too," I say, which makes him finally look at me. "Grace did us a favor. Hell, I should give her a pay raise."

"Don't joke about it."

"Why not? You must see the humor in the situation. My maid *killed* your mistress. It sounds like a terrible Lifetime movie."

"This isn't helping."

"You're right. We should get our stories straight before we're arrested."

He gives me a strange look.

"Brandi's been declared missing. Detectives will dig into her cell phone records, trying to triangulate her last known movements. They'll check surveillance footage. They'll find her—or what's left of her."

"And the murder weapon, linking her to Grace." Jack chews on his lip. "We'll have to hide her downstairs indefinitely. If she's ever found, we'll be the ones locked in a cell."

"Jack...that's insane."

"We won't hurt her. We'll fix up the basement, make it more...tolerable, and eventually, we'll let her out."

"What about the baby?"

Jack curses. "I forgot about the damned baby. We can do an anonymous drop-off at a fire station. As for Blake, he'll have to disappear. No way around it."

My throat tightens. "No."

"Better him than us," he says, his ears glowing red. "I don't like it, either. I never wanted to hurt my brother, but if I have to choose between him or us..."

"It won't work. They'll find Brandi, and once they do, they'll investigate how she ended up in the middle of the woods. Surveillance footage of the stoplight cameras she drove past will show your car, which will lead them to *us*."

"I'll tell the police it was stolen. Which it was."

"That's not good enough. They'll search for answers in her phone records. They'll discover you had a relationship, seize your phone, and once that happens...they'll figure out you were with her when she died and never called for help."

Jack freezes, his face bloodless.

"Please tell me I'm being insane," I beg him. "Tell me I'm crazy. That you didn't *pretend* to call nine-one-one and condemn that girl to death."

Heat rushes in my body as he slowly meets my gaze. His righteous glare throws gasoline on my rage.

"I did what I had to do. We arrived too late to help her, anyway."

"We didn't, though. If you'd called an ambulance, she would've gotten treatment as soon as they arrived. She would've been fine!"

Jack flails his arms. "Fine. Call me a killer if that makes you feel better, but you got us in this mess."

"*What?*"

"Yeah. You locked up that girl. You let Brandi in the house—"

"Let? She barged into our home after *you* gave the code for the gate!"

"Whatever. You knew it was coming to this," he shouts, the veins standing out on his neck. "The moment you shoved that girl in the basement, you crossed a line that can't be uncrossed. So please stop with the superior attitude, because it's getting really old."

Bristling, I watch him shove the leftovers back in the fridge.

"There has to be a solution that doesn't involve sentencing innocent people to captivity or death. I can't live with myself knowing we're destroying two lives just to cover up our mistakes."

Jack sighs, running a hand through his hair. "What choice do we have? If this goes to trial, our names get thrown in the mud. The media will paint us as abusive employees. It'll be a circus with my name in headlines for weeks. My father will never forgive us. That will send him over the edge."

"So? Let him freak out."

"He'll cut me off," he says, clutching the armrest. "We'll lose it all."

I sip my wine, my thoughts swirling. "That's not the end of the world. I can get by without the money. We'll be fine."

"You are in denial of how badly you've screwed us."

Heat scorches my cheeks. "We could go. Disappear, start over somewhere else."

Jack stares at me. "What about our careers, our friends?"

"Then we stay and face the consequences."

"Hell no."

"Yes. We need to turn ourselves in." I head out of the room, and Jack launches from the couch.

"I hope you're prepared for decades in prison!"

I stride to the basement door as he hovers over me.

"What are you doing?" he asks gruffly.

"Opening the door."

He seizes the doorknob, blocking me. "Wait."

"This is the right thing to do."

"Since when do you care about that?" he snarls.

My mind swims. "I've always been a good person."

"Don't be naive. You can't let them go."

I unlock the door. Jack grasps my arm, stopping me from turning the doorknob. He grabs it as it revolves on its own, then he's thrown backward. Blake and Grace yank on the frame, pulling until Blake's arm fits through. Then his torso. Breaking free, he tugs Grace with him.

Jack makes a wild grab for her. She dodges, sprinting toward the foyer. He takes off after her, and Blake tackles him. They tear into each other like beasts. Their mingled shouts and pained grunts echo. Blake rolls Jack onto his back, slamming his head into the floor. Blood bursts from Jack's nose, showering his chin and chest, and he screams. Still, Blake doesn't let up. He beats Jack mercilessly.

I watch the scene unfold, unable to move. I should feel something—fear, pity, concern—but I'm a spectator watching a movie.

Jack's hands slip from his brother's face, but Blake doesn't stop hammering every inch of his face. Blood sprays the floor as Blake unleashes hell on his brother. Jack's body heaves with each blow. Will Blake kill him? It seems likely. My apathy toward my husband's potential death scares me more than the idea of losing him.

"Stop," cries Grace, shaking his shoulder. "Let's go."

Blake stands, his fists greased with crimson. He wipes his hands on his slacks and allows Grace to steer him away. I'll probably never see her again.

I rush toward her. "Wait."

Blake pushes Grace behind him, teeth bared, but I only have eyes for her.

"I just want to say that I'm sorry and…you were the best thing that ever happened to me."

Her brows ripple, and Blake sneers. "I'll see you in court."

They exit the house. I step outside as they get into his car. The doors slam. I'm left alone, standing on the porch, as the taillights disappear into the night. The air is chilly, the stillness a stark contrast to the chaos of moments ago. My heart pounds, the adrenaline receding and leaving a hollow ache.

Jack lies on the floor, groaning and clutching his bleeding nose. It's as though I'm viewing it through a lens. I'm disconnected.

Slowly, I crouch beside him. His eyes are swollen shut, but he seems to sense my presence. I brush hair from his forehead. The warm, sticky feel of his blood clenches my stomach.

He groans, reaching for me. His grip is weak, his hand trembling.

"Shh." Why am I comforting him? Maybe it's out of habit, or maybe there's a small part of me that still cares for him. It's hard to tell anymore.

As I look at him, his once handsome face marred by cuts, I can't help but wonder about the choices we've made. They've led us to this moment, and now we're facing the fallout together. A chilling thought crosses my mind. Can our love ever be repaired? And even if it can, is it worth saving?

Only time will tell. All we have is the haunting uncertainty of the future. I lean my head against the wall and let the quiet envelop me. There's a long road ahead, and for now, it's enough to just breathe.

FORTY-ONE
GRACE

Free at last.

Blake pulls into a contemporary home nestled on a hillside overlooking the lake. It's not as imposing as Jack's mansion, but its understated elegance appeals to me. The exterior is a mix of cedar siding, glass panels, and concrete. It's a house that doesn't shout for attention, yet it commands respect in its quiet sophistication. Much like its owner.

Blake unlocks the front door. It creaks open, revealing a perfect balance between rustic charm and modern aesthetics. An open living area greets us, bathed in natural light pouring in from large windows, and serenity washes over me.

"Welcome home," Blake says softly, his hand resting on the small of my back.

Getting way ahead of yourself, buddy. I'm wary of staying here for many reasons. I still don't completely trust him. My feelings don't make sense. He promised me we'd get out, and he delivered. He's the reason I'm out of that basement.

Blake shows me around, pointing out the kitchen, the guest room, his voice straining with exhaustion. "Settle in. I'm taking a shower, and then...are you hungry?"

"Yeah."

He pulls out his phone. "What are you in the mood for?"

I wet my lips. "I could go for Mexican. Carnitas and horchata. Lots and lots of guacamole. Like, two extra sides."

He smiles. "Sounds good."

With a flick of his thumb, he completes the order. He heads down the hall. Left alone, I check out the guest room and collapse onto the mattress. It's so comfortable, I want to cry. My back had adjusted to the concrete bed at Naomi's, but this is nice.

After I wash off the day's grime, I find some of Blake's gym clothes on the comforter. I put them on and join him in the kitchen. Our takeout sits on the mid-century-inspired table. Blake smothers his burrito in green salsa and devours it.

I dig into the food, ravenous. I gulp down horchata, stuffing myself with tortilla chips and the spicy burrito. After what I've been eating at Naomi's house, it's heaven. Then Blake and I talk. It's light conversation. He probably needs more time to process everything. When the lights outside dim and my eyelids grow heavy, Blake suggests we go to bed.

"We could both use some rest," he murmurs. "Tomorrow morning we'll contact my lawyer. Okay?"

I nod, but the thought of talking to the police makes my stomach churn. How will we explain this? What about Brandi? *Damn*. I forgot about her. I head to my room and try to sleep, but the bed is too soft. It's not what I'm used to, and my brain won't shut up. After a while, I give up and search for Blake.

He's in his room, awake. He looks up from his phone as I enter, his brow furrowing.

"I can't sleep. Can I stay here?"

"'Course. Climb in."

He peels back the comforter, and I slide in beside him. The second I lie down, Blake's warmth envelops me. But then the enormity of what's happened, of what's still to come, crashes into me. My breathing hitches, and the baby kicks.

Blake holds out his hand. I take it, pulling him close. I'm safe. Slowly, tension melts from my body and I drift off.

◆

WHERE THE HELL IS BRANDI?

The next morning, I call the police with an anonymous tip, expecting local news to report that they've pulled her body from the forest, but it never happens. Her friends and loved ones continue posting on social media, pleading for her safe return.

My skin crawls with guilt. I can't explain why. She kidnapped me intending to murder me, which Blake reminds me of when I share my feelings. I spend hours curled up on Blake's couch, refreshing the news.

"Just talked to my lawyer," he booms as he joins me in the family room, stowing his phone away. "He says we should meet before filing charges against Jack and Naomi. What do you think?"

My throat tightens. "I don't know."

Blake frowns, joining me on the couch. "What's wrong?"

"I keep thinking about Jack's girlfriend—what I did to her. I'm a murderer."

His hand slides over my shoulder. "We're not even sure she's dead."

"That girl couldn't handle three minutes in the woods, let alone several days." I lean on the cushions, sighing. "My mom was right. I am a woman of low moral character."

"Don't say that," Blake insists, his voice gentle yet firm. "You didn't set out to hurt anyone. You were trying to protect yourself and your baby."

"She wasn't attacking me. I hit her while her back was turned."

"So? Were you supposed to trust the girl who threw you in a trunk? She was unhinged. She might've changed her mind and killed you."

"Yeah, but—"

"Stop blaming yourself. Yes, it's a terrible situation, but you didn't ask for any of this. You were a victim, too."

He's right, but I'm still responsible for another person's suffering.

"I wish I could turn back time," I whisper.

"We can't change what happened, but we can focus

on making the best of this. We'll make sure you're safe, and that Naomi and Jack face consequences."

"What'll happen to Naomi?"

He shrugs that off like a tiresome fly. "She'll be arrested for kidnapping, assault, unlawful imprisonment, and any harm she inflicted on the baby."

"And Jack?"

Blake's expression darkens. "He's complicit in what Naomi's done. Possibly more, if it's proven he played a larger role. It's hard to say what his sentence will be, but he won't avoid prison."

I nod, trying to absorb the information. Naomi and Jack in jail is a small comfort. They'll be held accountable for their crimes, but it doesn't erase my pain.

"And what about us?" I ask. "How can we co-parent after all this?"

Blake's gaze bores into mine with silent expectation. "We don't have to live separate lives, you know. You could stay with me."

"Like...as a roommate?"

"Not quite." A smile touches his lips and he leans in, kissing the top of my head. "It won't be easy, but I'm willing to try if you are."

I release a shaky breath. "Are you sure?"

"I am. I want to build a life with you."

The sincerity shines through his eyes, but I bite my lip. Everything has happened so fast. "But I'm nothing like the women you date."

"True," he admits. "But that's why I want you. You're strong. You're a fighter. Despite what you've been through, you've never given up. You've kept going.

That's...special. And I think you underestimate just how incredible you are."

My cheeks burn. Part of me is terrified to trust him, but I'm tired of being alone. I'm dying for a safe harbor for me and my child. Blake strokes my hand.

"Let me show you how good we can be together."

A ball of warmth glows in my chest. "I...I'll try, but I'm not committing to anything."

He smiles. "We'll take it slow."

Blake scoops me under my legs and back, swinging me into the circle of his arms. I bury my face against his neck, and then his fingers sweep under my jaw. He lifts my head and crushes his mouth against mine, sending a wild swirl through my stomach. My soul melts into the kiss.

Maybe we can create a future filled with love and happiness. I don't know what tomorrow holds, but for the first time in a while, I have a choice. And that makes me feel free.

FORTY-TWO
JACK

It's my last night in the States.

In a few hours, I'm leaving for Costa Rica. I would stay, but if I do, I'll be arrested and charged with Grace's imprisonment, which is ridiculous. I swear, the world is after me. I did nothing wrong. My only crime was sticking up for my mentally ill wife, but I'll be blamed for *everything* because I'm a man.

Men get all the blame these days. If we're not contributing to the patriarchy, we're incompetent jerks. Women are just as flawed, but no, let's hang Jack. My lawyers tell me I'm screwed. Nobody will believe my version of events.

After all, how could Naomi be the mastermind? She's a sweet, helpless little lamb. And that maid of hers? Totally innocent. Let's not forget my psycho ex-girlfriend, Brandi. She had no boundaries. She didn't accept the word no. God only knows why she kidnapped the maid.

My door pounds with a knock.

I open it, expecting my food delivery, but my father stands in the doorway. My insides twist like a pretzel as he gives me a thin-lipped smile.

"You look awful. May I come in?"

I turn around, swallowing hard.

Dad follows me inside, shutting the door.

"Want a drink?" I grunt.

"No, thank you. But help yourself."

I pour a finger of scotch, inhaling it as I gaze down at Seattle's busy streets. I'm at my high-rise downtown. After Naomi told me it was over, I left the house. Soon it'll be crawling with cops, anyway.

It could be worse. I've been waiting for the other shoe to drop for days. Grace hasn't yet filed a police report and Brandi is MIA, which makes me one lucky bastard. But my dad's presence is not a good development.

He pats my back, which is about all the old man is capable of in terms of affection. "I'm sorry to hear about you and Naomi. That's gotta be real tough."

"Yeah."

I inhale the rest of my drink. I haven't thought about our breakup. The names she called me still ring in my head. I never had the chance to respond to them, but I'd slap her if I could. She's as faithful as a rattlesnake.

"Why are you here?" I ask, facing him.

Dad sits at the breakfast table, drumming his fingers. "Your girlfriend's missing."

"I know."

"Her friends seem to think you might be involved in her disappearance."

"I didn't do anything."

"Of course." He grins, exposing his blinding veneers. "However, this puts me in a difficult position. Especially since it's not the *only* crime you'll be charged with."

I pour another shot.

"Blake told me about the maid. What a stupid thing you did to yourself. That has got to be the most moronic, the most braindead—"

"It's not my fault."

"That pathetic excuse won't cut it in court."

My cheeks flush with heat. I pound the drink, slamming it on the table. "I'm not a monster. What they're saying I did is exaggerated."

"Sure."

"I didn't touch her, for Christ's sake."

"That's true," he booms, clapping my back. "At least you spared me the indignity of being the father of a rapist. I've never been more embarrassed in my life."

"I wasn't even there when Naomi locked her up."

"But you didn't put a stop to it. Instead of letting her call all the shots, you should've put her in a mental institution. Now you're going to jail for a long time."

"I was trying to protect my wife."

Dad chuckles. "Yeah, you *protected* her."

"What the hell do you want from me?"

"Just to say goodbye." Dad folds his hands into steeples, staring at me over them. "For good. I'm cutting you off."

I expected it, but it stings. "I figured."

Dad glowers at me. "That means no more checks, no trust fund, and you'll never work at Luxe Pacifica again."

"I know."

Dad makes a face. "I'm not sure you do."

"You're here to piss over my carcass right before you cut me off forever." I wave my arm toward the door. "Take it all, and leave."

He sneers. "Useless drunk."

The chair scrapes the tiles as he gets up. He leaves without a farewell.

I glance at the semi-open doorway, hoping he'll change his mind and come back. Whatever. Everything will be fine. I read the writing on the wall weeks before this, and I'm prepared. Unlike Grace, I have money. A fake passport. Tens of thousands in cash, and enough squared away in a Swiss bank account.

My bags are packed.

I get up and close the door. Then I stumble around the apartment, crashing into walls. The booze doesn't ease my nerves. It fuels my rage. I keep picturing Brandi and the maid dying violent deaths. Even my wife screwed me over. To hell with her, too.

A muffled thump catches my attention.

I stomp into the bedroom and flip on the light. A dog-eared hardcover lies on the carpet. I put it on the shelf and pause, listening. Slowly, I move through the apartment. I search every corner, but find nothing else out of place. Maybe it's my imagination, or perhaps the alcohol is playing tricks on me.

I return to the family room and sink into a chair, ready for the long journey ahead. I need to call a taxi, but a nagging unease refuses to leave me. My phone slips out of my pocket and hits the tiles.

I bend over to grab it, and searing pain rips through my neck.

Warmth gushes forth. Dark rivers of crimson splash my shirt, as I clutch at the flap of skin gushing blood. *Oh my God.* I can't breathe. A dizzy spell overtakes me, and I crash to the floor. Slipping, I roll on my side.

Brandi stands over me, a knife in her hand. "Thought you could escape, huh?"

I gasp for air, my vision blurring. Brandi leans in closer, sneering. "You left me for dead, and for what? So you could run off with your maid? Did you think I wouldn't pay you back?"

I struggle to form words, choking. I *really* should've locked the door. *Dying. Need help.* I reach for my phone.

She kicks it away. "You ruined my life. Now it's my turn."

My strength fades. Darkness closes in. This is the end. My mistakes have caught up to me, and there's no escaping the consequences. Brandi's twisted grin is the last thing I see before the world dwindles to black.

FORTY-THREE
NAOMI

The food that passes as breakfast in this place is disgusting. Each morsel is a test of my willpower, but with a life budding inside me, I swallow down the calories. Jack's last gift to me was a baby, an irony that's both sweet and heartbreaking. I have already transferred full custody rights to my parents, who have promised to give me regular updates. At least my baby will never see the inside of a jail cell.

Thoughts of Jack haunt my solitude. Sometimes, the highlights of our relationship replay in my mind, reducing me to a weeping mess. But then I remember how he chipped at my self-esteem, how he never wanted this baby, and in those moments, I find a shred of gratitude for his absence. He can't control me anymore.

Life behind bars is a far cry from the luxury I'm accustomed to. The gray, cold cell, my new home, is a constant reminder of my fall. Visiting hours are the hardest. I watch other inmates reunite with loved ones, a bittersweet symphony of laughter and tears, while I'm reminded of my loneliness.

Prison gives me too much time to think. I reflect on my unborn child, the love I lost, and the mistakes I made. Regret gnaws at me, but I refuse to drown in self-pity over Jack's unfaithfulness or the woman who killed him. They say the best revenge is living well, and I could if it weren't for the guilt.

My parents have shared rumors that suggest Blake and Grace have found solace in each other. It's baffling, given Blake's usual type and Grace's naive innocence. But perhaps that's what he needs—a simple, devoted girl who sees no wrong in him. I love Grace, but her blissful ignorance *stings*.

She doesn't know the real Blake.

I can't sit back and let him hurt her. I need to warn her.

FORTY-FOUR
GRACE

Blake lounges on a sunbed, wearing sunglasses as he thumbs through a book. Sunshine gleams off his chiseled chest, his swim trunks hugging his hips just right. I can't help but stare.

My stomach twists into knots. The secret lodges in my throat like a shard of glass. I need to tell him. But I can't bring myself to break the peace of this moment.

Blake looks up from his novel. He takes off his glasses, revealing his soft, brown gaze. He smiles and beckons me over.

I nod, swallowing hard as I sit beside him. His arm wraps my waist, and I lean into his warmth.

"Happy anniversary, love," he murmurs.

His husky whisper warms me down to my toes. It's been two amazing years. A relationship that should've died a fiery wreck is stronger than ever. I'm married to the love of my life. We have a healthy toddler, Gianna. She is perfect.

Blake's dad passed away last year and left everything to him. He's at the helm of Luxe Pacifica. Best of all, the police caught Brandi. Apparently, she woke up the morning after we abandoned her in the woods and hitchhiked to Seattle. Then she bided her time, waiting for Jack to visit his apartment. Since her trial and sentencing, internet detectives have stopped harassing me, and Naomi is where she belongs—in jail. I'm so grateful that I no longer wake up to phone calls from strangers insisting I've murdered Jack Hamilton.

"Happy anniversary," I echo.

I'm no longer the wide-eyed girl Blake married, but he still makes me feel like I'm walking on clouds. His finger curls around my chin. Sighing, I let him pull me into a consuming kiss.

When we part, he rests his forehead against mine, a sigh escaping his lips.

I force on a smile, the words I need to say threatening to spill out. But I swallow them down. I can't tell him now. Not when the sun is shining so brilliantly and he's looking at me like I hung it in the sky. I just want to enjoy this moment, even with the storm of uncertainty looming overhead.

Blake's touch glides to my hand, his gaze alive with affection. "I never expected to marry a girl I met at the bar."

I lean into him, my head resting on his bare chest. "Well, I never imagined I'd get hitched to a guy who can't handle his tequila."

"Hey, I can handle my tequila just fine."

"Sure. That's why you ended up proposing to a potted plant that night."

His laughter rumbles through me. "You're exaggerating."

"I am. But you were pretty drunk."

"True, but I was more nervous."

I grin. "Really?"

"Yeah," he grunts, running his fingers through his hair. "I had no idea what you'd say, and I needed you to say yes. Thank God you did."

"So you've always been this hopelessly romantic?" I nudge him with my elbow.

"Not at all. I was prepared for a fling." Blake shakes his head, smiling. "Life, it's just so unpredictable...full of surprises. Some so wonderful, you fall in love."

His words pass through me, as soothing as the balmy breeze. He knows how to cool me off and make me melt. It's making it hard to confront him.

"Should we check on Gianna?" I ask.

"We've only been here an hour."

I glance at the hotel behind us. "I suppose."

Blake takes my shoulders and kneads my muscles. He hired a nanny to come with us, a nice girl we vetted out.

Blake kisses my back, and I tense. "Something wrong?"

I fight the boiling in my chest, but it's no use. I can't go through the whole vacation ignoring it. "Blake..." I begin, my voice just above a whisper. He looks at me, a question in his eyes. I take a deep breath, steeling myself.

"Yeah?" He brushes a strand of hair behind my ear. His touch is grounding and terrifying.

"I…I visited Naomi in jail. Right before we came here."

He sighs. "Why would you do that?"

"Because I never got closure."

"Did you get it?"

"Somewhat. She told me things."

Judging by the way he swallows his cocktail, he's aware of what's coming.

"I'll bet she did," he mutters.

"Like Janice was a private investigator." I cross my arms as his fingers whiten on the glass. "Is that true? You spied on me?"

"Yes."

"Why the hell would you do that?"

Bristling, he sets the drink down. "I hired her after you contacted me, okay? I wanted to make sure you had a place to stay. I know that's creepy, but I…I had to keep a close eye on you, especially after you claimed you had no support."

"Why not offer me help?"

He grimaces. "My lawyer advised me not to."

"So you paid Janice to give me a room…and spy on me?"

"Yes, and I'm sorry. It was wrong."

I let his words sink in, fuming. At least he isn't denying it. Despite his good intentions, it's hard to shake that he watched me without my knowledge. "I understand that you were protecting me, but that violated my privacy."

"I'm sorry. I should've told you."

"What else have you done?" I already know, but I want to hear it from him.

Blake rubs his forehead, pained. "I asked Naomi for a favor. I explained that I'd screwed up and needed her help. That I'd owe her if she gave you a job and took care of you. She created the job post and made it as appealing as possible, and I had Janice pass on the link."

"So Naomi wasn't lying."

"I know it's bad, but I swear to God. I had no idea she'd react the way she did. I assumed she'd treat you like a sister, like she promised."

"She told me everything," I grind out, glaring at him. "You wanted me in her home. To *control* me."

His neck flushes. "What?"

"She said you seeded her with doubt for weeks. Whenever she called you with information, you questioned my parenting ability. Telling her that someone should intervene. That it's a crime that low-income women have to resort to relying on people like her." My voice trembles as I search his face for the truth. "Did you say those horrible things?"

"Absolutely not."

"Why would she lie?"

He lets out a humorless laugh. "Sweetheart, Naomi is out of her mind."

"But you did ask her to take me in?"

Blake covers his face with his hands, his wedding band winking in the sunlight. "Yes. That part is true."

"Why would you manipulate me like that?"

"You had no health insurance, and I hated that you

lived in the Blade. It's not safe there. I wanted you out of there, and I had a strong rapport with Naomi. I knew she'd help me. I know that's insane, but I wasn't thinking rationally. I had to keep you close and at arm's length at the same time."

"So you didn't put me there to mess with her?"

He lifts his head, his brow furrowing. "For what purpose?"

"To make her have a psychotic break."

"Why would I do that?"

I shrug, crossing my arms. "To royally stiff Jack, so he'd lose his share of Luxe Pacifica."

He frowns. "She told you that?"

"I figured that out on my own."

Blake's entire face turns red. Desperation leaks into his words. "We're together. What does it matter how it came to be?"

"I need to know the truth."

"I knew your presence would annoy Jack, that the disruption might distract him from the company, but I never saw it going this far."

"You *used* me."

"I messed up," he grinds out. "When Janice told me that Jack was being an asshole, I realized I'd made a terrible mistake. Then I tried convincing you to leave, but you understandably turned me down. If I'd known what was happening, I would've pulled you out of there."

Blake's confession hits me like a ton of bricks. His normally vibrant eyes are dulled with remorse.

"I never meant to hurt you," he whispers.

"You lied to me. You manipulated me. That *is* hurting me."

"I regret it every day. I wish I could take it back."

I glare at him, the man I love, the father of my child. My husband, who despite his mistakes, has always been there for me. Anger, betrayal, and sadness swirl inside me, but they're overpowered by another emotion—understanding. He was raised by a fleet of nannies and his psychopath father. Am I surprised he ended up this way?

I rise from the chair, overlooking the sparkling Mediterranean Sea. The salty breeze caresses my burning cheeks. Distant waves crash against the shore as I sort through my feelings. Blake's revelation is shocking. His manipulation caused me pain. But I know the man he is now. He loves me unconditionally and treats Gianna like she's the center of his universe.

I think about the past two years, the happiness we've built. Our love isn't perfect. It's complicated, but it can also withstand the harshest storms. Still...

"Why did you keep all this from me?"

When I turn around, remorse is etched in every line of his face. His uncertain gaze meets mine.

"I...I was terrified of losing you."

"I'm not going anywhere. We'll work through this. But no more secrets, okay?"

He nods, sighing.

As I take his hands, hope sparks in my chest. We have a long road ahead of us, filled with apologies and forgiveness, but we'll stroll it together. Because I still love him, flaws and all.

I pull him into an embrace. "I love you."

He holds me tightly. "I love you, too."

The sun dips, casting a warm glow around us, and it hits me. I'm not just Mrs. Hamilton, the privileged woman living a life of luxury. I'm also Grace, a girl who's learned the strength of love and the beauty of second chances. And for that, I wouldn't change a thing.

ACKNOWLEDGMENTS

I owe a lot of people thanks for this book. I am fortunate to have crossed paths with people from diverse walks of life, spanning the spectrum of wealth. You know what? Money doesn't guarantee a picture-perfect family. Far from it. In fact, the most dysfunctional family I've ever met was also the richest, and they make the Hamiltons look sane.

Theresa, your support and encouragement have meant the world to me, and I can't thank you enough. And Kevin, my partner-in-crime, thank you for holding my hand through yet another book release. Love you to the moon and back!

Jess, you're a total legend. I owe you. You've been there for me every step of the way, offering guidance, and feedback. I don't know what I'd do without you. A special thanks goes to Bettye Underwood and Christine LePorte, the editing dream team. You both have polished this book to perfection, and I'm forever grateful for your sharp eyes. And major props to Llywellyn for the cover that's sure to turn heads.

To everyone I've mentioned and all the others who've supported me, thank you from the bottom of my heart. This book wouldn't exist without you, and I'm beyond humbled and appreciative of your presence in my life.

ALSO BY RACHEL HARGROVE

Thrillers

Not a Normal Family

The Maid

Sick Girl

My Sister's Lies

Contemporary Romance *as Blair LeBlanc

The Guarded Heart

ABOUT THE AUTHOR

Rachel Hargrove is from Montreal, Canada. She earned a BA in English and Comparative Literature at San Jose State University and worked as a data analyst in a biotechnology company. When she turned 26, she left her career in tech to write fiction full-time. Rachel now lives in Seattle.

Rachel's debut psychological thriller *Sick Girl*, was released in March 2018. She is represented by Jill Marsal of Marsal Lyon Literary Agency. Rachel can be reached at admin@rachelhargrove.com

Printed in July 2023
by Rotomail Italia S.p.A., Vignate (MI) - Italy